FOR YOUR LOVE

Janice Sims

ARABESQUE

★BET

BOOKS™

BET Publications LLC
http://www.bet.com
http://www.arabesquebooks.com

ARABESQUE BOOKS are published by

BET Publications, LLC
c/o BET BOOKS
One BET Plaza
1900 W Place NE
Washington, DC 20018-1211

Copyright © 2002 by Janice Sims

All rights reserved. No part of this book may be reproduced, stored in a retrieval system, or transmitted in any form or by any means without the prior written consent of the Publisher.

If you purchased this book without a cover, you should be aware that this book is stolen property. It was reported as "unsold and destroyed" to the Publisher and neither the Author nor the Publisher has received any payment for this "stripped book."

All Kensington Titles, Imprints, and Distributed Lines are available at special quantity discounts for bulk purchases for sales promotions, premiums, fund-raising, and educational or institutional use. Special book excerpts or customized printings can also be created to fit specific needs. For details, write or phone the office of the Kensington special sales manager: Kensington Publishing Corp., 850 Third Avenue, New York, NY 10022, attn: Special Sales Department, Phone: 1-800-221-2647.

BET Books is a trademark of Black Entertainment Television, Inc. ARABESQUE, the ARABESQUE logo, and the BET BOOKS logo are trademarks and registered trademarks.

First Printing: July 2002
10 9 8 7 6 5 4 3 2 1

Printed in the United States of America

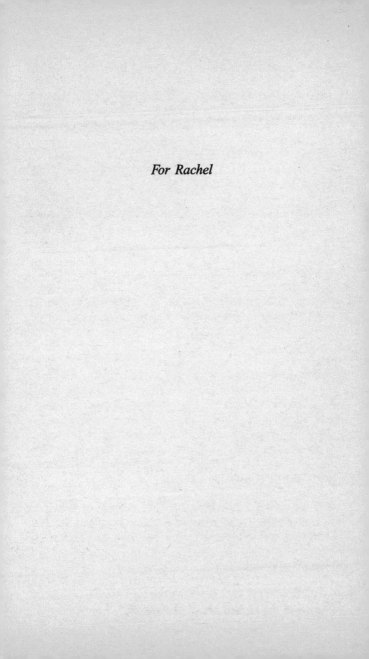

For Rachel

Part One

A black girl I am, but comely, O you
daughters of Jerusalem, like the tents
of Kedar, like the tent cloths of Solomon.

—The Song of Solomon

I want you the way Adam wanted Eve . . .
David desired Bathsheba . . .
King Solomon craved Makeda.

—The Book of Counted Joys

Prologue

Ethiopia, 1529 A.D.

The doors of the monastery were thick, therefore the abuna, or archbishop, did not at first hear the frantic knocking. He was roused by the second round, however, and groaned softly as he coerced his old bones to a sitting position on the hard, lumpy bed.

Short and thin, his scrawny body was covered from neck to ankles by a rough nightshirt made of wool. His rheumy eyes looked hopefully in the direction of the fireplace. Not an ember glowed in the ashes. Luckily, he wore knitted socks to bed. Bless the women of the neighboring village for making them. His poor feet would freeze in the winter months without them. Moonshine coming through the single window helped him find his way to the door. "I'm coming," he said, as he pulled on his robe.

"Abuna, priests from Aksum have come bearing the Ark!" cried a youthful voice that he knew belonged to Habte-Mikael, the acolyte who attended him.

The abuna's heart was suddenly racing. He threw the door open wide. Light from the fat candle Habte-Mikael held high in his right hand illuminated the old man's face. "Where are they?" the abuna asked breathlessly, barely able to contain his excitement.

The acolyte, a good-looking lad of seventeen, handed him the candle. "I cannot let you to go downstairs like that, Abuna. You will surely catch your death of cold." He went and fetched the abuna's slippers, bent and placed them on his master's feet. Then he took the candle and led the way down the dark corridor. The air in the monastery was damp and cold due to the stone walls. Built near a lake in the late 1300s, more than two hundred years ago, the underlying strata upon which it stood had been gradually saturated. It was not uncommon to find puddles in the cellars.

"Ahmed Gragn and his marauders must be drawing closer," the abuna mumbled, as they descended the stairs that led to the great hall. "Our people have never been conquered. I pray God will be with us this time, as well."

"Yes, father," Habte-Mikael dutifully agreed. His mind was on the object he'd seen downstairs. The priests had bundled it in several cloths. You could barely make out its shape underneath all of its wrappings. He wondered if the abuna would allow him to remain, or immediately dismiss him so that the priests' business could be conducted in private. He hoped he would be allowed to stay. He'd longed for this moment. He fairly trembled in anticipation. To actually be in close proximity to the Ark of the Covenant! God had ordered the Israelites to build it as a proper place for keeping the Ten Commandments. It was rumored that the two stone tablets upon which God had written his laws still lay in the bottom of the chest. Perhaps disintegrated into dust by now.

The reason the priests had carefully bundled the Ark was to protect all those nearby from its power. In ancient times, only priests—the Kohathite Levites—were allowed near it. Habte-Mikael had read an account in the Holy Scriptures explaining how King David had ordered the Ark to be carried to Jerusalem in a wagon instead of in the advised manner: upon the shoulders of the Levites.

The oxen pulling the wagon were somehow upset and Uzzah, the young man walking behind it, not wanting the Ark to touch the ground, reached out and grabbed hold of it. He fell dead a moment later.

King David had been so angry at God for taking the life of Uzzah, he had allowed the Ark to remain in a private home for three months. However, when he saw how blessed the household was due to the presence of God in the form of the Ark, he soon returned and took the Ark back with him to reside in Jerusalem.

The acolyte marveled at the arrogance of the men in the Holy Scriptures. If King David had not gone against God and transported the Ark in an ill-advised manner, Uzzah would not have died.

Emboldened by his thoughts, Habte-Mikael asked the abuna, "Master, have you ever beheld the Ark?"

"Only the priests allowed in the holy of holies are granted that great honor," the abuna said, his voice filled with awe. Now, he supposed, that responsibility had fallen on him. The Ark had come to his monastery for safekeeping. He must not let the people down. Even though the people were not allowed to look upon the Ark, its presence in Ethiopia served to magnify the people's faith in God. They naturally believed their nation was favored by Him. The Ark had remained within their borders for centuries.

"Do you know the story of how we came to be entrusted with the Ark's safekeeping?" the abuna asked his pupil. Any good acolyte should know the legends surrounding the Ark of the Covenant. That is, if he desired to become a full brother.

Habte-Mikael solemnly nodded. "Yes, Abuna. King Solomon's son Menelik, by her majesty Makeda, Queen of Sheba, found favor in his father's eyes. However, there were also those in King Solomon's court who were jealous of the king's devotion to his son. Menelik was thought unworthy because his mother was not of their religion.

"To keep the peace, King Solomon regretfully asked Menelik to return to his home country. King Solomon ordered several young men from the royal court to accompany Menelik home. Without either King Solomon's or Menelik's knowledge, several of those men took it upon themselves to steal the Ark and bring it to Ethiopia."

The abuna laughed at the foolishness of those long-ago men as he took up the story the young acolyte had begun. "They did not realize they were being led by God. Soon after, Jerusalem was invaded and Solomon's temple destroyed. But because the Ark had been transported to Ethiopia, it was safe. And has been ever since.

"The Ark brought blessings to Israel when it was in its possession," the abuna continued. "However, God did not allow the Ark to be used by the faithless or the disobedient. The Israelite army never lost a war when the Ark was carried into battle according to God's instructions."

Momentarily they arrived in the great hall where candles had been lit in built-in sconces along the walls. The other thirty-three monks had also been awakened, and stood around in various stages of undress, some of them having forgotten their robes. There were no females present. Females were firmly forbidden to set foot on the monastery's grounds. Females of any species. They didn't even keep female goats.

The abuna stepped forward and was immediately embraced by a tall monk about thirty years of age. He wore ceremonial robes signifying that he alone was permitted into the holy of holies once a year to offer up prayers for the people. "Abuna Samuel, greetings from his majesty Emperor Lebna Dengel. Ahmed Grahn has declared a jihad against the Christians of Ethiopia. The emperor thought it best that the Ark reside here at Lake Tana, where your walls are impenetrable, until the heathens have been soundly thrashed."

"We are honored to be so blessed," the abuna assured the emissary from their emperor. He turned and clapped his hands twice, requesting immediate attention from his fellow monks, who were huddled together muttering among themselves about the miraculous turn of events. "We have prepared for this day, brothers, and now it is upon us. Each of you will go about his assigned task. Get to it."

Regarding the representative from Aksum once again, Abuna Samuel said, "As you know, we prayed this night would never come, that our nation would not be overrun by barbarians. However it's best to pray *and* be practical, therefore we've prepared the inner room of the sanctuary according to the specifications set forth in the Holy Scriptures. Come, brother, and judge whether we have done a good enough job."

Slowly they walked down the long hallway leading to the main chapel. Finally they arrived and the double doors were held open by two of the soldiers who had accompanied the retinue from Aksum: men in the bloom of youth, their physiques chiseled by the martial arts. Abuna Samuel and the emissary strode ahead of the priests carrying the Ark, still wrapped in its many cloths, upon their shoulders. Wooden poles fit through holes in rings at the base of the sacred chest. The Ark was made of acacia wood and overlaid inside and out with pure gold. The cover was solid gold, and mounted on it were two cherubs kneeling and facing each other, their heads bowed and their wings extending up and over the entire length of the Ark. No one knew the identity of the artisan who had lovingly made it.

Once inside the chapel, Abuna Samuel walked to the back of the room and drew aside a pair of intricately patterned damask curtains. Hidden behind these curtains was a golden-hued door. Opening it, he motioned for Habte-Mikael to light the candles already placed in the built-in sconces on the walls, then moved aside and allowed the emissary to precede him inside the sixteen-by-sixteen-foot room. There were no windows. The walls and the ceiling were covered with murals depicting events from the Bible, the most beautiful of which was a Madonna and Child, both with warm brown skin.

"You have an artist in residence?" asked the mesmerized emissary. He wore a contented smile as he walked around the room. "I have not seen such workmanship since I was in Athens ten years ago."

"The artist is none other than Habte-Mikael, here," the abuna said, grasping the young man by the arm and pulling him to stand before the emissary. "His is a God-given talent." He could not have been more proud if Habte-Mikael had been his own son.

"For one so young," the emissary said, "he shows great depth of feeling. The pain on our Lord's face in the Crucifixion is truly exquisite, and gazing upon the Madonna and Child, one can *feel* the love Mary has for the baby Jesus." His gaze fell on the acolyte, whose eyes were downcast out of respect. He moved forward and tilted the boy's head up. The emissary's eyes narrowed. "Well done, young Habte-Mikael, *gift of Michael*. Did you know that is the translation of your name?"

Habte-Mikael could look the emissary in the eyes for only a second or two. With his gaze lowered once more, he replied, "Yes, sir. My mother named me that because before I was conceived she feared she would never have a child. Alas, I am all that she was given by God."

The emissary continued his perusal of the murals. "God works in mysterious ways. He did not give your mother many sons and daughters. Only one. But that one was born with this talent. A talent that glorifies God."

This said, he again regarded Abuna Samuel. "I am certain the Ark will be perfectly safe here."

The abuna smiled his pleasure.

The Ark was safe at the monastery on Lake Tana for many years. Like any national treasure, its safety was of tantamount importance to the Ethiopians. Up until the present day, with each emperor's incarnation, the Ark has been moved from one safe place to another. It now rests in Aksum behind a walled compound guarded by government soldiers armed with AK-47s.

Numerous learned men have come bearing papers setting forth their credentials to examine the Ark for authenticity. But the Ethiopians maintain that the Ark in their possession is real enough for them, and no amount of carbon dating will make it more real. They accept its authenticity on faith.

Of course, faith is not enough for some men.

One

He won't come, Dr. Solange DuPree thought as she sank deeper into the oversized tub. Fluffy, coconut-scented suds tickled her chin. She blew bubbles away from her mouth. Did she want him to come? Yes. *No!* Maybe.

Dark brown eyes narrowed in determination. Yes, she wanted him to come knocking on her door. It was the reason she'd come to Ethiopia with Toni and Charles, wasn't it? Her presence here in Addis Ababa wasn't essential to the process of ransoming Toni and Charles's daughter. She could have given the goddess, the item Yusef Makonnen wanted in exchange for Briane Shaw, to Toni and that would have been the end of her participation in the drama. But then she would have missed being in the same place as Rupert. And she'd dearly wanted to see Rupert Giles again.

He'd made a promise the last time they'd been together in Miami, where all of this had started for her. He'd said that after his job was done, he intended to properly "call on" her. Rupert was British, so she didn't know exactly what he meant by that. However, the possibilities were delicious to ponder.

Scooting up in the tub she reached back, placed a small

air pillow beneath her head and relaxed against it. Her problem was she analyzed everything to death! A man was attracted to her. She was attracted to him. How many times in the past two years had that happened? Nil. She'd closed off a part of herself after her last relationship. She'd had a lot of soul-searching to do.

To begin with, she bore some blame for the disastrous conclusion of her last relationship. She and Dr. Nicholas Campion had been dating nearly a year. Then, out of the blue, he proposed—and Solange panicked. For months she'd put off telling him about her condition: she could not conceive. She'd been born with ova that would never be viable. When she told Nick, he was understandably upset at not being told before. Solange took this as a rejection. After a few days, however, Nick calmed down and tried to see it from her perspective. Her condition was extremely personal. It wasn't something you'd confess to just anybody. Only someone whom you trusted implicitly.

Nick tried to reassure Solange that it didn't matter. They could adopt. Or, if she wanted to experience carrying a child to term, they could go to a fertility specialist. With borrowed ova and his sperm, there was the possibility that she could get pregnant.

But Solange was afraid to try again with Nick. His initially violent reaction to the news made her wonder how he'd cope with any number of other problems that might crop up in their life together. No marriage ran smoothly. She was well aware of that, since her own parents divorced when she was thirteen. Now the only time she saw her parents in the same place, at the same time, was at weddings and funerals.

Rejection brought out the worst in Nick. She didn't want *him?* When he was being so magnanimous about her frailties? Hot, young anthropology professor (with tenure) that he was, didn't she know he could get any

nubile female within a hundred-mile radius? She should
be jumping at the chance to marry him!

No matter how much Solange protested to the contrary,
Nick would not accept that it was over between them.
Solange finally had to get a restraining order before Nick
would stop phoning her, sending vicious faxes and dis-
turbing E-mail, and leaving dead flowers on her front
porch. In the note that came with the flowers he'd written,
"Since what makes you a woman has withered up and
died, you should have something that reminds you of that
fact." It was his cruelty that was the clincher for her.
She'd left him for good.

Rising, Solange stepped out of the tub onto a thick,
white cotton bath rug. One hundred and thirty pounds
dripping wet, five-feet-four-inches tall, she had a well-
toned yet sensuously voluptuous body. Skin the color of
toasted almonds. Eyes a deep velvety brown, quite remarkable in contrast to the tone of her skin. Men would
say they were her best feature, until they lowered their
eyes to her mouth. It was full and heart-shaped, the lower
lip a smidgen fuller than the upper. She was not given to
pouting, it simply wasn't in her. But it was a mouth made
for getting one's way with men. One barely perceptible
jutting-out of that lower lip would do it.

Dr. Solange DuPree had retired her repertoire of feminine wiles some time ago, however.

Until Rupert Giles blocked her sunlight.

That's what he'd done that day. She'd been walking
across the lawn of her building on the campus of the
University of Miami, trying to get to the ambulance that
was carrying Jack Cairns, the night security guard who'd
been attacked by unknown assailants, to the hospital.
She'd discovered him that morning when she arrived earlier than her colleagues, as was her habit. But now a tall
dark-skinned man stood in her path and wouldn't let her
pass.

She had been instantly intrigued by his height. He was a strapping six-feet-four-inches tall, or more. An entire foot taller than she was. Then he'd removed his sunglasses and she saw those burnt-caramel-colored, almond-shaped eyes. To cap it off he'd opened his mouth and spoken in a British accent. "Dr. DuPree, you can't do the security guard any good by getting in the way."

She had believed him to be a police detective. She had been deceived.

After drying off, Solange strode naked into the walk-in closet and removed the sheer white-lace negligee from its hanger. Back in the bedroom, she put it on the bed, then went to the bureau to get a bottle of lotion. Squirting a small amount into the palm of her left hand, she placed her right hand over it so that both palms were covered in the coconut-scented lotion and then smoothed it over her arms, legs, shoulders, and mid-section. Then she put on the negligee; its hem came to just above her knees.

Going to sit at the vanity, she picked up a hairbrush and began brushing her shiny, blue-black hair away from her face. Staring at her reflection in the mirror, she paused in mid-brush. What exactly was she preparing for, anyway? Rupert was back in her life—she'd just had dinner with him.

But at no time that evening had Rupert pulled her aside and whispered, "I can't wait to get you alone," in her ear. She had definitely been on pins and needles all night in expectation of some kind of declaration.

They had sat on pillows around a low, round table, sharing a last meal with Toni Shaw, Charles Waters, their daughters Georgie and Bree (the ransomed daughter, returned a bit dehydrated but otherwise unharmed) and their significant others—Georgie's husband, Clay, and Bree's boyfriend, Dominic. The mood had been jubilant.

Solange had sat beside Rupert. A thrill shot through her each time he touched her arm for emphasis, or once, her cheek, when he was demonstrating the way the culprit, Vera Chong, had disguised herself when trying to flee the country. "She used a huge rubber band around her hairline which drew up the sagging skin, making her appear younger than she was. Then she placed a blond wig over her normally dark hair. Of course Salah Makonnen, being an expert in hair and makeup, saw through her disguise like that!" He ended with a snap of his fingers.

Yeah, Solange thought now, *what was up with all that touchy-feely stuff if he didn't mean business?*

She continued brushing her hair away from her face. It was chin-length and blunt-cut. In her line of work, she needed a style that was relatively carefree. All she did was wash it, blow it dry. A monthly visit to a salon kept the cut looking sharp.

Placing the brush on top of the bureau, she rose. As she did, she caught the reflection of the goddess in the bureau's mirror, then walked purposefully over to it and picked up the box it sat in. The eighteen-inch carving of the unnamed African goddess was hewed from ebony wood. It shone with the patina of age. Solange had gotten it from an elderly African woman who owned a fetish shop in Bujumbura, the capital city of Burundi. With it came the warning, "Do not touch the goddess unless it's your desire to bear children." Until tonight, Solange had allowed superstition to override her common sense, and had not done so.

Where had superstition gotten *him?* All his millions hadn't precluded his falling for a con woman's game. Following her instructions, he'd hired four mercenaries to steal fertility gods and goddesses from the four corners of the earth. The last one had been in Solange's possession. That's how she was drawn into his sick, twisted scheme.

Why had Yusef done it? Because his wife was infertile,

and they'd gone to every reputable fertility expert, with
no positive results. He'd been desperate and crazy. *What
some people would do for love.* From all indications, his
wife Salah seemed to be standing by her man, come hell
or high water. She would not leave his side.

So, there they were: Bree was back in Dominic's arms.
Yusef Makonnen was in jail, but with all his lawyers he'd
undoubtedly be sprung in no time. And she was standing
in the middle of her hotel room with a wooden goddess
clutched to her chest, daring the goddess to work her
magic.

"If you can cause a child to grow in *my* womb you
truly are the real deal, old girl," she said with a laugh as
she gazed down at the wood carving.

At any rate, she vowed then and there not to allow fear
to rule her life any longer. A piece of wood wasn't going
to grant her her heart's desire. That would take a miracle.
One miracle and one willing male . . .

Suddenly she heard a noise on her balcony. She'd
opened the sliding glass door earlier, to allow fresh air
to circulate; now she was afraid some hooligan was trying
to get into her room via the balcony. Quickly placing the
goddess on the bed, she ran to the sliding glass door and
saw Rupert, dressed entirely in black, climbing over the
railing with a rose between his teeth. Letting out a yelp
of panic, Solange turned and sprinted back into the bedroom for her bathrobe. She could hear Rupert laughing
at her as she fled. "I had to slip past security and bribe
the couple in the room below to allow me to use their
balcony. She was for it, he was not. She won," he said,
as he walked further into the room. "But, I finally made
it. As promised!"

Busy tying the sash on her robe, Solange re-entered
the bedroom laughing. "I do not believe you! You're nuts,
you know that? You could have broken your neck!"

Rupert responded by going to her and pulling her into

his strong arms. "Mmm, you smell good." He leaned closer. His deep voice went an octave lower. "But you feel even better than you smell. Give us a kiss, will you?"

Smiling, Solange tilted her head back, meeting his eyes. "Where's the champagne?"

Rupert reached behind him. Quasi-spy that he was, he knew a thing or two about smart inventions. Solange hadn't noticed the leather strap going across his chest. He unclipped it on the right side and the entire piece came loose. A chilled bottle of bubbly had been safely carried in a leather pouch on his back. He removed it and handed it to Solange.

Taking the bottle, Solange grinned again. "I'll get the glasses." Hotels always provided glasses for their guests. So what if they weren't crystal wineglasses? She had a man in her room who'd climbed onto her balcony to get there. She'd drink it directly out of the bottle if need be! She turned out of his embrace to go get them.

Rupert made himself comfortable on the couch in the large suite while Solange went over to the cabinet that held a miniature refrigerator. On top of the cabinet were two glasses wrapped in plastic.

"I have to tell you, you had me worried," she said, as she removed the plastic from both glasses. "I was waiting for you to say something, anything, that would indicate your intentions. But, no, nothing!"

"I couldn't keep my hands off you," Rupert said, inclining his well-shaped head toward her. "I would say that's some indication as to my intentions." He rose, unable to just sit there while she was clear across the room.

Solange loved to watch him move. How cool his gait was, so smooth. Confident. She wondered if he'd ever felt inadequate in his life. Like she was feeling right now. She'd willed him here. Now, what was she going to *do* with him?

There was no doubt Rupert thought of her as a woman

of the world. What was it he'd said in her bedroom in Miami, when they'd kissed for the first time? "I won't make love to you, although I want to. It wouldn't be the right thing to do. Not now."

How about now? Solange thought. *Would now be a good time?*

She moved over to the sink adjacent to the cabinet to open the bottle of champagne in case there was spillage. Rupert came up behind her just as she was about to pop the cork. "Allow me," he said.

She handed him the bottle. Her hand trembled a bit.

Rupert pretended not to notice. He adeptly removed the cork, holding the bottle over the sink. A little foam escaped over the side, but not much. Solange held the glasses while he poured. When both were three-quarters full, Rupert set the bottle on the cabinet's top and accepted a glass of champagne from Solange. He held it up in a toast. Solange followed suit.

"To the pursuit of Dr. Solange DuPree. May the best man win." His golden-brown eyes held a mischievous glint in them.

Solange didn't know what to say to that and drank deeply instead. Rupert refilled her glass even though it was still half full. Narrowing her eyes at him, Solange said, "You're not trying to get me drunk, are you, Mr. Giles?"

"You've uncovered my plot, doctor. I'm going to ply you with wine, have my way with you, and slink away under the cover of darkness."

"You scoundrel!" Solange cried, feigning shock. "Why I'll have you know I'm . . ."

". . . not that kind of girl," Rupert finished for her. He set down his champagne. Taking hers as well, he set it near his, atop the cabinet next to the champagne bottle. Grasping her by the shoulders, he looked at her intently. "I don't want to make love to you, Solange." He grinned.

"That's a lie. I *do* want to make love to you. Just not that, alone. I'm saying this badly."

He released her and took a step backward.

Solange's heart was pounding in her chest. Could he be about to say something completely hokey? She hoped so. Where were the men who weren't afraid to let down their guards long enough to risk being thought of as less than cool?

She waited for his next move, her dark eyes hopeful.

Rupert sighed and smiled slowly. "You make me want to run away! Just ditch everything and do what I want to do for a change. And what I want to do is spend the next few weeks getting to know a lovely archaeologist with the most beautiful brown eyes I've ever seen. Stay with me, Solange. Let's see Ethiopia together." Rupert paused. His eyes raked over her face. She looked confused. Her eyes widened and when she opened her mouth to speak no sound came out. "Ah . . ." she finally said. Then, "Mmm . . ." A contemplative hum, and that was all.

Rupert took that as a maybe, and went on, "You told me you were studying the ancient kingdom of Kush. I know archaeologists do a lot of research in dusty old books, but you would eventually have to get out in the field, right? Then, here you are! I looked it up on the Net: The modern-day location of the ancient kingdom of Kush is said to rest in parts of Ethiopia, northern Sudan, and southern Egypt."

"I'm well aware of that," Solange said, smiling at him. She was impressed.

"But you don't know me," Rupert said, guessing at her next objection. He paced. "This is your opportunity to *get* to know me." He looked her straight in the eyes. "Have you ever done any backpacking?"

"Yes, across Europe and part of West Africa," Solange informed him. Amusement was evident in her eyes. There was no hindrance to her remaining in Addis if that was her wish. She was not currently teaching any classes at the university because she was taking a three-month sabbatical to complete her research on Kush and publish a paper on her findings. That was the nature of academia today: It was publish or perish. Instructors were no longer deemed suitable simply because they could inspire students to academic heights. They also had to prove to their peers that they had the right stuff by being published in reputable journals.

As she ruminated, Rupert was still talking. "I'll outfit us both with camping gear. In villages with good accommodations, we'll get lodgings. Separate rooms, of course. And since it was my suggestion, I insist on paying for everything."

"That isn't fair," Solange protested. "If I decide to stay, I'll pay my own way."

Rupert smiled at her. "Hasn't anyone ever told you not to look a gift horse in the mouth?"

"I don't like being in debt to anyone," Solange told him, adamant in her stance. "Especially not to . . ."

"A man?" Rupert said sweetly.

"Will you quit that!" Solange cried, referring to his habit of finishing her sentences. It was uncanny how he knew what she was thinking. They hadn't known each other long enough for him to know what she was going to say next! "It's just plain rude to interrupt someone when they're speaking."

Rupert feigned an attack of the trembles. "Ooh, you *are* a teacher. I'm duly chastised, Teach. I'll be silent while you think about my suggestion." He stood there with a smile on his lips, his brows arched in a questioning pose.

Solange put her hands on her hips, pursed her lips and tapped her right foot, thinking.

"Does that bode well for me?" Rupert joked. "All that

fidgeting? Will you stand on your head next to get the old brain cells stirred up?"

Solange laughed and hit him on the upper arm. His biceps felt as hard as a rock. She couldn't resist a little squeeze before allowing her hand to fall back to her side. Rupert drew her into his arms. Bending his head, he said, "May I do this while you're thinking?"

With that he quickly placed his mouth over hers. His breath was warm and clean. He tasted like peppermint. Fresh and cool, in spite of the warmth of his tongue entering her mouth. They were both tentative at first, then insistent. Her right hand came up and grasped his hair, which was slightly damp. She knew then that he'd bathed, too, before climbing onto her balcony. The thought that he'd been showering while she was soaking in a tub, both of them with seduction in mind, made her sigh and fall deeper into the kiss. He felt as good as she remembered. Better!

Rupert had wanted to kiss her soundly ever since he'd laid eyes on her again at Lideta Airport yesterday, following the capture of Vera Chong. But they'd never gotten the chance to be alone. Toni Shaw and Charles Waters both seemed intent on keeping them apart. Rupert didn't know why the local police's acceptance of his credentials wasn't enough for Toni and Charles. It was as if they'd appointed themselves Solange's surrogate parents. If Toni wasn't by Solange's side, then Charles was. After dinner tonight, Rupert had pulled Charles aside, given him the phone number of his boss in London and urged him to phone if he needed further proof that he was who he said he was. Charles admitted that that would go a long way in setting his and Toni's minds at ease about Rupert's interest in Solange. They'd both taken an instant liking to her, and didn't want anything bad to happen to their new friend. Charles apologized for being over-protective, but in light of the recent abduction of their daughter, they felt the need to be cautious. Besides, Solange had come to Addis Ababa with them and they felt responsible for her.

Deep down, their concern touched Rupert. But he wasn't going to let anyone get in the way of his and Solange's budding relationship. It had been a long time since any woman had interested him to this extent. He was compelled to learn everything about her that he could. He sensed in her a contradiction. She was cerebral yet inexperienced.

Solange turned her head and broke off the kiss. She smiled at him. "You're very good at this." An understatement, to be sure. Her entire body was singing his praises. Her nipples had hardened and were pressing against the material of her negligee. Her female center was throbbing. She was tingling all over.

Rupert kissed the side of her mouth. "We're equally good at this. Makes one wonder what else we're equally good at." He smiled down at her. "Well, what's the verdict?"

Solange gently squirmed out of his embrace. "Has any woman ever been able to say no to you after a kiss like that?" She didn't wait for his reply. "I'm going to sleep on it. I'll let you know in the morning."

Rupert's face didn't mirror his disappointment. He had half-expected her to say no. Her wanting to sleep on it was a kind of reprieve.

He went and planted a chaste kiss on her forehead. "Fair enough. Good move for me. You'll dream about me, and in the morning you'll decide you want more of those kisses."

Solange walked him to the door. "Have you always been so cocky?"

"It's self-taught. Something I learned to do after being rejected by so many women."

Solange laughed heartily. "Going for the sympathy vote, huh?"

"Did it work?" he asked hopefully.

"No." She relished the stricken expression on his handsome face even though she suspected he was faking it. At the door, she tiptoed and kissed him long and deep. "A little something to remember me by in case my answer is no in the morning."

Rupert looked genuinely dazed as he turned and walked through the door.

Two

"Gaea, wake up, I need your levelheaded advice," Solange said. She was sitting on the bed in her hotel room, nervously crossing and uncrossing her legs. Several thousand miles away in New York City, Gaea Maxwell-Cavanaugh pulled herself into a sitting position in bed beside her husband, Micah. Micah, eyes still closed, moaned softly and groped for her. After his hand found her thigh he contentedly fell back into a deep sleep. Gaea smiled, let the hand stay there and spoke into the handset. "What's up, Pudge?" Solange had been chubby as a kid. The nickname had followed her into adulthood.

"I'm in Addis Ababa," Solange announced.

"What are you doing in Addis Ababa?" Gaea cried, confused. "More research on Kush?"

"Sort of. Here's the skinny," Solange said, telling her best friend the condensed version of how she'd ended up in Ethiopia. ". . . I'm thinking of staying awhile," she concluded a few minutes later.

"With Rupert Giles?" Gaea laughed, stuck on Rupert's name. "You're pulling my leg about the name, right? That's not *really* his name."

"No, why would I do that?"

"You don't know?" Gaea asked, incredulous.

"No. Explain it to me. It's a perfectly wonderful name." Solange's tone was a tad indignant. Toni Shaw had had the same reaction to Rupert's name.

Gaea laughed again. "It just happens to be the name of a character on one of my favorite TV shows, *Buffy the Vampire Slayer*," Gaea informed her popular-culture-ignorant friend. "Actor Anthony Stewart Head portrays Rupert Giles, a British scholarly type who's actually kind of a hunk, if you ask me. I take it your Rupert Giles is a looker too? Lord knows, with a name like Rupert he's got to have something going for him."

"It's more than that," Solange said. "There's something mysterious in his eyes that makes me want to dig further. Sure, I'm afraid of getting involved with anyone after what happened with Nick. But I'm so tired of being alone."

"You're not alone, sweetie," Gaea said, offering consolation across the miles. "You'll always have us." "Us" was Gaea, husband Micah, and their son, seven-month-old Micah, Jr., whom everyone called Mikey. Gaea was a marine biologist. She taught at Benson College, a historically black college in upstate New York. She was also an integral part of a Powers-Benthic Corporation project. The company was constructing an underwater station, similar to a space station, to study marine life. Micah was the head attorney for Powers-Benthic.

"I know," Solange said, still sounding sad. "And I love you with all my heart."

"But you want something to call your own," Gaea said softly. "I could kick Marie for not showing you the love you deserved when you were a child."

"Let's not get on the subject of my mother. I learned to do without her love a long time ago. I'm not even going to tell her what's going on."

"You can't just disappear for days without telling her where you are. She'd worry. Believe it or not, she loves you. She simply doesn't know how to show it. You have to take into account her experiences in Haiti. The hardships she had to endure. All of that had to scar her emotionally," Gaea said reasonably.

"I know people who've gone through worse and still manage to love and appreciate others," Solange said, not cutting her mother any slack. Gaea's folks, for instance. They hadn't had easy lives either, but they knew how to love. If not for Cameron and Lara Maxwell, she wouldn't have known what it felt like to be loved unconditionally. Thanks to them, and Gaea, she had the capacity to love. The ability to express that love, and the desire to give it away. She thanked God for the Maxwells every day of her life.

"Maybe you'll feel more sympathetic toward your mother when you have children of your own," Gaea suggested.

"We both know that isn't going to happen," Solange guffawed. In keeping with her new resolution to move forward and not allow her infertility to sideline her life, she had decided to find humor in it.

"You're only thirty-four. There's nothing the matter with your uterus. They're making remarkable progress with fertility procedures nowadays. I'll give you some of my ova. You just concentrate on the sperm donor, I mean the husband." Gaea laughed too. "Honestly, it was a slip of the tongue."

"You were right the first time," Solange said, still laughing. "At the rate I'm going I'll never get married. I'll have to go to a sperm bank and make a withdrawal."

"Stop it," Gaea begged. "I'll wake up my men." Micah rolled over in bed. And she could hear Mikey's soft snoring across the hall in the nursery. They kept his door open so they could hear him if he should need them.

"So, you're staying in Ethiopia with a guy you don't know from Adam," Gaea said, getting back on track. "And you want my opinion? I say you should do what your heart dictates. In your job, you've traveled the world.

I don't worry about you when you go on a dig. You're a survivor and I never doubt that you'll be perfectly fine wherever you go on the planet. I *do* worry about you when you phone me raving about a cute guy, though. I don't want you to get hurt again. But, this much I know is true: nothing worth having in life is ever gotten without taking a few risks. And there's no better—or worse, depending on how you look at it—way to get to know someone than to travel with him. You need anything for the trip that you might have difficulty finding over there? Like tampons, condoms, a back-up toothbrush? Deodorant? I can airmail those things to you tomorrow. No problem."

"Ever the practical one."

"Well, I know I wouldn't want to be in a foreign country without my wet wipes," Gaea joked. She had extensive experience traveling the globe and knew how useful the wet towels could be when you were unable to bathe for days. "A girl's gotta think of personal hygiene. You can get pretty rank without access to water."

"You know I always pack my wet wipes," Solange told her. "Along with my water purifying kit, Pepto-Bismol tablets, and tampons."

"What about communications?"

"I'm sure we'll find a phone somewhere along the way." She wasn't *that* sure.

Gaea sighed. "Call me if you get the chance."

"You lied, you *are* worried," Solange said.

"I'm concerned," Gaea admitted. "It wasn't long ago that Ethiopia and Eritrea were fighting along their borders. They signed a cease-fire in June, so maybe they're at peace now, but you be careful anyway. All right, I'm finished being the mother hen. Have a good time. Give Rupert my number and tell him if you should ever be incapacitated in any way he is to phone me, pronto. I'll notify your parents. Oh, and one more thing."

"Yes, mother?"

"If an Ethiopian man makes an unsolicited pass at you, you have to slap him at least twice in quick succession to let him know you mean business. Slapping him once is just a turn-on."

Laughing, Solange said, "And where did you pick up that bit of information?"

"In a sleazy joint in Addis Ababa in '97. Went there with Oliver Bekele, remember him? He used to have a huge crush on you."

"Of course I remember Oliver. Whatever happened to him?"

"He teaches at U.C.-Berkeley. Married a nice woman and they have a little girl now."

Solange lay back on the bunched-up pillows on her bed. "Good for him."

Micah opened his eyes and smiled at his wife. "Pudge, I assume?"

Gaea nodded in the affirmative. She reached down and gently touched his cheek.

Solange heard Micha's muffled voice in the background. "I'll let you go. I just wanted to run this by someone I trust. Someone who would tell me if I'm out of my mind to do this. Give my best to Micah. And kiss Mikey for me. Good-bye, you lucky, lucky girl!"

"Bye, Pudge. I love you!"

"Love you, too."

They rang off, and Solange picked up the goddess, which had been lying on her bed all this time. Gazing down at it she said, "What am I going to do with you? I can't lug you around Ethiopia for the next few days."

"Have you thought this through?" Toni asked later that morning, when Solange went to Toni and Charles's suite to say good-bye and ask a favor of Toni. She'd found Toni there alone. "Rupert seems like a nice man, but you've just met."

Toni was wearing a sand-colored lounge outfit that billowed about her five-foot-eight-inch frame. Her short black hair had a few strands of silver in it, and she wore it in a style that needed little more than combing with one's fingers to make it fall back in place. Solange doubted that Toni had even bothered doing that this morning. Her beautiful brown face was devoid of makeup. "Chuck and I had Clay check him out. He does work for a prestigious insurance firm out of London, that much is true. But Clay couldn't find anything on him prior to that position. Do you know what that means?"

They were standing in the middle of the suite. Toni hadn't even offered Solange a seat before launching into her protestations about Solange remaining in Ethiopia with Rupert. Solange stood staring at Toni.

"You checked him out?" she asked, puzzled and a little miffed. "Why would you go to so much trouble? Has he done anything to make you suspect him of something?"

Toni came and grasped Solange by the shoulders. "Solange, Rupert wanted us to. He gave Chuck his boss's number in London, and encouraged Chuck to phone Mr. Latimer. Chuck went a step further, that's all." She smiled. "I apologize. We shouldn't have done any of this without first speaking with you. But we were concerned. We wouldn't want anything to happen to you. I know we have no right to snoop into Rupert's background. And we can't tell you how to live your life. But ever since I learned Rupert's name I've not been convinced he is who he says he is."

"Because he shares the name of a character on a popular TV series?"

"Then you know about that?"

"I know. It's coincidental, Toni. Nothing more."

"I hope so," Toni said, as she dropped her hands and

turned away to walk over to the bar. She poured herself a glass of bottled water. "Can I get you something?"

"A glass of water would be nice," Solange said. She joined Toni at the bar where they sat on bar stools and turned to face each other.

"There was a doubtful note in your voice when you said 'I hope so'," Solange said, after they'd both drunk from their glasses.

"It seems as if his records have been expunged, Solange," Toni told her. "That only happens if a person has been involved in something dangerous. Maybe Rupert is part of a witness protection program and had to change his identity. Or perhaps he was a spy and he left the company. Their identities are changed to protect them and the agencies they formerly worked for."

Solange laughed. "A spy?"

"Bear with me," Toni said, not finished. "Think about it. All of the skills he used as an intelligence agent could be utilized in his present job. He has to be able to work alone. You heard how he tracked the men Makonnen hired, from Cairo to Miami. You saw how he dealt with the two of them who came to your house. Kicked their butts without breaking a sweat. The man has skills."

Narrowing her eyes at Solange, Toni paused. "What am I doing? If you're anything like my daughters, all my protests are falling on deaf ears. There's something about him that draws you to him and nothing I say is going to deter you from finding out what that 'something' is. Am I right?"

"I'll be careful," Solange promised. "I'm willing to take a chance on him, though."

Toni sighed heavily and rose. Looking Solange in the eyes, she said, "I thought I'd give it a shot. I guess we'll have one less passenger on the plane back to Boston."

Solange rose too and went to embrace Toni. "Thanks

for being concerned. I appreciate it more than you can know."

Toni hugged her back. "We've adopted you in our hearts, young lady. If there's ever anything we can do for you, all you need to do is ask."

Ending the embrace, Solange said, "There is the matter of the goddess. Would you take her home with you? I'll come and pick her up after my trip."

"I'd be happy to," Toni said. "Just make sure the little bugger is in its box and I don't have to touch it."

"I've touched it, Toni. There's nothing to that old woman's warnings," Solange said.

"Get back to me on that a few months from now," Toni said with a wry grin.

Rupert was thirty-eight years old and never in his life had he encountered a woman who enjoyed her food as much as Dr. Solange DuPree.

They were sitting at a window table in the restaurant of the Sheraton. It was a fine establishment. He'd noticed several British influences on the menu, plus a few dishes that were definitely American. Like the burger. The hotel aimed to please its wealthy foreign guests. He aimed to please the woman sitting across from him. If she'd let him.

Solange was lazily consuming a plate of delicate pasta with clam sauce. Occasionally she would close her eyes and sigh softly, as if eating the pasta were an orgasmic experience. Surely her in that dress, a lovely sheath in deep red that came to her knees and hugged every curve of her body, was enough of an orgasmic experience for him to have to cope with in one night. But, no, she had to entice him with those lips as well.

Each time she sucked the pasta between the opening

in her lips he found himself wishing he were the pasta. Lucky pasta.

He was going to need a cold shower after dinner.

"Rupert?"

"Mmm?"

"I said we need to talk about something before leaving tomorrow morning. Where were you?" Solange impatiently cut into his daydreaming, a bemused smile on her lips.

"You have a very . . . unusual way of eating pasta," he said, his voice cracking a bit.

"Oh, I'm sorry. Are my manners extremely bad?" she asked, putting her fork down. She honestly thought she'd somehow offended his British sensibilities.

"Not at all. Watching you eat is tantamount to foreplay."

Solange's eyes stretched in surprise. Smiling, she said, "I suppose that's better than being caught with asparagus in my teeth."

Rupert leaned close to her ear. "Much better." He bent down further to plant a kiss on the side of her neck. He inhaled the heady fragrance that was her body heat coupled with a scent that had to have been inspired by the Orient. It was spicy and sweet. Subtle, yet powerful. Like its wearer, no doubt.

Solange blushed down to her toes. Though it wasn't visible, the effect left her warm and slightly weak. They looked into each other's eyes a long while.

At last, Solange's brain unfroze and her ability to speak coherently returned. "Talk?" she reminded him of her earlier request.

"I'm listening," Rupert murmured, but his gaze never wavered.

"Toni thinks you're Tom Cruise."

He laughed. "I don't look anything like Tom Cruise."

"In *Mission Impossible*. The occupation, not the physical characteristics. She thinks you're a spy. A former spy, to be more accurate."

One of Rupert's eyebrows had the uncanny ability to rise while the other remained in a fixed position on his face. "What gives her that impression?"

"They couldn't find anything on you prior to your position with your present company. That and the fact that you have moves reminiscent of Jackie Chan's."

"Oh, that," he said, still amused. "I started studying the martial arts when I was a kid. My father is also an aficionado. After my schooling I enlisted in the Royal Air Force and was recruited into a special forces group while in the RAF. The SAS or Special Air Service was the force that captured the terrorists who took hostages at the Iranian embassy in London in 1980. They're considered to be the best special forces commandos in the world. But that's the closest I've ever gotten to being a spy." He laughed again at the notion. "Toni has a very vivid imagination. But I know that from her books."

Solange blushed all over again, and reached for his hand. "You read romance novels?"

"You haven't done your homework, doctor. Toni Shaw writes romances under the pseudonym Serena Kincaid, but she uses the name Julia Wentworth when she pens mysteries. I prefer her mysteries, although her romances aren't half bad either."

"Then you *do* read romances," Solange exclaimed, pleased by the discovery.

"I've been known to pick up a love story every once in a while."

"What's your opinion of them?"

"I think the authors tend to make the males too perfect. None of us is perfect. It gives the readers exalted views of the male sex, something the average male can never live up to. In those novels we're depicted as studs in the bedroom, indefatigable heroes who never give up or, in the case of the bedroom, out. Women who read romances will be sorely disappointed if they're looking for a man like the heroes in those books. Let's face it, they don't exist."

"You're wrong," Solange said. "Readers of romance novels aren't comparing men we know with the men we find in books. We know men aren't perfect. It's all fantasy. An escape. Like watching a film. A reader can imagine herself in the heroine's place for a little while. Then she closes the book, puts her children to bed, and makes love to her husband. He may not be built like the stud in the book, but he is warm and alive. What's better, he loves her, and she loves him.

"Besides," she continued. "I wouldn't be here with you now, while my friends are winging their way back to the States, if I expected you to be perfection itself."

"What?" Rupert said, sounding surprised by her insinuation. "I'm as close to perfection as any male has ever been: I chew with my mouth closed; I floss before bed each night, brush after every meal. Clean my neck, because my mother says if you don't you—"

"Might as well plant potatoes," Solange spoke up, pleased to be finishing his sentences for a change.

Rupert laughed. "Mothers are the same the world over."

"Obviously," Solange said, pushing her plate aside.

The waiter must have been waiting for some sign that they'd completed their meals, for he swooped in and politely asked if they were finished and if they would like coffee or dessert.

Rupert looked at Solange. "I don't, but if you'd like something . . ."

"No," Solange replied, smiling at the waiter. "Thank you."

"My pleasure, madame," he said, and made short work

of clearing the dishes from the table. Once his arms were loaded, he said, "I shall return with the check."

Solange bent and retrieved her bag, which she'd stashed beneath the chair earlier. "I thought we could talk about our itinerary. I like to plan where I'm going."

"Must we plan everything down to the last detail?" Rupert asked. "I thought we'd simply be spontaneous."

Solange removed the guidebook on Ethiopia, Eritrea and Djibouti from the bag, then put it back beneath her chair. "I'm all for spontaneity. But there are a few places I really don't want to miss seeing." She flipped through the book until she came to a section on monasteries. Scooting closer to Rupert, she showed him a picture of one of the island monasteries on Lake Tana, the largest lake in Ethiopia. "Don't laugh, but it's rumored that the Ark of the Covenant was kept there for a time. Blue Nile Falls is near there, I thought we could kill two birds with one stone."

Rupert took the book and read the paragraph next to the picture. Momentarily, he looked up at her. "It'll take us a couple of days to get there from here. But Debre Libanos is only a day-trip away. We could stop there first and keep heading north all the way to Aksum, where they say the Ark is today."

Solange smiled at him. "You know about the legend?"

"That the Ethiopians are in possession of the Ark of the Covenant? Of course, I do. It's only folklore, though. A fairy tale the Ethiopians have told for so long they believe it themselves."

"It's the reason I'm an archaeologist," Solange told him, her voice low.

"The Ethiopians claiming they have the Ark of the Covenant?" Rupert asked, puzzled.

"No, the very thought that what they say might be true. The wonder of it all. I saw *Raiders of the Lost Ark* when I was fourteen years old. It was the year after my parents divorced. I was a shy, chubby teen who'd gone inside herself to escape the pain of a broken family—then, all of a sudden, I had a purpose. I wanted to be Indiana Jones."

"I'm sorry about your parents, that must have been hard on all of you. I never knew my birth parents. I was adopted when I was a baby."

Solange smiled warmly at him. "Where are your adoptive parents from?"

"Sussex," Rupert replied. "They are the palest white folks you'd ever want to see." His eyes were filled with humor. "What? You expected me to say the Islands? They were Peace Corps volunteers in Guyana when my mother came to them with me in tow. I was a toddler. She told them she was without a husband and could not keep me. Her father was a stern disciplinarian and told her she had to either give her child away or go away herself and never return. She was eighteen years old. Where could she go? What could she do? My adoptive mother has told me that story since I was five. She said she always wanted me to remember my birth mother. The woman who loved me enough to give me away."

Solange was enthralled. "Is that all you know about her? You never found out who your father is?"

Rupert shook his head. "No."

"Have you tried to locate your mother?"

"She died shortly after she gave me up. My parents say she drowned," he said, his gaze lowered. "I suspect she killed herself rather than live with the recriminations of an unforgiving father."

Tears shone in Solange's eyes. "Do you know what she was called?"

"Maryam," Rupert said softly.

"That's beautiful," Solange said.

The waiter arrived with the check. Rupert peered at it, then got out his wallet and gave the waiter several Birr notes, plus a generous tip. The waiter thanked him and left.

"You're so lucky to have been reared by parents who loved you. It doesn't matter what color they are," Solange told him.

"Oh, I know they loved me," Rupert told her. He rested his right elbow on the table and absently smoothed a brow as he continued. "They weren't very good at showing it, though. Demonstrative, I mean. They were scholars. The Peace Corps was a diversion for them. A test to see if they could survive outside of academia. I don't believe they ever considered having children until my mother brought me to them. Then it dawned on them that they could excel at something else—being parents. I became their next pet project. They used to have me quote Shakespeare when they had guests. I suppose I was quite the oddity, being the only black kid for blocks."

Solange was amazed by how closely his experiences as a child mirrored her own. Although her parents had been her biological ones, they were unable to express love for her. She was primed for excellence from birth. Her parents spoke French and English at home and she was expected to be proficient at both. A "B" on her report card was a calamity. Punishment was no TV for three months, and no going to the movies with her best pal, Gaea, which she loved to do every Saturday afternoon. She couldn't date until she turned eighteen. Her mother lived in fear that she would get pregnant before graduating high school, never guessing that she lost her virginity at seventeen to a jock who showed her a little affection. It was not something she was proud of. She'd learned a lesson—that sex and love do not go hand in hand.

"Did you resent them because of how they treated you?" Solange asked. She needed to know because she'd come to the conclusion a long time ago that the way you live your life is dependent upon how you react to what life throws at you. Will you grow stronger, or will you crumble? Will you moan and groan about the glass being half empty, or exult at it being half full?

"No, I figured they behaved the way they did due to conditioning. And I was always taught where I came from. I think they wanted me to have a sense of pride in my people and in myself because they knew they were helpless when it came to schooling me in a culture they naturally knew nothing about. We went to Guyana for a month once a year, where I played with children who looked like me. My first crush was on a girl I met at Strabroek Market. It's Guyana's main market and it's a gathering place. Even at night there are people hanging out there, listening to music. Teens, checking each other out. Old men playing dominoes and cards until the wee hours."

"Sounds great," Solange said, smiling. "Is it still there?"

"Yes, of course," Rupert said. "It's an enduring institution."

"I love the African and Caribbean markets," Solange said. "My parents are from Haiti. I don't know what happened to them there, but they never went back. I visited for the first time when I was twenty-five." She closed her eyes, remembering. Looking at Rupert again, she continued, "You read about a devastated nation in the newspapers. See footage of Haitian boat people. Yes, the country is destitute. It's been so long since the people have had a good government. But, you know what? The people themselves are not broken. I have never seen any people with more hope for the future. That's why I try to do all I can to help Haitian immigrants where I live. Some fellow professors and I have even set up a scholarship fund for deserving Haitian students. It's not much, but at least it's doing something. My parents have been completely Americanized. They don't even talk about their childhood in Haiti."

"They could have a reason for not wanting to talk about it," Rupert suggested.

"I'm their only child. They could at least tell *me*," Solange said, with a sad glimmer in her dark eyes. "They've never told me how they lived their lives prior to coming to the U.S. That's important to me. Whether we want to admit it or not, our parents' past impact our present. I guess that's why I have so much anger inside. Both are closemouthed on the subject. It's frustrating." Tears shone in her eyes for the second time that evening. "I need to know who my grandparents were. How they died. What they did for a living. But my parents are so secretive, I sometimes feel like they must have done something horrible in their past lives and that's why they don't talk about it."

Rupert reached for her right hand, brought it to his mouth and kissed the palm.

"Maybe the horrible thing was done to them," Rupert said. "I don't know my birth parents' histories either. It's the one thing I regret in life. I know I shouldn't let it bother me. I've created a pretty good life for myself. I love my adoptive parents. I love what I do for a living. Still, there's some part of me that's left unfulfilled. Until I know who my parents were, I believe my spirit will be restless."

"Yeah," Solange cried, smiling. "You've got it. That's exactly how I feel. And my mother doesn't understand when I try to explain my need to know where she came from, *who* she came from. She says that's her business. It's her life and she's not obliged to share it with anyone, not even her own daughter. Unfortunately that's my father's pat answer, too. Which is why I believe the two of them are hiding something."

She sighed. "Still, on the whole, I'm a happy person.

I love what I do for a living, I have great friends and I enjoy living in Miami."

Rupert regarded her with a contemplative smile. "I told you I wasn't seeing anyone when we were in Miami. How long has it been since you seriously dated anyone?"

Solange's smile slowly faded. That was her least favorite subject. Men were brief visitors in her life. If only Nick's stay had been even briefer. "My last relationship ended two years ago. Since then I've been wary. Nick didn't take it well when I broke up with him. He stalked me for a while. Would send dead flowers with sick notes attached. That sort of thing." She looked him straight in the eyes. "After that I didn't date much at all. None of them got past dinner."

"So, it's been a while," Rupert said softly, expecting that Solange would get his meaning. "It's been a while for me, too. I travel a lot. It isn't easy to get to know someone when you could fly out of town at a moment's notice. Plus, I have this quirk: I don't sleep with anyone I don't feel something for. And emotions only grow with time. Which is why I wanted us to spend some time together. I know I'm physically attracted to you. But I want more than that."

Solange tried not to let the astonishment she was feeling show on her face. A man who required an emotional connection before sleeping with someone. That was novel.

Inwardly, she breathed a sigh of relief. "I agree." She reached across the table and clasped his hand. "Shall we make a pact? We won't make love until both of us can no longer take it, and expressing how we feel about each other is not only a need, but a necessity."

Rupert gently squeezed her hand and smiled anew. "Deal."

They rose shortly afterward and, hand in hand, left the restaurant.

An Ethiopian gentleman in his late thirties glanced in their direction as they passed his table on the way out. He set his coffee cup down on its saucer, and followed the petite woman with his gaze. She was lovelier than he'd imagined she would be. Gault had neglected to tell him she was attractive. Not that it mattered. He had an assignment. Never, in the past twenty years, had he ever shirked his duties in the service of Theophilus Gault.

He lit a small cigar and pulled on it. Dr. DuPree and the unknown man she was with were long gone now. He was not concerned because he'd lost sight of them. The hotel clerk he'd bribed had told him they were spending the night there and, starting tomorrow, would be taking day-trips around the area. They were not giving up their rooms for three weeks. To his way of thinking that meant they would not be traveling too far afield. Following them would not be difficult.

Picking up his glass of port he swirled the liquid around in the glass before raising it to his lips and drinking what was left of it. His brown eyes sparkled with excitement. If he could get close to Dr. DuPree this assignment might not be as mind-numbing as he had first anticipated.

Three

"Lucy in the Sky with Diamonds," Solange sang, the Beatles song. She was named after that. She got as close to the large glass case as she could. The mummified bones she was looking at belonged to a hominid—a kind of half-human, half-ape creature that some believed was Darwin's missing link. Dubbed Lucy when it was found in a dried-up lake near Hadar in north-east Ethiopia, it was also known by the Ethiopian name, Denkenesh (*you are wonderful*).

"Lucy's discovery was significant because before that scientists figured mankind did not begin to walk until their brains evolved to a larger size. But with Lucy, who had a small brain, they learned that mankind stood and walked before developing a large brain. Though she was tiny, she was unmistakably human from her pelvis and her legs to her jaw, which was shaped much like our own jaws are today. Dissimilar to the box-like design of an ape's jaw."

Rupert stood smiling down at her. "Intriguing. I will have a minor degree in archaeology by the end of our time together."

He leaned closer to her. Solange was dressed in a pair of khakis and a long-sleeved white shirt. Ethiopians dressed conservatively, and visitors were looked upon as respectful if they did likewise. Rupert breathed in the scent of her hair, a flowery aroma reminiscent of honey-suckle.

He wished they were alone, but they were far from alone in the National Museum in Addis. Tour guides led tourists from exhibit to exhibit, explaining the significance of each one. Students were ushered through the museum by their teachers, with sharp instructions not to touch anything. To the left of them a little girl was kissing a glass case. The air was cool in the large, airy building. Marble floors abounded and one tended to speak in whispers because voices carried in the cavernous space.

Solange and Rupert had been in the museum for more than two hours. Solange could have stayed all day. "You know, I've heard that that's not the real Lucy, but a plaster cast. The real bones are kept elsewhere in the museum. I suppose the real bones are too valuable to be put on display. It's a darn good cast, though."

A boy of about twelve or thirteen brushed against her. The room was crowded, but not so crowded that he couldn't have passed her without contact. Solange felt his hand slip in and out of her back pants pocket. She reached out with lightning-quick reflexes and grabbed his thin wrist. "Hold it." She didn't have anything in her back pocket except a few Birr notes in small denominations that she planned to use for tipping. But she wasn't going to stand for being pick-pocketed without protesting.

The boy wore the traditional head wrap of the Muslim male. His dusky skin was as smooth as a baby's. He obviously hadn't hit puberty yet. The expression in his golden-brown eyes was indignant. "Ana mish fahem," he cried. *I don't understand.*

Seeing what was going on, Rupert grabbed the boy's arm, allowing Solange to let go of him. "Of course you don't understand," she said, as she pried his hand open and removed her pilfered Birr notes.

She peered up at Rupert. "Shall we move this outside?"

"Good idea," he said. To the boy he said, "Ismak eh?"

The boy had calmed down. If they were going to call security and have him tossed out, they would have done it already. He took them for softhearted foreigners. Foreigners felt guilty when they saw you begging on the street. They would either give you money or buy you a meal. He preferred the money. "Ismi, Tesfaye." His name really wasn't Tesfaye, but it was a common name and they would believe him. Lying was a minor sin compared to what he'd seen others do on the streets.

He didn't give the big man any trouble as he and the woman led him toward the front of the museum. But when they got to the entrance where the fee was taken, the man behind the glass window took one look at the boy and shrieked, "Thief!"

The boy would have bolted if Rupert hadn't been holding him with a firm grip. Instead, Solange approached the man and said in low tones, "What's the problem?"

Dressed in a dark blue blazer and dark trousers, the uniform of the museum, the man pointed at the boy. In halting English, he related his problem with the boy in accusing tones. "This is the seventh time he has used stealth to gain admittance. I am busy with a visitor and he slips past. I didn't even see him this time. He is slippery as a snake, that one." He narrowed his eyes at the boy. "A good beating is what he needs."

Solange handed the man the wadded up Birr notes she still held in her hand. "What if you take this and call him paid-up for all those times he came in without paying first?"

The man looked down at the notes, then back at the crazy foreigner. That amount of money would pay for cigarettes for an entire month. "Very well," he said gruffly. "But next time I see his face I shall call the authorities on him."

Solange thanked him and beckoned to Rupert, who pulled the boy after him. When Solange and Rupert's backs were turned, Tesfaye stuck his tongue out at the ticket seller. The man clenched his teeth in frustration and waved a fist at the boy, but didn't move from behind the glass enclosure.

Outside on the colonnade in front of the museum, Solange turned to Tesfaye. "Are you hungry?" she asked in English. "And don't tell me you don't understand English. If half of what that guy in there said is true, you're an old pro."

"I speak a little," Tesfaye hedged. He gave her a wary look. "What are you called, pretty lady?"

"Save the flattery," Solange said, squinting at him. "If Rupert lets go of you, will you run off or will you stay? We would like to discuss a business proposition with you."

Rupert looked puzzled. "We would?"

"We'd like to hire you as our guide. But only at a reasonable price. And only if you're not constantly trying to rip us off."

Tesfaye nodded in the affirmative. "I will not run away." He had them. They were more gullible than he'd first judged them to be if they thought he was a suitable guide. Sure, he knew this city like the back of his hand. He'd been born here and had lived on the streets ever since he was ten years old. He knew how to survive. It definitely wasn't by working as a guide for a mere pittance. Not when you could score big and not have to work nearly as hard. What was this crazy foreigner trying to do, convert him into a do-gooder? Do-gooders didn't survive long on these streets. They wound up dead in the gutter with no one to cry over them. He'd spent five years in the orphanage with little hope of being adopted. Social

Services had made a half-hearted effort to locate him. He used to see them in their conservative attire walking the streets hopefully presenting his photo, asking everyone if they'd seen him. The lower the people they questioned were on the socio-cconomic scale of the city, the less information their questions garnered. There was an unspoken code on the street: You didn't inform on a fellow street rat. It had been a long time since he'd seen anyone from Social Services looking for him.

Some of the children were made orphans by the AIDS epidemic. He'd heard there were 900,000 AIDS orphans in Ethiopia. That wasn't his story, though. His parents had been killed by soldiers along the Ethiopia-Eritrea border. He had been five years old at the time. The soldiers had spared him only because they figured he was too young to identify them. They were wrong. Their faces were indelibly etched in his memory. His older brother, the real Tesfaye, hadn't been so lucky. He was only nine years old. But they'd gunned him down as mercilessly as they had killed the children's parents. "Tesfaye" hadn't trusted another adult since that day. He'd been on the streets two years and had not met one adult whose behavior could inspire his trust.

He looked at the two he was presently with: one an American, judging from her accent, the other British. He'd expected the woman to be fawning over him by now, but instead she was frowning down at him while the man still held him firmly.

"Would you at least agree to talk about it over a meal?" she asked, her eyes cagey. He would have to watch her. Women were often more intuitive than men were and not as easily tricked when it came to listening to his sob stories, of which he had a healthy arsenal.

He had to think for a moment. Oh, yes, they'd offered him a job as their guide. He smiled at the thought. He'd lead them right into hell.

His stomach growled. "I agreed not to run," he reminded her sharply. He had to establish the fact that he was tough from the beginning. No one took advantage of him. And if she was looking for an apology for stealing her money, she would be sorely disappointed. She had been careless to put it in her back pocket.

The woman gave a nearly imperceptible nod to the man and he let go of Tesfaye. Tesfaye had been leaning away from the man and nearly toppled when he was let go so abruptly. But he righted himself without taking a tumble.

Standing up straight, he looked up at the woman who was only about three inches taller than he was. "I suppose you want me to 'guide' you to a restaurant now?"

Solange pursed her lips. The little con artist. He spoke English as well as she did.

"That won't be necessary," she said. With a glance in Rupert's direction, she said, "By the way, I'm called Solange and this is Rupert."

"I spotted a very nice-looking street-side cafe on the way here," she said, as they began walking down the brick-paved road. "Near the Piazza." The National Museum was east of the Piazza, which was in the center of many places to stay, eat, shop, and visit in Addis Ababa. "Tell me about yourself, Tesfaye," she said conversationally. "How old are you?"

"How old are *you?*" the boy parroted. He comfortably walked alongside her with his hands folded behind him. Rupert hung back, watching the two of them.

"I'm thirty-four," Solange answered easily. Age was just a number to her.

"That's old," Tesfaye said, stretching his eyes at the mention of such advanced years. "My mother wasn't that old when she . . ."

"Your mother?"

"She's twenty-seven, and very beautiful," he said, changing his story.

"Judging from her handsome son, I have no doubt she's lovely," Solange said sincerely.

"She is," Tesfaye vehemently cried. His voice faltered.

"Do you have any brothers or sisters?" Solange asked, changing the subject.

"Do you?"

"No. Sometimes I wish I did have several. But I'm an only child."

"So am I," Tesfaye said, with a crafty smile in her direction.

They were at a crosswalk, and waited while the traffic passed, then crossed the street with a hoard of other pedestrians. The day was clear and bright. If Solange didn't know better she would have thought she was walking down a street in the Miami business district. Addis Ababa was a thriving city with modern buildings, wide boulevards and traffic jams. On the other hand, those tall buildings sometimes stood next to historic churches built two or more centuries ago and palaces of past kings that were just as impressive on the outside today as they must have been when they were first built. The people were the same: ultra modern in some instances and throwbacks to another era in others. She saw men in dark business suits, men in shammas—white, light cotton togas oftentimes worn over slacks and a shirt. They were worn in both Ethiopia and the neighboring Eritrea.

Tesfaye was wearing a sort of modified shamma that came to the tops of his shoes, a battered pair of brown leather slippers.

They passed a woman sitting in the alley close to the street. Before her, spread on a blanket, were dried leaves. There were six men bending and picking through the leaves. They paid her, stuffed the leaves in a pouch they carried for that purpose, and sauntered down the street.

It was as easy as buying a pack of cigarettes, and probably not as deadly.

"You want some chat?" Tesfaye asked Solange. "It'll make you feel mellow."

Solange knew of the mildly intoxicating leaves. Chewing them was popular in Djibouti and Ethiopia but it was illegal in Eritrea, a predominately Muslim country.

"No, thanks, I'm feeling pretty mellow already," Solange said without a note of censure. To each his own. There were few ethnic groups, she'd learned in her career as an archaeologist, that didn't practice ways to dull or heighten their senses.

"How about tej?" Tesfaye asked. "Have you tried the honey wine yet? It's delicious."

Solange smiled. "You're interested in the job then?"

She'd paused in front of a street-side cafe. Tesfaye assumed this was the place she'd chosen for them to have a midday meal. He didn't want to miss the meal. "Trips outside the city will cost more. You pay for lodging."

Solange stuck out her hand.

He cautiously took it and they shook. "I reserve the right to quit anytime I wish."

"Of course," Solange agreed. "All free men have that right."

Later that evening, as Solange and Rupert walked back to the Sheraton, Rupert was surprisingly pensive. Solange was used to him leading the conversation. They'd had a full day of sightseeing, with Tesfaye on his best behavior.

They'd visited St. George Cathedral and Museum in the Piazza. St. George was Ethiopia's patron saint. Both Haile Selassie, Ethiopia's last emperor, and Empress Zewditu, the ruler before him, were crowned at the cathedral. Visitors could see the garments they wore during the coronations. Solange enjoyed the murals in St. George the most. Especially those of famed Ethiopian artist,

Afewerk Tekle. The mosaic of Christ with his arms out-stretched had taken her breath away.

"What do you think of going to the Merkato tomorrow?" Solange asked. "Maybe we can get an early start. I hear the place is a sight to see." The Merkato was the largest open-air market in eastern Africa.

"Oh, now you ask my opinion on something," Rupert said evenly.

Solange stopped walking to turn and look into his face. Others walked around them. "You don't want Tesfaye with us?"

Rupert grabbed her by the arm, turning her back around. "We can walk and talk at the same time. I'd like to get back to the hotel for a bath and a decent meal."

Solange resumed her pace. "Why didn't you speak up if you thought hiring Tesfaye was a bad idea? You didn't have to sit there like a bump on a log."

"That isn't the point. It's true. I don't trust the little bugger. I think he'd much prefer stealing than working. And he'll probably lead us to some secluded spot where his friends will pounce on us and leave us for dead. But that's still not the point."

"What *is* the point?" Solange asked impatiently.

"The point is, you and I are travelling together." Rupert calmly laid it out for her. "A decision like that should be made together. I would not presume to tell you what our itinerary will be, nor how much money to spend in the markets. Whom we hire to guide us, if indeed we need a guide, should be something we both agree on."

Solange nodded slowly. She was not dense, she knew she should have spoken with Rupert prior to making the offer to Tesfaye. She'd acted on impulse. She liked the boy. He was a little rough around the edges, but she supposed if she'd had to fend for herself at his young age, she would've grown a tough hide, too. "You're right," she softly admitted. "I apologize. But please don't nix the idea. I think we could all learn something from each other."

This time it was Rupert who paused in his steps. He gave her an astonished look. Then he smiled. "You're one of those bleeding-heart liberals I've heard about, aren't you?"

"Am not!" Solange cried, and punched him on the shoulder. "You take that back."

Rupert laughed heartily. Passing pedestrians peered at him as if he were ripe for the loony bin. "You are. I bet you take in stray kittens. Hand out your last dollar to beggars on the street. Are a regular contributor of food and clothing to homeless shelters. I'd be willing to wager that you've never passed a Santa Claus ringing his bell next to a Salvation Army kettle without dropping a few dollars inside. Am I right?"

Narrowing her eyes at him, Solange huffed, "So what if you are? What's wrong with being generous when we're blessed with so much?"

Rupert's smile faded. His tone was cold. "People like you get hurt. I know because I used to be just like you." With that he picked up his pace and Solange had to nearly run to keep up with him all the way back to the Sheraton.

It was dark when they arrived at the hotel. A small crowd was gathered around the singing fountain out front. The singing fountain effect was achieved by multicolored floodlights trained on jets of water while ethereal music floated on the night air. Tourists came from all over the city to witness it.

Solange stood there a few moments, composing herself. Rupert went ahead inside. She was glad to be out of his presence for a while. He could be overpowering when taken in large doses.

She hugged her bag close to her side, marveling at the rainbow-hued lights and the sounds of the water jets crashing into each other. The music was superfluous to her. The sound of running water always soothed her.

"Beautiful, isn't it?" a man's voice said close to her right ear.

She hadn't even noticed his approach. He was a few inches taller than she was and perhaps a few years older. His brown skin was pockmarked but his face was not unattractive. He smiled, revealing dimples in his cheeks. "My name is Danyael." She knew it was customary for Ethiopians to give their first names only upon meeting. Did that make Americans more suspicious, because they wanted the first name *and* the last name?

She returned his smile. "Solange."

"You are French?" He launched into rapid French, which Solange could barely follow. She spoke the language passably. But when someone spoke it too rapidly she got lost. Her parents would be ashamed of her ineptitude; they'd spoken it around the house with the express purpose that she grow up speaking it as well as they did. That had never happened.

"I'm American," Solange hastily informed Danyael. "And I'm late for an appointment. So, if you'll excuse me."

Danyael politely stepped aside. "Of course. Perhaps we will run into each other again. I'm staying here."

"Perhaps," Solange said, and beat a hasty retreat.

Rupert met her at the entrance. "I see you're becoming friendly with the natives."

Solange stuck her nose in the air and glided past him. "He was just a pleasant fellow who found the singing fountain as entertaining as I did."

They walked companionably toward the bank of elevators off the lobby.

"Oh, was that why you lingered? You were enjoying the view? I thought you were pouting because I accused you of being a softy."

"I don't pout, Mr. Giles. If I'm unhappy with you I'll tell you I'm unhappy with you. So, there. Are you always so disagreeable when you're tired and hungry?"

"Yes," Rupert immediately replied.

Solange laughed. "Well, at least you're honest."

Rupert smiled at her. "I've given it some thought. The boy stays. It's possible you'll feel more comfortable with a chaperone."

The elevator doors slid open with no one inside. They stepped onto the conveyance.

"Having the boy around is going to cut into my time," Rupert told her as he pulled her into his arms. "I think that's what upset me."

"Mmm," Solange said. That hadn't occurred to her. The purpose of this trip had been for them to get to know each other. Now they had a kid tagging along. She tiptoed and planted a kiss on his chin. "I acted on gut instinct. There's something about Tesfaye that intrigues me."

Rupert pressed her a bit closer to him. "I'm not intriguing enough for you, you have to invite trouble?"

"He was very well-behaved today," Solange reminded him.

"Even the most incorrigible of con artists can behave well for a day, if there's something in it for them."

The elevator stopped on their floor. Rupert allowed Solange to precede him and they walked down the carpeted hallway to their connecting rooms. Solange paused in front of her room door. Turning, she looked Rupert in the eyes. "If he tries anything, he's gone. But can we agree that if he conscientiously gives this job his best shot, we keep him on? At least for the excursions in and around Addis?"

"All right. Agreed," Rupert said rather reluctantly. He brightened. "Hey, maybe he'll be satisfied with your watch and we won't even see him tomorrow morning."

"What?" Solange felt her left wrist. The reliable Timex

with the brown leather band was gone. Her brows knit together in confusion. "How did he *do* that? I didn't feel a thing."

"You were too busy saving his thieving soul," Rupert said, smiling.

Solange sighed. She was too weary to give the loss of her watch much thought right now. After a bath and a good meal, she'd ponder what best to do about Tesfaye. If anything. Rupert was probably right: Tesfaye was a lost cause.

Rupert pulled her in his arms again for a sympathetic squeeze. She gave him a wan smile and gently pushed out of his embrace. Glancing down at her wrist out of habit, she looked over at him hopefully, "What time do you have?"

Rupert went to consult his watch, and realized his timepiece was gone as well. "I'll skin the little pickpocket," he fumed, blowing air between full lips and turning to look around them as if he expected Tesfaye to come walking down the hallway at any moment. An intense frown made lines appear on his forehead.

Solange laughed and handed him his watch. "To prove we weren't 'mommy's girls' my friend, Gaea, and I ran with a rough crowd in high school. Thank God we both learned that what others think of you isn't nearly as important as what you think of yourself before we got a record. Still want to get to know me better? After all, I have a criminal past." She didn't pause for his answer. "I don't know what happened to make you so cynical. Maybe you'll tell me about it over dinner tonight. Or maybe you'll think twice about our stay here in Ethiopia. Maybe it wasn't such a good idea. I am an unknown quotient in your well-ordered calculations on life. Beware. I have other things I have yet to reveal to you. I have not led a neat, uncomplicated life. I am not innocent, and you can't mold me into someone you will feel more comfortable with. I'm liable to do anything, and say anything."

Rupert pulled her roughly into his arms and kissed her soundly. When they parted he gazed down into her upturned face. "Meet me downstairs in thirty minutes. And don't be late."

With that he turned and went to his own room next door.

Solange unlocked her door and slipped inside. She leaned against the door for a few minutes, dropped her bag on a nearby chair, then ran and launched herself onto the bed, laughing. Rupert Giles was proving to be a worthy sparring partner. She liked that in a man.

Four

"You look beautiful," Rupert said a few minutes later, as he and Solange approached each other in the lobby. Solange smiled warmly. She had on the remaining dress she'd brought with her: a black tube dress that you could scrunch up or pull down, depending on where you wanted the hem. It traveled well. All she had to do was roll it into a tight ball, and shake it out and hang it up once she arrived at her destination.

The dress had a square neck that plunged, but not too deeply. It had long sleeves that fell past the wrists, onto the tops of the hands. Trendy, with classic lines. It was the little black dress for the twenty-first-century woman.

She wore her short hair slicked back and had applied a crimson lipstick. In her ear lobes were the only diamond earrings she owned, one-carat studs. Her shoes were pumps with three-inch heels and pointed toes. They were not made for walking or dancing. She'd done both in them and had lived to regret it.

"Good, you brought your wrap," Rupert said, as he directed her toward the hotel's exit with a gentle but persistent hand at the small of her back. "The concierge suggested The Hard Luck Café as a place to get a good burger. Are you game?"

A grilled burger sounded good to Solange about now, so she nodded her acquiescence. "I could go for a burger as long as it's cooked through to the center."

Several taxis waited at the curb at the Sheraton. A driver jumped from behind the wheel of one of the mid-size cars and held the door open for them. "Where to, sir?"

"Do you know The Hard Luck Café on Bole Road?" Rupert asked.

"Yes, of course. It's a short drive from here," replied the middle-aged man.

Solange got in the back and slid over. Rupert got in after her and the driver closed the door, then trotted around the front of the car and got in. "A most beautiful evening," he said in heavily accented English. Then he fell silent, pulled away from the curb and turned his attention to his driving.

The cab was clean and had a faintly spicy scent, as if the driver had been burning cinnamon incense inside. The windows were up to guard against the chilly night air. The temperature was presently around forty-five but was expected to dip below freezing before morning.

Rupert put his arm about Solange's shoulders, drawing her close to his side. "Are you warm enough? That wrap looks thin to me."

He was dressed in black slacks, a long-sleeve deep brown silk shirt, a rich cocoa-hued leather jacket and black leather boots. Impeccable as always, but extremely fly. He removed his jacket. "Here, put this on."

Solange was glad to take it. "I feel so foolish," she said, as she draped the jacket about her shoulders. "I should have worn my coat, but it didn't go with the dress."

Rupert smiled as he pulled her close again. "I'm flattered that you risked frostbite for me." He bent his head and briefly kissed her cheek close to her mouth. His breath was warm on her skin. Solange turned her head to the right and their mouths met. Their breath mingled as she said, "I believe they frown on public displays of affection."

Rupert promptly pulled the jacket up over both their heads, thereby obscuring the driver's view of them in the backseat. With her lips on his mouth Solange felt his muscles form a smile, rather than saw it. "We're alone now," he said, before fully covering her mouth with his in a slow, passion-filled kiss.

If kissing were an art, Rupert would be a master. He knew not to rush the act, but to hold off, not to press too firmly down, but to increase the pressure only when she indicated she wanted more. His tongue did not plunder, but enticed.

Solange had never been this near to swooning in her entire life. In fact, she'd always been a complete skeptic when other women told her a man's kiss could render them weak and helpless to resist. Until she met Rupert Giles.

Rupert was no less affected. He prided himself on being somewhat of an expert on kissing. Women were not inanimate objects with no feelings. You had to approach them with gentleness and finesse, allowing them to lead you. It was his opinion that a man could get turned on more easily and with less stimuli than a woman. Therefore it was unwise for a man to try to lead in this situation. He would reach his goals much quicker and with less drama if he simply played it cool and observed her actions.

Solange moaned softly and deepened the kiss. Rupert's right hand was holding the jacket up. His left was cupping her shapely bottom. Soon, Solange was sitting on his lap and atop a prodigious erection, felt through his slacks. She broke off the kiss.

"Maybe we should tell him to take us back to the Sheraton," she said breathlessly.

Rupert firmly took her by the arms and deposited her

on the seat next to him. Solange smiled knowingly and placed his jacket in his lap.

"Thank you," Rupert said.

"You're welcome."

They sat apart the remainder of the ride to The Hard Luck Café.

"Oh, no," Rupert said, shaking his head as they entered The Hard Luck Café.

The music was pumped up to an ear-splitting volume. Young bodies writhed together to the funky beat. The language of the singer was unidentifiable due to the screeching of the dancers who were being led by the disc jockey, a person of unknown gender with a bald head and an excessively made-up face. His/her bright pink jumpsuit was in direct competition with the flashing colored lights when it came to migraine-producing potential.

"Scream!" the DJ encouraged.

"This is not my style." Rupert had to yell to be heard over the pandemonium.

"Looks like fun," Solange yelled back, surprising him. She took his hand. "Come on, every song can't be this loud."

Rupert wanted to be able to talk over dinner. At this rate, they'd be yelling at each other all evening. But if the lady wanted to observe the youth of Addis Ababa in a frenzy, then so be it.

Luckily, the dance floor was somewhat removed from the tables. He looked around wondering if they had to wait to be seated, saw no sign that this was indicated, and led Solange to a table as far away from the dance floor as he could get.

Across the room, seated at a table with five of her newfound friends, Samantha Gault quickly crouched be-

hind the guy with the broadest shoulders when she saw
a man with her father's build enter the restaurant.

The guy, Christian he'd said his name was, turned and
looked at her with a quizzical expression on his good-
looking face. "What is the matter? Did you lose an ear-
ring?"

"Yes," Samantha said. She felt around on the floor as
if she were indeed looking for lost jewelry. Christian
joined her on the floor. He smiled at her. "Are all American girls as dotty as you are?" He smiled. "Neither of
your earrings is missing."

Samantha touched both ear lobes. She grinned
sheepishly and slowly rose. "I guess I've had too much
tej, huh?"

Christian pulled out her chair for her, and sat down
next to her. Leaning close to her in order to be heard, he
said, "You want to tell me what's going on?"

He was an engineering student at Addis Ababa University. His father was an engineer as well. His mother
taught at a local church school. Many well-off Ethiopians
go abroad when seeking a college education, the majority
returning to work in a civil service job. He'd chosen to
stay in Addis but he wished to live in America one day.
Meeting Samantha Gault, who was a recent graduate of
Howard University in Washington, D.C., could be a
stroke of good luck for him.

"I thought I saw my father come in a second ago."

"Ah," said Christian. "How would your father know
you're here?" he asked reasonably.

"He has his ways," Samantha said. Her eyes darted
about the room, but she was calmer now. If that had indeed been her father who had come in with a beautiful
woman on his arm, he would have been seeking her out
right now. She could imagine him going from table to
table, looking into the startled brown faces of all the
young women present.

Her father was still a handsome man at fifty-six. Tall, imposing, physically conditioned from pumping iron and jogging. The man was more disciplined than anyone she'd ever known. Though he was handsome, his hawk-eyes, a caramel brown with dark centers, could be cutting when he wished them to be. He'd struck fear in many hearts with just a look. Including her own.

He loved her, and she knew it. As an only child, that love could sometimes be a bit much though. Because he loved her so much, he was always fearful of some calamity befalling her. Samantha supposed her mother's death had something to do with that. He had become more controlling since her mother succumbed to the effects of a burst aneurysm three years ago. It had all been so sudden and cruel. Francesca, called Frannie by her doting husband, had been thirty-nine when she died.

Samantha sat up straighter in her chair and smiled at Christian. "You're right. He'd never find me here." She rose. "Excuse me for a moment, would you?"

Christian rose, as any gentleman would. "Of course."

He watched her as she walked away swinging her small purse, a tall shapely girl in jeans, a plush hooded pullover in shocking red, and stacked boots. He didn't know any local girls who had such panache. He was already half in love with her.

Samantha made her way across the room, heading in the general direction of the ladies' room. The DJ had taken a break, and the song playing now was Mary J. Blige's "All That I Can Say." She smiled at the thought of the hip-hop diva's music being played in a dive in Addis Ababa. It was a small world.

She paused to watch the couple who'd just come in get up to dance to Mary's upbeat tune. The man was nearly a dead-ringer for her father in his youth. Theophilus Gault was perhaps a shade darker than the anonymous brother, but the resemblance was uncanny. He had good moves for a big man. His companion, a petite beauty, seemed a more seasoned dancer. She was enjoying herself, throwing her hips as adeptly as a belly dancer. They were good together. They must be lovers. Her mother used to jokingly say that if a man was a good dancer, he was usually a good, lover, too. Her father would have had a conniption fit if he'd known how candid her mother had been with her about sex. He wanted to keep her as far away from the dreaded subject as possible.

Reluctantly moving her gaze from the couple, Samantha continued across the room toward the back of the building, where she'd seen the sign denoting the facilities. She let out a soft groan as she turned the corner. The line in front of the ladies' room door was even longer than usual.

While Samantha was standing in line, the cell phone in her purse rang.

She let it ring.

"This is really good," Solange said after biting into her burger, relishing the freshly barbecued taste, and swallowing. No American accoutrements like lettuce, tomato, or mayonnaise. This burger was half an inch thick. The bun wasn't exactly a bun, just two slices of homemade bread that had been buttered and toasted. The only condiment was awasi, a kind of mustard sauce, slathered all over the top of the beef burger. Solange had cut hers in half to make certain the meat was cooked through. There was the slight possibility of picking up a parasite from uncooked meat. She did not wish to get sick so far from home.

"Have you noticed," Rupert said after swallowing, "that no matter where you find black folks the world over, they all love to eat grilled meat?"

Solange laughed shortly. "And consider themselves pros at cooking it. Everybody's uncle has a secret sauce."

"Every neighborhood has a place where you can buy barbecued meats, whether it's a shack thrown together with plywood and grass on an impoverished island somewhere, or a beautifully appointed restaurant in New Orleans, Louisiana."

"You've been there?" Solange asked.

"A few times, on business," Rupert answered.

"It would probably be less of a chore for you to tell me where you *haven't* been," Solange said, referring to his globetrotting.

"Antarctica," Rupert said with an enigmatic smile.

Solange sat watching him. Half the time she couldn't tell whether he was telling the truth or pulling her leg. At any rate, the man was eye candy. From those gorgeous light brown eyes in that dark chestnut-colored face, to his strong chin with the dimple in it. His hands were what got to her, though. Big, masculine hands. Long fingers. She loved it when he touched her. He simply didn't do it enough. Perhaps his non-demonstrative adoptive parents' attitude had rubbed off on him. She hoped not because if there was one thing she liked it was being touched, and often.

They finished their burgers in silence; the only forms of communication that passed between them were glances and smiles. Thankfully the DJ had toned down his/her repertoire, playing both western music and Ethiopian fare that was more conducive to diners keeping their food down. At the moment, an Enrique Iglesias song was being piped through the sound system.

Solange rose when her plate was empty. "Excuse me, I need to find the ladies' room."

"I believe it's in the back near the double doors that lead into the kitchen," Rupert said, rising too. He helped her with her chair and then sat back down. He knew exactly where the restrooms were because he made a point of checking the layout of every building he entered. It was a wise thing to do when you might need to exit quickly. Not that he expected to have to do that tonight. It was difficult to break out of the habit when you were on vacation.

Vacation. He hadn't been on a real vacation since he started with the firm. He supposed that those who didn't travel much might envy him his schedule of hopping one plane after another for destinations deemed exotic by most standards. But he was becoming weary of all the traveling. He enjoyed the investigative aspects of his job, but he would have liked to be able to go home every night. Perhaps to a petite woman with mocha-colored skin and brilliant brown eyes, a warm smile, and open arms.

He was daydreaming about Solange meeting him at the door when a feminine voice said, "Would you dance with me?"

She was tall, and in her early twenties, if that. He rose. "It's kind of you to ask, but I'm with someone."

"I know. I've been waiting all evening for her to go to the ladies' room. I figured if I was patient her bladder would speak up sooner or later."

Rupert considered himself too old to be flattered by her attention. He was nearly forty, whereas she was just out of the cradle as far as he was concerned. He liked her attitude, though.

"It's just that you're the tallest man in here," she continued, undaunted. "And as you can see, I'm probably the tallest woman. We tall folks have to stick together."

Rupert gave in. The song playing was by Shakira. It was upbeat and had a Middle Eastern rhythm ideal for jumping around the dance floor. If Solange came back from the ladies' room before the song ended, at least he wouldn't be caught with a beautiful woman in his arms.

"All right," he said. "But take it easy on me, I'm an old guy."

"Fabulous. I'm Samantha Gault from the good old U.S.A."

"Rupert Giles, from the U.K."

Samantha laughed as they began grooving to the music. Tilting her head back, a movement that made her long auburn hair cascade down her back, she said, "It's okay if you don't want to tell me your real name."

"That *is* my real name," Rupert assured her.

"Come on, I watch Buffy and pals every Tuesday night."

"I don't know to what you're referring," Rupert said, straight-faced.

Samantha frowned but continued dancing. "I gather you don't watch much TV."

It was true. He owned a set but rarely switched it on except for the occasional rugby match or to catch the late news. "You would be right."

"Okay, see," Samantha explained. "You have the same name as a character on a show about a white chick who was born a vampire slayer. Rupert Giles, on the show, is her watcher. You know, the dude who trains her."

"Vampires?" Rupert said. "Who would watch a show with such a ludicrous premise?"

"Millions of people," Samantha said with a laugh. "It's a fun show. Doesn't take itself too seriously, fast-paced, and Buffy kicks butt on a regular basis. That's very empowering for women to watch, you know? Seeing a woman who can defend herself and who doesn't rely on a man to rescue her at every turn. That's very cool."

Samantha felt a tap on her shoulder. She turned to find Solange smiling at her.

"Would you mind if I cut in?" Solange politely asked.

"Not at all," Samantha said with a genuine smile. She

bent close to Solange's ear. "Where did you find him? He's to die for."

"I didn't find him, he found me," Solange said as she walked into Rupert's open arms.

"Lucky girl," Samantha tossed over her shoulder as she left the dance floor.

"I can't leave you alone for five minutes," Solange joked when she felt Rupert's arms move snugly around her waist. She laid her head on his shoulder.

Rupert blushed. "She's a child."

"That was no child. That was a woman." She looked him in the eyes. "A woman with impeccable taste in men," she added with a mischievous grin.

Rupert smiled and bent his head to reward her with a kiss for being so understanding.

It was after one in the morning by the time they got back to the Sheraton. Rupert took Solange's key and unlocked her door for her. Placing the key in her palm, he said, "I really hate to say good night. It's been a wonderful day."

"Even with my hiring Tesfaye and getting my watch stolen?"

Rupert smiled. "Life with you, so far, is definitely not boring."

Solange took off his jacket and handed it to him. "Thanks for the loan. It has your fragrance on it, a combination of your cologne and you. It was a strangely erotic experience wearing it."

"Will you always talk to me like that?" Rupert asked sincerely. He held the jacket in his left hand and gently traced Solange's jawline with the other. "Will you always truthfully tell me how you feel about me?" His tone was serious all of a sudden.

Solange moved closer until her thigh was touching his. She was tired after a long day. But the weariness had given her a mellow feeling, almost like being intoxicated.

Or perhaps it was being in Rupert's presence all day. They had learned things about each other that it took some couples months to learn. He was not perfect. He could be short and irritable when things didn't go his way. As petulant as a spoiled child. She wasn't perfect either. She made snap decisions that had the potential of coming back to bite her in the can. She led with her heart. He liked to observe before committing himself.

She looked into his eyes. "I wish I could promise you I'll always be honest with you. But we both know I'd be lying if I did."

"Give me one reason why you'd lie to me," he said, his gaze intense.

"I'd lie to you if I knew the truth would hurt you," Solange said without hesitation. "And that's the truth. I rarely lie for any other reason."

"I'd rather hear the truth," Rupert said. He sighed and straightened up. "I'm a big boy. You don't have to lie to me to protect my feelings. Lauren did that and it ruined everything."

"Lauren?"

"The reason I'm cynical," he reminded her. "Earlier you wanted me to tell you why I tend not to wear my heart on my sleeve. It's because of her."

"Mmm, I see," Solange said, her hand on the door-knob. "Can we move this conversation inside? It's getting very interesting and I'd like to get out of these shoes. They're killing my feet."

Rupert peered down at her feet and snorted. "Why do women wear such instruments of torture?"

"Because they make men's eyes bug out," Solange said with a sexy grin. She opened the door and went inside. Rupert followed.

"Your legs are lovely without the lifts," Rupert informed her as he closed and locked the door behind them. "So don't wear them for my benefit."

Solange was already sitting on the bed removing the offending pumps. "Ah," she softly moaned, "that's better."

Rupert deposited his jacket on a nearby chair and joined her on the bed. "Let me have them," he said.

"My fect?" She was ticklish and didn't allow just anybody near her feet.

"Yes, my dear, your feet. I'll massage them for you."

For a moment, she was tempted. When Rupert had said *I'll massage them for you* in his British-accented voice, she'd had a vision of his doing a lot more than massaging her feet. It was entirely unfair that he could make a phrase as innocuous as *I'll massage them for you* sound sexy as all get out.

She rose and wiggled her toes in the carpeting. "Thanks for the offer, but they're feeling better already."

Rupert rose and before Solange realized what he had in mind, he'd swept her into his arms and dropped her, bottom first, onto the bed. "Now you've got me curious," he said with a squint in his eye. "Why don't you want me to see your feet? Take those tights off. I've got to see your feet. What? Do you have webbed feet? Hammer toes? Fungus growing on them? Do they smell?"

Solange wasn't going to sit still while her feet were being maligned. He tried to grab her by the ankles and she kicked at him long enough to give her time to scoot over to the other side of the bed and stand up again. "No, no, no, and no," she said of his libelous assertions. "There is nothing the matter with my feet. I just don't want you to massage them, that's all."

Rupert calmly removed his own boots and set them aside. Straightening back up he regarded her with a steely gaze. "I shall not rest until I touch those piggies."

He slowly walked toward her, trying to assess where she'd try to seek refuge—the bathroom, or would she be desperate enough to try to make it out the door?

Solange, on the other side of the bed, feinted to the left. When Rupert lunged in that direction she quickly went to the right and around the bed. She had a clear path to the bathroom and went for it.

Rupert, however, was twelve inches taller and a seasoned athlete. By the time she'd taken six steps he had imprisoned her in his strong arms and lifted her one hundred and thirty pounds up and across his left shoulder.

He firmly held her legs together in a steel-like vise. Solange pummeled his back with her hands. "Put me down, you foot fetishist."

"I'm going to put you down," Rupert said calmly.

He gently placed her on the bed and pinned her to it with his body weight. With their faces only inches apart, he said, "Come on, we all have little imperfections. So what if your toes are ugly."

"Ugly?" Solange cried, indignant. "Get off me, you big lummox, and I'll prove to you that I have perfectly normal feet."

"You won't run again?" Rupert asked cautiously.

"You'll just have to trust me."

Rupert pushed himself up with both arms and rose. He stood a few feet away from her as Solange carefully raised the hem of her dress, revealing the fact that her "tights" as he had referred to them, were actually a pair of stockings.

Pointing to a spot across the room, she said, "I want you to stand over there."

Rupert obediently went to stand six feet away from her.

Satisfied, Solange placed one well-shaped leg on the bed and, beginning at the top of her thigh, slowly rolled down one stocking and removed it, then switched legs and removed the other one. This done, she sat primly on the bed and crossed her bare legs.

"You may approach," Solange said, with mock disdain. He owed her an apology.

Rupert did so, his eyes drawn to her small brown feet. They were exquisitely formed, as far as he could tell. Her toes were not overly long, nor too short. The nails were even and obviously well cared for. Apparently she didn't go in for nail polish. They were unpainted, neatly filed to a smooth finish, and had healthy white tips as if she'd had them professionally done. He raised his eyes to hers. Solange pursed her lips and raised her brows, waiting for an apology.

"Well?" she said. "No hammer toes, no smelly feet, no fungus among us."

She went as far as to wiggle her toes seductively in his direction, taunting him.

Rupert stood there chewing on his bottom lip, thinking. If there was nothing physically wrong with her feet, why had she been so reluctant to allow him to touch them? Unless . . .

"You're ticklish," he announced with some satisfaction. A smile formed at the corners of his mouth and rapidly spread across his handsome face.

Solange's eyes widened in horror when she heard the dreaded "t" word. Unfortunately, that was a dead giveaway. Rupert knew then that he'd guessed correctly.

She got up and sprinted for the bathroom.

Rupert easily caught her as she tried to pass him. "Come now, sweetness, I would not do anything to you that doesn't give you pleasure. I'm a British gentleman. We don't get off on that kind of thing. Your tootsies are safe with me." He held her securely with her back to his chest. "Calm down," he murmured softly.

Solange breathed a sigh of relief and relaxed in his embrace. Turning in the circle of his arms, she looked lovingly into his eyes. "Thank you, Rupert. You don't know what I've been through. Nick used to tickle me until I was nearly in tears. It was later in the relationship that I learned he had a cruel streak."

"I am tempted," Rupert confessed, his eyes sweeping over her face, "Just to hear you laugh. You have a delightful laugh. But if you derive no pleasure from it, neither do I. There are more pleasurable things we can do together."

"The reason you came in got lost in that silliness," Solange said as she turned out of his embrace and took a step backward. "You were going to tell me about Lauren."

His eyes instantly took on a sad aspect.

Solange quickly said, "I'll understand if you'd rather not talk about it."

"It's all right. It's been more than two years since Lauren and I went our separate ways." He walked over to the window and gazed down at the city. Although the skyline didn't rival London's, the lights were quite magnificent to behold.

Solange didn't join him at the window, but sat on the bed with her feet curled under her. She watched his back stiffen. Apparently, talking about Lauren was difficult for him to do. It took a great deal of willpower not to go to him, throw her arms around his neck, and insist that he not put himself through the pain of remembering.

A full two minutes passed before he spoke again. "She's the only woman whose hand I ever asked for. I did it the right way, too. Went to her father and asked his permission. Of course, her father was happy to oblige. He and his wife were immigrants from Suriname. Lauren had been born in London, and she was an only child. They understandably wanted to make a good match for her. As far as they were concerned, I was perfect for her. Plans for the wedding were implemented quite swiftly. Then came the day the parents of the bride and groom were to meet for the first time. As I've told you, my parents are not demonstrative people. They are very conservative. A high old time to them is tea at the Ritz and a matinee afterwards. However, they had met Lauren and thought highly of her. They were especially happy for me because I'd never before brought a girl home to meet them. They later told me that they were beginning to think I was ashamed of them. But I've never been ashamed of them, Solange. It sometimes felt awkward introducing them as my parents at Parents' Day when I was in school. However, that was because I was the only black child with white parents and we rather stood out. When you're a child, the worst thing you can do at school is to be different. And, boy, was I different."

He turned back around and smiled at her. He momentarily lost his train of thought when he saw her sitting on her haunches on the bed, a look of utter interest in her brown eyes. She was truly listening to every word he said.

This knowledge made him a little self-conscious, as if he had to suddenly weigh his words more carefully. Then he caught himself. They had agreed to be honest with each other. He'd speak from his heart.

He walked toward her as he continued, "My mother, Helena is her name, spent the better part of a day preparing tea for Lauren and her parents. Let me preface this by saying Lauren's parents and my parents had this in common: they were all modest people who lived well within their means and were not impressed with one's station in life. However, there are experiences that people are exposed to in everyday living that predisposes them to a certain way of thinking. When my mother opened the door that day, Lauren's parents' faces went ashen underneath their brown skin. My mother could have been a ghost or some vile creature from the pits of hell from the look on their faces. You see, Lauren had not told them my parents were white. And Lauren's parents had been

servants in a house owned by a white British family before they came to England. They had been treated badly
by this family. Too polite to say anything, Lauren's parents went through the motions of having tea with us that
afternoon. They barely consumed a thing. I learned later
that they had been too upset to eat. My mother, who is
sensitive in that way, noticed how uncomfortable her
guests were and bent over backwards, offering one thing
after another when her cakes and her cucumber sandwiches went untouched. I could tell she was mortified.
My father, Benjamin is his name, is the type who makes
the best of a situation. He went on chattering about anything and everything. What a brilliant student I'd always
been at school. How I excelled in sports, all things any
father would say about a son. Two hours into the visit,
Lauren's poor father could take it no longer. He uttered
something in Hindi, which I could not translate for my
confused parents, but to which Lauren replied, 'I couldn't
tell you. You would not have found him suitable. I'm a
grown woman, I should be able to choose my own husband.' Her father said something else in Hindi whereupon
both he and his wife got up, bowed to my parents and
myself, and strode out of the house. The next day, Lauren
returned my ring saying she couldn't marry me. She
wished me well, but if she married me against her parents' wishes they would disown her."

"How old was Lauren?" Solange asked as she swung
her legs from beneath her and got to her feet. Rupert had
stopped at the foot of the bed. She went to him and gently
took his right hand in hers.

"Well past the age of consent. At the time, Lauren was
a thirty-year-old physician with residency at a respected
London hospital. Yet the ties that bound her to her parents
were stronger than the ones that bound her to me. To her
way of thinking, if she'd told them my adoptive parents
were white from the beginning, they would have disap-

proved of me right off the bat. She had hoped that after they learned to love me, the color of my adoptive parents' skin would not matter. She didn't know the deep-seated resentment her parents had for white people. She didn't know how terribly they'd been treated all those years ago in Suriname at the hands of hateful whites. Did they hate all whites? I don't think so. However, they certainly couldn't abide them in the family."

Solange put her arms around him and held him tightly. She felt the thump of his heart against her ear. Heard the muffled sound. It would be so easy to fall in love with this man. He was strong yet gentle. Kind in many ways. Honest even when it made him look bad.

"Do you love her still?" she asked against his chest.

"Once I love someone I don't stop loving them. She was a victim of her own fears. I don't blame her for what she did. I don't hold any grudges because she gave me up with such apparent ease. How do I know what she was feeling when she gave my ring back?" He looked her straight in the eyes. "I have accepted that we were not meant to be together, and my passion for her has waned. I still care for her, though, and wish her only happiness."

"Stay with me tonight," Solange said in a voice barely above a whisper. "What I mean is, when I'm really keyed-up like I am tonight, I sometimes have a difficult time drifting off to sleep."

"Ah," Rupert said, as what she was getting at dawned on him. "You'd like me to stay until you fall asleep."

"Would you mind?"

He smiled slowly and bent his head to kiss her between her brows. "Not at all."

Solange smiled her thanks and turned and hurried into the closet, where she quickly pulled the little black dress over her head, hung it up, and rummaged in the lingerie drawer in the closet for a moment. Good thing she'd brought the sole pair of pajamas she owned. They were electric blue and had yellow lightning bolts on them.

When she returned to the bedroom Rupert had removed his long-sleeve silk shirt, revealing a white T-shirt underneath. Solange had known he was in good shape. She'd felt his muscles rippling whenever he held her in his arms. That was nothing compared to seeing his arm, chest, and stomach muscles up close and personal, though. She tried not to stare as she walked over to the bed and turned down the covers.

Rupert was busy folding his shirt and laying it across one of the chairs in the room. That done, he unbuckled the belt at his waist and unzipped his slacks. "Is it all right if I get down to my skivvies? They're not too brief. I'm a boxers man."

Boxers, Solange thought. *They're no more revealing than a pair of shorts.* "I want you to be comfortable," she said, and sat on the edge of the bed to watch.

Rupert finished unzipping his slacks, pulled them down, and stepped out of them.

Solange had earlier joked with him about women wearing high heels because it made men's eyes bug out. It was her turn to catch her eyeballs before they fell out of her head. Rupert's legs were long and muscular, the calves large and beautifully shaped, obviously from running. The thigh muscles bulged, the veins sticking out in all the right places. The man was beautiful all over. Well, she hadn't seen him entirely naked. But what she had seen was definitely worth gawking at.

He'd taken off his socks while she was changing and she couldn't help glancing down at his feet to see if they were as gorgeous as the rest of him. He was six-feet-four. His feet suited his body. They were big and masculine. Brown like the rest of him. They didn't appear as if he wore socks continually and never allowed his feet to see the light of day. His nails were clean and neatly trimmed.

No razor-sharp toenail attacks in the middle of the night. She smiled at that.

Rupert caught her smiling at his feet. "What?" he asked, curious.

"You have nice feet."

"And they're not ticklish. You can rub them all you like."

"Maybe later," she said, rising. "I'm going to wash my face and brush my teeth. I have an extra toothbrush if you'd like to brush."

"I would, thanks," Rupert said, and followed her into the bathroom.

Solange immediately went to the medicine cabinet, got the extra toothbrush, and handed it to him. Then she grabbed a tissue and began removing her lipstick.

"This is a pleasure for me," Rupert said as he spread toothpaste on his toothbrush. "I've never actually seen a woman remove her makeup before."

Solange glanced at him by looking at his reflection in the mirror. "Then pay close attention." She went over her lips once again with the tissue. "Voila! I'm done. Now all I do is wash my face with soap and water."

"What about all that gook you see advertised on TV? Foundation, mascara, blush, all sorts of concealers?" Rupert asked, confused.

"Powder and foundation make my skin look chalky and unnatural. I just go natural. I never needed mascara because my lashes are already very dark, long, and curly. But don't get me wrong, should I ever think I need makeup to look my best I'd be the first one in line at the makeup counter at Belk's."

"Belk's?"

"It's a popular department store in Florida."

"I see," said Rupert.

Solange reached into the medicine cabinet and got the

dental floss. She unwound a long strip and tore it off. "Do you floss before or after?"

"Before," he said, taking the floss and following her example.

They stood there flossing at the sink.

Finished, Rupert began brushing while Solange spread the Colgate on her toothbrush. She kept stealing glances at the way his biceps moved each time he ran the brush's bristles over his strong, white teeth. She had it bad if he was turning her on while brushing his teeth. It was such a mundane routine. She'd never thought watching Nick brush was particularly erotic. She must be horny. In which case having Rupert sleep over might not be such a bright idea.

Rupert was finished brushing and gargling by the time Solange remembered she was supposed to be brushing her teeth. She'd been in a time warp while watching him. Rupert splashed warm water on his face and dried off with a spare hand towel. He grinned at her. "I feel much refreshed, thank you."

Solange paused with the loaded toothbrush in the air. A toothbrush that had yet to enter her mouth. "Your teeth are perfect, too. Is there anything on you that isn't perfect?"

"I'll show you something on me that isn't at all perfect when you come to bed, little girl," he said cryptically, and left her alone in the bathroom.

Solange brushed with vigor and hastened to wash her face and run a brush through her hair. She looked at her reflection in the mirror. Bared her teeth. They were not perfect. They were too short, but they were definitely clean.

She did not consider herself beautiful. She had a widow's peak that gave her a sophisticated appearance, even when she didn't feel the least bit refined. Her face was heart-shaped, as were her lips. High cheekbones accentuated her wide, deep set brown eyes. No, it wasn't a beautiful face, but it was distinct. Unusual. And she liked it, which was what counted.

"Here I come," she said as she ran and jumped onto Rupert who had been minding his own business going through the boob tube guide the hotel provided to their guests. There was no HBO or Showtime, but there was a DVD player and a list of DVDs from which the guests could choose. All they had to do was phone the desk and someone would bring them the movie they'd chosen—for a price.

Rupert, who wasn't much of a TV watcher, would never go to all that trouble just to watch a film. He threw the magazine onto the nightstand next to the bed and grabbed hold of Solange. She had apparently gotten her second wind. He saw by the expression in her eyes that she was in a playful mood.

He fell back against the pile of pillows at the head of the bed with Solange on top of him. She was such a tiny thing that her weight on his chest was not uncomfortable.

Solange thought she was too heavy for him, though, and slid down onto the bed on his left side. They were facing each other. His right hand lay on the indentation of her waist. "You're my first," Solange joked.

"The first man you've ever gone to bed with without being intimate?"

"The night isn't over yet, but yes," she joked again.

"I can see you like word games. What if I show you another type of game?"

"I love to learn," she told him with a flirty smile.

"All right. The name of my game is Find the Wound."

Her expression went from playful, to surprised, to intrigued. Rupert took her left hand and placed it on his chest. "The object of the game is to find the places on my body that are not smooth. Those jagged places that should not be there."

Solange was silent for a moment. "Okay," she softly said.

"Close your eyes," Rupert instructed.

Solange closed her eyes. He raised his shirt and placed Solange's hand on his bare chest. "Now move your hand over my chest, stopping only when you think you feel a spot that shouldn't be there."

Solange slowly ran her hand across his pecs first. Then she touched each collarbone above the pectorals, gradually moving downward across his nipples. His chest was hairy, so that was also a tactile delight. She was careful to feel along both his sides as well. Nothing so far. With her eyes closed she felt as if her other senses were heightened. The warmth of his hard body, the smell of his skin, the feel of his muscles against her fingertips, all became sensory pleasures. How many times had she taken for granted the feel of someone else's skin against hers? It didn't have to be a lover's. Hugging a friend should never be something one does in a mindless way. That hug should mean something. Giving a baby a bath should not be looked upon as a task, but as an opportunity to connect with another human being. She remembered giving Mikey a bath when she'd visited Gaea and Micah a few months after he'd been born. She had relished that time, knowing she'd never get the chance to bathe a child of her own. Gaea had left her alone with Mikey, as if that time were her gift to Solange. That's the kind of friend Gaea was, she was willing to share her joy with Solange.

Tears formed at the backs of Solange's eyes now, as she recalled holding Mikey after his bath. He was a happy baby. He grinned all the time, showing nothing but gums. God how she loved that little boy.

Solange paused at a three-inch-long scar. The scar was raised, only two inches below Rupert's rib cage. Solange opened her eyes and looked into Rupert's. She sat up and pulled his shirt up farther until she was looking down at the scar. It was a shade lighter than the rest of his skin. "How did you get that?"

"It was done with a hunting knife. It was in the middle of the night, on a beach where we were not wanted," was all he'd say.

Solange bent her head and kissed it. Then she straddled him and kissed his chin.

"How is this conducive to sleeping together without sex?" Rupert asked of her actions. "Because, as you can undoubtedly feel . . ." His member was hardening even as he spoke. ". . . your proximity is doing things to my body."

Five

"Quick, say something to make me angry," Solange said desperately. "I can't make love when I'm angry." Rupert was absolutely right, at this rate they'd be naked in no time flat. She had been presented with the opportunity to test her willpower, and she was failing miserably. Blast her overactive glands.

She reached underneath her head, retrieved the bottom pillow and shoved it snugly between them, separating their lower halves. "There, that should help."

"Doesn't help," Rupert told her, his eyes caressing her face. "I still want to kiss you like crazy. I should leave before it's too late."

"The British Empire was built on the backs of brown people," Solange said, hoping to get a rise out of him. "Africans and Indians. What's more, if not for the slave trade, Britain wouldn't be the power it is today."

"You have to do better than that," Rupert said. "Because I happen to agree with you. But what can I do? It's home. I don't see you immigrating to Canada. The U.S. also reaped benefits from the institution of slavery."

"Okay, okay," Solange said, getting worked up now. "I'll allow that. I've got one for you: Unlike the U.S., which has the blues as a wholly American invention, the U.K. does not have a form of music it can call its own. You are borrowers. Look at the Beatles. They've admitted their sound was inspired by black rhythm-and-blues singers like Little Richard. And in some circles, African-American musician Billy Preston is known as the fifth Beatle."

"That's blasphemous!" Rupert cried, sitting up in bed to glare at her. "How dare you say that about the Holy Quartet! They were creative geniuses. Even today they're revered the world over."

Solange sat up with a huge grin on her face. "No disrespect intended," she said. "Everybody's inspired by someone." She got up on her knees and leaned toward him in order to look him in the eyes. "Did it work?" she asked.

Rupert hooked her around the waist with one strong arm and pulled her down on top of him. "Not in the least."

Solange's smile faded. She was lost, like all those women who'd told her it could be this way. Her mouth descended on his. He lowered both hands to her waist, giving her the option to back away if she wanted to. She didn't.

The taste of him was intoxicating. She had never known a man to give of himself this way. Her pleasure was uppermost in his mind. Unlike some men, who tried to gain the advantage by guiding the intensity of the pressure, he allowed her to pursue him, to lead him, show him exactly how she wanted to be kissed.

With only a hint of a movement, she indicated she wanted him on top and he gently rolled her over until he was straddling her. Solange moaned deep in her throat. Her arms were around his powerful neck. She turned her head, momentarily breaking off the kiss. Arching, she threw her head back. Rupert kissed her throat.

"Tell me to go."

"Why, when I want you to stay?" she asked breathlessly.

He pressed his lips to the area between her breasts.

The top button on her pajama top had come undone. Solange unbuttoned the last four.

Rupert could not hide the immediate physical reaction he had at the sight of Solange's full breasts. Solange felt his erection at once.

Rupert bent and laved the nipple of her right breast. Solange tensed, her center throbbed, and she bit her bottom lip when the desire to cry out seized her. Rupert's hot tongue gave her no surcease. "God, you're tasty." *And extremely responsive,* he thought. She would wear him out when the time came.

But the time wasn't now. She was exhausted, which made her more vulnerable. When he took her he wanted her well rested, and with all her faculties. There would be no self-recriminations the next morning, as he knew there would be tomorrow when she awakened and realized she'd made love to a man she'd only met five days ago. He couldn't put her through that. Even though he wanted her so badly he was in pain right now.

He slowly gave the left nipple as much attention as he had the right one, then raised his head to meet her gaze. "As much as I'd love to stay, I think I should go."

"But . . ."

He hastily kissed her slightly swollen lips. "Believe me, it's for the best." After kissing her forehead, he gingerly got off the bed, for he was still erect.

Solange sat watching him as he put on his clothes. She would not ask him to stay again. She'd already told him she wanted him to stay. It was up to him whether or not he took her up on her offer. Besides, they were not animals who had little control over their natures. Their eventual coupling would be that much sweeter. They could wait.

She got up to see him to the door. By the time he'd gotten his pants on, Rupert could walk in an almost normal manner. She smiled when her eyes lowered to the bulge in his pants. He was a stronger person than she was if he could deny that baby what it craved.

"Good night, sweetness," he said with a rather regretful smile.

"Good night," Solange said. She pulled him down for what was rapidly becoming her standard good-bye to him—a deep, soulful kiss. "You can dream about me," she said.

Rupert limped out the door.

Solange closed it, a satisfied grin on her face. That'll teach him to get her all worked up, and then leave.

"Samantha Gault, do you know what time it is?"

Samantha nearly jumped out of her skin. It had been a long time since her father had waited up for her. But there he was, standing in the foyer like a big, furious sentinel.

She closed and locked the door and walked farther into the villa. Actually, she was surprised that Theophilus Gault hadn't changed the security code in her absence, ensuring that when she'd tried the code, the entire household would've been thrown into chaos. He was slipping in his old age.

Her father reached over and turned on the light in the foyer. Samantha squeezed her eyes shut against the sudden glare, then gradually opened them again. "What is this going to be, an interrogation?" She walked past him, her heels clicking on the marble floor. "Can we take this to the kitchen? I'm dying for a Diet Coke."

Theophilus followed his recalcitrant twenty-one-year-old daughter to the kitchen, which took all of two minutes in the huge villa. The house sat nearly twenty minutes north of Addis Ababa. It belonged to a longtime associate of his with whom he'd conducted business in Ethiopia on numerous occasions. He'd been given the use of it for the next two months. Which was all the time he needed for his purposes.

In the kitchen, Samantha went straight to the refrigerator and got a can of Diet Coke. She looked across the room at her father, who was leaning against the doorjamb with an irritated expression on his face. Six-foot-three and solidly built, Theophilus had dark brown skin that defied aging. His curly hair was black with a touch of gray at the temples. He wore it very short and tapered at the neck.

He pierced her with a look from his golden-brown eyes. "What good is that cell phone if you refuse to answer it?" he bellowed. "I was worried sick that you'd been kidnapped or worse." He moved farther into the kitchen until he was standing directly in front of her. He was six inches taller than Samantha and she had to crane her neck to look him in the eyes.

"I can take care of myself," she said with confidence. She would not back down. She was, after all, his daughter. He'd taught her that if you believed in something fervently enough you should never back down. The hard part was distinguishing between the causes to champion and the ones to let go of. "I just graduated, Daddy. I want to have fun. I went to Addis Ababa University this afternoon and met some students around my age. They were kind enough to show me around. We ended up at a club where we danced, drank tej, and talked most of the night. That's all. One of them drove me home, a guy named Christian. He's majoring in engineering and wants to come to the U.S. when he graduates."

She went and flopped down on one of the stools at the kitchen nook. Swiveling around, she said, "You told me to go discover Addis Ababa."

"That was twelve hours ago," he said, his voice lower but no less threatening.

He sat down across from her. Sighing, he took the Diet

Coke can from her and set it on the counter. Grasping both her hands in his, he said, "Samantha, you're the only person on this earth who still has my heart. My parents are gone. My Frannie is gone. When someone has lost so much, they tend to hold tightly to what's left to them. So don't come in here trying to make light of your behavior. We're in a foreign country. This isn't D.C., where you know the streets like the back of your hand. You have no friends here you can call to bail you out of a sticky situation that you'd rather your father didn't know about."

Samantha was tired. On the entire drive home Christian had been trying to get her to change her mind and go home with him. She sincerely doubted his mother knew what a horn dog her son would grow up to be when she'd named him after the son of God. Still, he had to be somewhat of a gentleman. He hadn't put her out of the car in the middle of nowhere when she'd rebuffed his advances. He'd driven her all the way home and given her a deflated peck on the cheek.

Her physical exhaustion coupled with the mental exhaustion of having to listen to Christian's pitch for sexual bliss had worn her down. She actually felt remorse for making her father worry about her.

She rose and put her arms around him in a tight hug. "I'm sorry, Daddy."

"Just don't do it again," Theophilus said, his tone weary.

He held her at arm's length. "I'm going to bed. I'm getting too old for these late-night vigils." He kissed her forehead and turned away. When he was in the doorway he turned and said, "Oh, yeah, Julian phoned. He wants you to call him, no matter what time you get in."

Samantha's eyes narrowed in pique as she picked up the Diet Coke can and followed her father out of the kitchen, flicking off the lights as she passed the switch on the wall.

Julian Underwood was the man she'd been dating the past eighteen months. He'd asked her to marry him, but Samantha didn't want to get married. She'd been accepted into the law school at Howard, and it would be years before she'd feel she could devote herself to a marriage. Julian was one of the leading defense attorneys in the Southeast. It had not escaped her notice that Julian was ambitious. He knew that Samantha would eventually take over Gault Technologies, a Fortune 500 company. When she did, he'd be a shoe-in to become managing counsel for Gault Technologies.

Samantha didn't know how she was going to break it to Julian. She wasn't going to marry him. Now or ever. Witnessing the love her parents had shared had left her with a slight fault as far as the Julians of the world were concerned. She needed to love and *be* loved. Julian had a practiced charm. He was an excellent escort and looked well on her arm at the social functions she was obliged to attend on her father's behalf. However, when they were alone and no longer center stage, Julian had not a remote notion of what it took to interest a woman like Samantha. For even though she'd been brought up the privileged child of a powerful couple, she didn't relish the things one might expect her to. What Julian didn't know, and what many people who knew Theophilus Gault didn't know, was that he'd been born poor. It was her father's passion for the American notion that a man made his own way in the world that Samantha valued above material things. Give her a man who knew what it was to struggle for something and get it. That was the man for her.

Samantha and her father walked the darkened hallways in silence. They paused at the door to her room. "You're not going to marry him, are you?" Theophilus said quietly.

He had not voiced his opinions. He knew if he were opposed to the union, Samantha would obstinately fight for it. But he didn't think Julian would make a fitting partner for his daughter. She needed someone stronger. Someone as strong as she was.

"No, Daddy. I might consider it if I thought he loved me. But Julian loves things. He doesn't love people. If I want to be ignored, I'll adopt a cat."

Theophilus laughed. "You have a dry sense of humor, just like your mother's."

"On that note," Samantha said as she tiptoed and kissed his cheek, "I'll bid you good night, sweet prince."

Smiling, Theophilus continued down the hall to his room.

Samantha entered her suite and went to sit on the edge of the bed to remove her boots. She was almost looking forward to telling Julian it was over between them, as if a big weight would be lifted from her shoulders as soon as she was free of him. Julian would demand an explanation. He liked everything spelled out for him. It was one of the things about him that irked her, his wanting to know the reason behind her every action. The first time he'd ever stayed the night at her place, he'd wanted to know why she squeezed the toothpaste in the middle when it made more sense to squeeze the tube from the bottom and work your way up. You wasted less toothpaste that way. He was so rational it sometimes drove her crazy. She was not averse to order, just his unswerving devotion to it. A person had to cut loose sometimes or else life would lose its flavor. Her life with Julian would be all vanilla. A girl had to have chocolate sometimes.

Which made her think of that tall drink of water she'd met tonight at The Hard Luck Café. He had it going on, and then some! She frowned as she walked around the bed to pick up the phone on the nightstand next to the side of the bed she slept on. She wondered if she'd been attracted to him because he'd reminded her of her dad. They say women are attracted to men who are similar to their fathers, their first male object of affection. She put the thought out of her mind and dialed Julian's number. Why was she wasting time thinking about Rupert Giles? It was more than apparent that he and the woman he had been with were totally into each other. Samantha didn't go after men who were already involved with someone.

"Hello?" came Julian's alert voice.

"Hello, Julian."

"Sam, where have you been?" he had perfect diction. He sounded like a Shakespearean actor to Samantha. The longer she'd dated him the more this became evident to her. She had to be fair, though. Julian's voice in and of itself was not irritating. She'd simply grown weary listening to it tell her how best to behave, how to dress to impress, whom it was more advantageous to know, and who to avoid at all costs. Thank God she hadn't listened to him when he'd suggested her best friend, Beverly, was a bad influence on her because Beverly was only one generation from the projects, as he put it.

Remembering that got her ire up. "Julian, I'm sure you'd want me to tell you if I had any misgivings about us."

"Of course, darling. Fire away. What's the matter? All brides-to-be get cold feet. It isn't your father, is it? He's not opposed to the marriage?"

"Julian, my father has never chosen anyone for me. He believes I'm intelligent enough to make my own choices, and if I told him I wanted to marry you, he wouldn't do anything to try to prevent it. Not unless he dug up some dirt on you." Her voice trailed off. She knew her last statement had sounded like a question, so she hurriedly continued, "Which he . . ."

"I swear that child is not mine!" Julian cried, before she could complete her sentence.

Samantha had been about to say, "Which he hasn't." However, Julian's comment was much more intriguing.

"It's not?" she asked, playing along to see where he was going.

"It's true, we had a fling. But a paternity test was done and it was determined that I couldn't possibly be the father."

But I bet you sweated it out until the verdict came back, Samantha thought derisively. "It's not as if you were seeing her at the same time you were seeing me," Samantha put out there. She was fishing, and hoped he wouldn't detect the ploy.

"Okay," Julian said. "Technically, you and I were dating, but we hadn't become intimate yet. Remember, you said you had to know me at least six months before you'd feel comfortable enough with me to make love to me."

"Julian, are you saying you were having sex with her while you were seeing me?" Samantha said, her tone even.

She stood and paced the room. Anger made the adrenaline start flowing. She had to work off some steam, so she kept walking as she spoke into the cordless handset. "I'm waiting," she said, sounding for all the world like her father when he was dressing down an employee who'd royally screwed up.

Julian sighed and spoke with as much conviction as he could muster. "Sam, you're not a child. Men do it all the time, date two women. One puts out, but the other one has that 'something' you're looking for in a woman, so you invest your time in her. You were the special one, Sam. The one I didn't want to lose. If not for your father's snooping, you would never have found out about Desiree."

"Desiree? Desiree Garcia, your secretary?"

"Yes, I thought that would be in the investigator's report to your father," Julian said, sounding confused.

"Undoubtedly it would have been if Dad had actually

had you checked out," Samantha said. "But he didn't. *You* spilled the beans, Julian."

Julian was silent on his end for a while. Then he quietly said, "There's nothing going on between Desiree and me. I didn't dismiss her because she needs the job. She's a single mother."

Samantha was surprised when her eyes brimmed with tears and big droplets spilled over, running down her cheeks. If she didn't love Julian, why had she felt lied to when she'd learned he'd been sleeping with his gorgeous secretary when they were . . . "How long?" she asked.

"How long, what?"

"How long did you sleep with her after we met? Right up until the time I invited you into my bed? You'd just as well be honest about everything."

Julian was silent for so long, Samantha thought their connection had been severed.

"Julian, are you there?"

"I don't see how knowing that has anything to do with us now, Samantha."

"It shows your intentions, Julian. Did I actually mean something to you? If I did, you would have stopped having sex with Desiree soon after you and I met. But if you didn't, that means you were hanging on to your sure thing."

"You've lost me, Samantha." He only called her Samantha when he was upset. Otherwise he referred to her as Sam, or darling, or sweetheart.

"You were hedging your bet. Hanging on to your good thing in case our relationship didn't work out. I'm not judging you if you did that, Julian. I need to know everything, though, before we can go forward with this relationship. Tell me the truth."

"All right. I don't want to hurt you, Samantha, but yes, I continued seeing Desiree even after you and I made love." He continued before she could digest his admission. "I'm sorry, but I was working on the biggest case of my career and I had so much bad energy floating around, I had to expel it in some way. I was insatiable, if you recall. I could have made love to you 24/7, Samantha, but you weren't available. So I would go to Desiree and she'd never deny . . ."

"That's enough!" Samantha said. "That's quite enough. It's way more than I bargained for when I asked the question."

He had the temerity to ask, "You're not jealous of Desiree because she's uninhibited, are you? Because, baby, you're very good in bed. Just a little inexperienced. You'll mature into a wonderful lover someday."

"Not under your tutelage," Samantha said. "Go screw yourself, Julian."

She hung up.

To think, she'd given up her virginity to that slimeball. As far as she was concerned he could *intuit* that it was over between them when the movers showed up at his apartment to collect her mother's antique sofa and armoire, the only two pieces of furniture she'd contributed to the household when they'd moved in together eight months ago.

She felt like waking her father and having an all-night gabfest. Instead she went into the bathroom and stood under the hot spray of the shower for a long time. After that, she went to bed and slept like a baby. She slept as if the weight of the world had been lifted from her shoulders.

One cup of Ethiopian-grown coffee was enough for Solange. But Rupert didn't seem to be able to get enough of the dark, rich, strong brew. He was on his fourth cup when Solange looked up and spied Tesfaye being escorted to their table by an employee of the hotel.

"Sir, Madame," the man said after he and Tesfaye had reached them. "This boy says he has been hired as your guide. I assure you the hotel frowns on street urchins who make nuisances of themselves. If he has misrepresented himself in any way I'd be happy to show him the door."

Solange smiled at the indignant hotel worker as she rose to put an arm about Tesfaye's slim shoulders. "This young gentleman has been a godsend," she told the man from the hotel. "You *can* do something for me, though."

"Anything, Madame," he said, eager to please.

"Mr. Giles and I have finished breakfast, but our man here might like to have a bite to eat. Would you please send a waiter to our table right away?"

A disbelieving expression crossed the man's face for a millisecond. "It would be my pleasure," he said, and quickly strode off.

Rupert sat there brooding behind a pair of dark glasses and sipping his coffee. Apparently the caffeine hadn't kicked in yet. Or he was curious as to how Solange would approach the subject of her stolen watch. At any rate, he simply observed as the drama unfolded before him.

Solange sat back down and graciously gestured to the empty chair next to her.

Tesfaye pulled the chair out and sat down. He'd made an effort to clean up. His shamma was whiter than it had been yesterday. His headwrap was also more pristine. Solange glanced down at his hands. They were clean as well. He'd definitely given some thought to his appearance. She wondered what he had in store for them today.

Tesfaye tried not to stare at the opulent surroundings. He adopted a bored expression, but it was difficult to maintain when his eyes rested on something he'd never seen before, like the cart laden with various mouthwatering pastries, less than four feet away, being pushed from table to table by a waiter.

Solange had caught that look of longing. When the waiter stopped at their table she said, "I'll take one of those, please." She pointed to the largest pastry on the cart. It was golden, flaky, had apple filling, and was drizzled with icing.

The waiter happily placed the pastry on a plate and handed it to her. Solange placed it in front of Tesfaye. "To hold you until you can order breakfast."

Tesfaye didn't have to be coaxed. He picked up the sweet and bit into it with gusto. He looked at Solange with something akin to ecstasy in his almond-shaped brown eyes. He took several more big bites, chewed, and swallowed before saying, "Why are you so nice to me?"

"Do I have to have a reason to be nice to you?" Solange returned.

Tesfaye didn't say anything else until he finished his pastry, but while he ate he watched Solange. She was dressed as she had been yesterday, with a long-sleeve shirt and a pair of slacks plus the brown leather boots. Her short hair was combed away from her face. She wore no jewelry.

Tesfaye licked his fingers after he'd finished his pastry. Solange handed him a cloth napkin. He promptly put it in his pocket.

"Put it back," she sternly ordered.

He pursed his lips as if to say, no great loss, and placed it on the table. Then he reached inside his shamma and withdrew her watch. Holding it in the palm of his hand, he said, "I found this on the ground last night after we separated. Does it belong to you?"

Solange smiled warmly and took the watch. "Yes, it's mine. Thank you for returning it, Tesfaye. That was very sweet of you."

He could not tell by the tone of her voice whether she was sincere. Her eyes were wholly innocent-looking. She was either as good a liar as he was, or she truly didn't suspect he'd stolen it right off her wrist.

The man, however, choked on his coffee.

Six

It didn't take Solange long to find out that the map of Addis Ababa in her trusty guidebook was of no use to them. There were few street signs. She discovered that most residents navigated the city by using local landmarks that had been around for years, such as large churches and palaces or enormous modern buildings. Solange, for one, was pleased to have Tesfaye with them.

The day was sunny and bright. Although the weather could drop to below freezing at night from October to January, the days were pleasantly cool but not excessively so. A jacket was sufficient to keep warm.

Most of the time Solange and Rupert walked behind Tesfaye, who enjoyed being the knowledgeable one. He pointed out anything he thought might be of interest to them. He took them to several museums, including the Ethnological Museum, part of Addis Ababa University. It was in the former palace of Ethiopia's last emperor, Haile Selassie. The palace was home to the library of the Institute of Ethiopian Studies; a walk upstairs took them to the Ethnological Museum, thought to be the best museum in the country.

Solange and Rupert slowly walked past the exhibits of arts and crafts and black-and-white photos of the various peoples of Ethiopia, including the Dorze people, who live in huts shaped like giant beehives.

They learned that the people of Ethiopia speak eighty-three languages and two-hundred dialects. It wasn't surprising that the country was so ethnically diverse. Solange and Rupert perused photographs on the walls that showed the Oromo, Amhara, Tigrayan, Gurage, Hurari, Somali, Afar, and Sidama peoples participating in everyday life. It was a pictorial tribute to the people of Ethiopia.

Solange noticed that Tesfaye had the features characteristic of the Afar people, who lived in Eritrea's southeast and Ethiopia's eastern sections. They had rich, darkly tanned skin and dark hair, as well as long noses, thin lips and, like most African peoples, very high cheekbones. Tesfaye had never removed his head wrap so Solange had no idea whether he had curly hair underneath it; but otherwise he could pass for an Afar. In the copy beneath the photos of the Afar people, Solange read that they lived in an area that was considered one of the most inhospitably arid environments on the planet. Living that way had made the Afar fiercely proud and independent.

She glanced at Tesfaye who was standing a few feet away from her, eyeing the bag of a white woman who had left it open with the strap of her camera hanging out. She was talking animatedly with the man at her side.

Solange went and touched Tesfaye's shoulder. "I think we've seen enough of this museum. Are there any interesting churches nearby?"

"I will take you to them, but I won't go in with you," Tesfaye said at once.

"All right," Solange said. She would not ask him why he didn't want to go inside a church, that was his business. She was content to have gotten out of the Ethnological Museum without Tesfaye five-finger-discounting that woman's camera, and possibly her wallet. She couldn't fault the woman, she herself had been just as careless.

Christianity was said to have begun in Ethiopia in the

fourth century. It wasn't until the fifth century that a group of Greek missionaries began founding monasteries in the northern part of the country. Around that time, the Bible was translated from Greek to Ge'ez, the language of the Ethiopians.

Nearly fifty percent of Ethiopia's population today still practiced Orthodox Christianity. The country had such a strong spiritual foundation that you couldn't walk very far in any direction without coming upon a church.

It took them barely half an hour to reach the Trinity Cathedral, the biggest Orthodox church in the country. Tesfaye ran into the churchyard, the final resting place of several patriots who'd opposed the Italian Occupation that had begun with an invasion in 1935. "I'll wait for you out here," he called over his shoulder.

Rupert took Solange's hand and joked, "Alone at last!"

Solange shushed him. "Don't say that too loudly, you'll hurt his feelings."

Rupert laughed at her assertion. "Believe me when I say that boy is here only because he has something up his sleeve. Luckily, it's not your watch."

They lingered outside a moment because once they were inside the church they had to lower their voices considerably or not speak at all. A sense of decorum and respect was encouraged while visiting the churches. Photography wasn't allowed in many of them, and modest dress was expected.

"Speaking of watches, he returned mine. I'll give him the benefit of the doubt," Solange said with a winsome smile.

Rupert shook his head and took her hand, pulling her toward the very tall, handcarved door that served as one of the entrances. Many Ethiopian churches had three separate entrances. One for men, one for women, and another that both sexes could use. Once inside, however, the males went to one side of the cathedral while the females had to go to another. No mixing of the sexes during services.

Solange was looking for the sign indicating whether or not photography was allowed. Luckily photography was, but flash photography was not. She used high-speed film in her camera and it didn't require a flash in order to capture an image.

There was a group of tourists in front of her and Rupert. She paused, waiting for them to move on so she could get a better shot of the ceiling, which was thirty or more feet high. The only sounds in the cathedral were the tourists' shoes clicking on its stone floors and the murmur of their voices.

"The architecture is a combination of styles," Rupert said. "I can see the Italian influence, even the Islamic. Imagine that. Aren't they supposed to be the enemy?"

Solange was lining up a shot. "This is a country of contrasts, don't you think? On one hand, you have street children, and on the other, since the late fifties Addis has been considered Africa's diplomatic capital."

"I see what you mean," Rupert agreed. "Even though the city has the look of a world capital, it's not unusual to see a goat herder ushering his charges down a main thoroughfare." They commenced walking down the long aisle.

"Exactly," Solange said. "Last night when we were coming home in the taxi I could have sworn I saw a giant bat arcing over the tops of a clump of eucalyptus trees. I wanted to yell for the driver to pull over, but I didn't want you to think I was nuts."

"Don't worry about my thinking you're nuts. I want you to feel free to chase bats, if that's what you want to do," Rupert joked.

Solange stopped walking to photograph several interesting murals of various notable events in Ethiopia's history, among them Emperor Selassie's impassioned speech before the League of Nations asking for help to expel the invading Italians.

They came to the throne room, wherein sat two intricately carved thrones that had belonged to the last emperor and empress. They were carved from ivory, ebony, and marble. To the side of them were four smaller thrones belonging to their children.

Solange once again paused to take photos. "Emperor Selassie was the first black royal I ever heard of," she said.

"He was undoubtedly the most famous," Rupert said.

"To black Americans he was the evidence that our past did not begin and end with slavery. Some of us had been kings," Solange said, with a catch in her voice. "That does a lot for your self-confidence. I must admit, unless I did the research myself, I was not taught much black history in elementary or secondary school."

"You?" Rupert said. "My history courses were lily white!"

Even though their conversation was lively, they remembered to keep the volume of their voices low. Solange took photos of the tall, wide nave and narrow aisles. This cathedral wasn't much different from the European cathedrals she'd visited years ago. Except here the murals depicted black saints, as did the stained glass windows.

Solange slipped into a pew. The backs were high and ornate. She had to sit up very straight in order to see over the pew in front of her. Rupert had no such problem.

"It must be nice being tall," Solange groused.

"Why are we never satisfied with the physical attributes God gives us?" Rupert returned. "You're perfect just the way you are." He smiled down into her upturned face. "You're just the right size for me to pick up and carry off caveman style."

"Aren't you afraid God is going to hear you speaking in that manner in His house?"

"God can hear me anywhere," Rupert said, his smile not wavering. "God was there in your bedroom with us last night."

"So you believe God is omnipresent?"

"I believe God is everything good. And what happened between us last night was good."

"What's your definition of sin?" Solange wanted to know. She'd been reared Catholic by parents who required her to attend mass but were not very devout themselves. She did not resent them for their hypocrisy. Quite the contrary, she enjoyed the rituals of the church. When she was a girl it was her dearest wish to be an altar boy. Of course, since she wasn't a boy she wasn't qualified. She'd been crushed when Father Demetrius had gently told her she could not serve.

The church and religion in general were mysteries to her. She loved mysteries.

Rupert squinted, thinking. "Sin to me is when someone makes a conscious choice to harm someone else, or himself. Of course, I'm not an authority on sin. I've led a rather monastic life myself."

A chill ran up Solange's spine when he said that because there had been a panicked expression in the depths of his eyes. No humor sat in them at all. She had the feeling he was about to reveal something important to her and then, with the lowering of his gaze, he'd changed his mind. That look, though, was imprinted in her mind. She would never forget it. Her imagination came into play also. What Toni had said about Rupert's past being expunged ran through her thoughts. Could he have actually been a spy?

"I'm ready to leave if you are," Solange said, after what seemed like a long break in their conversation.

It was the first time Solange had felt truly uncomfortable in his presence.

Rupert said nothing, but rose and allowed her to precede him out into the aisle of the cathedral. When her back was turned, he momentarily closed his eyes and silently blew a relieved sigh between full lips. That was close.

What was it about churches that made you want to confess your deepest secrets?

After they'd descended the steps of the church, he stood back and watched Solange as she greeted Tesfaye, who was waiting for her at the bottom. The smile she gave the boy was absolutely devoid of guile. She was growing to care for him. Just as he knew she would. He didn't sense any genuine affection in the boy for her, though. What he saw in the boy's gaze when he looked at her was cunning.

But that could be because he himself was not being entirely honest with her. He was able to recognize the same deceit in someone else.

"Let's call it a day, shall we?" Solange was saying to Tesfaye. She took several Birr notes from her bag and handed them to him. "You've done a wonderful job today."

"What time will you need me in the morning?" Tesfaye asked.

Solange looked back at Rupert for his input.

"Half an hour earlier than this morning," Rupert told him. "That way you can breakfast with us and we won't have to wait while you eat your meal. Deal?"

Tesfaye's face brightened. "I shall be there." With that, he took off in a sprint toward the south.

Solange stood looking at him a moment, then turned her attention to Rupert. Their eyes met. She was trying to see if vestiges of that look lingered. No, it was gone. In its place was admiration, pure and simple.

"I don't know what you see in that boy, but being around him makes you happy so I won't give you any more grief about his tagging along. And I'll try to control my jealous streak."

They began walking north, in the general direction of their hotel. "Jealous?" Solange said. Her golden-brown skin looked kissed by the sunlight. The sunlight also brought out the brown streaks in her hair. The wind lifted it off her neck, and Rupert's heartbeat accelerated crazily when she peered into his eyes and said, "You don't have anything to be jealous of. I'm yours for the asking." Her eyes narrowed somewhat. "But after leaving me high and dry last night, you're going to have to ask very nicely."

Rupert laughed. "I believe I'm the one who suffered the most last night. I tossed and turned all night, regretting not making love to you."

"All that regret," Solange quipped. "And, according to your definition of sin, not one sin committed."

"You never did say what your definition of sin is," Rupert pleasantly reminded her.

Solange bit her bottom lip as she gathered her thoughts. Going back to her Catholic upbringing, sin was a very real denominator that could be multiplied in an instant. She tended to agree with Rupert's definition to an extent. Sin was indeed an act committed with conscious thought. But was sin always maliciously done?

What about original sin? Did Adam consciously disobey God and eat of the forbidden fruit, or did he do it because his wife had done it before him and he made a conscious choice between God and Eve? Solange had always thought that the original sin was committed because of love. Adam's desire to remain at Eve's side. There was the possibility that if he didn't follow her in sin, they would have been split up, with him remaining in the Garden of Eden and Eve being cast out. So in Solange's estimation, Adam sinned out of love. Eve sinned out of ignorance. If she had been fully aware of

the consequences, perhaps she wouldn't have chosen to
eat the forbidden fruit, either.

That's subversive thinking, young lady, Solange could
clearly recall Father Demetrius saying after she'd shared
her views with him at the tender age of thirteen. She'd
never again told him how she honestly felt about church
doctrine.

"I believe sin is anything that keeps our souls from
rising to the heights of Heaven," Solange said. "I agree
with you when you say that it's the intentional harm done
to someone, or yourself. I'm going a bit further by also
saying that stunted-thinking can be sinful. Disbelief in
your ability to rise above sin is a sin."

"Oh my God," Rupert said. "You're not only a bleeding heart liberal, you're an optimist!"

"You say that like it's a dirty word," Solange said with
a grin.

They were standing at a crosswalk waiting for the light
to change, along with about twenty others. "Life is hard,
sweetness, and anyone who doesn't accept that is in for
a rude awakening," Rupert told her matter-of-factly.

"Life *is* hard," Solange readily agreed. "It's even
harder if you don't believe that it can get better. Hence,
I'm an optimist, and proud of it."

"Well, I'm a firm believer in the notion that life can
always get worse," Rupert said. "So I try to enjoy it while
it's moderately livable."

"You're not trying to tell me you're a present-focused
person," Solange said aghast.

The light changed and they crossed the street. Rupert
knew what she was getting at. If he were a present-focused
person he would have made love to her last night instead
of walking out her door.

"What you are is a sensitive guy masquerading as a
man of the world," Solange said, her voice low. "You

want me to believe you are not affected by Tesfaye, and you don't wish to help him. But deep down you like him."

"I don't detest him, but *like* is too strong a word."

"What is it? You don't like children?"

"Of course I like children. I want a house full of my own. But that boy is not my responsibility. He's the responsibility of his own people. What good would it do him to have two foreigners fawning over him? He's going to be back to fending for himself soon enough. We aren't doing him any favors by coddling him. And we aren't doing other tourists whom he'll meet after us any good either. He'll expect them to pay him too much for his services as well. And when they don't, he'll try to take it. That's the harm in the behavior of liberals, your soft-heartedness renders those you care so much about worse off than when you stumbled upon them."

Solange had stopped in her tracks to glare at him. "It's obvious we're never going to agree on politics. I don't believe every child is our responsibility. However, I do believe that one person can make a difference in this world. I do know for a fact that if not for my best friends' parents I would have been incapable of loving anyone, because my own parents were sorely inadequate in that department. The Maxwells were a very good influence on me. And maybe my taking time with Tesfaye will make a difference in his life. Who knows? I just know that simply because life is hard is no reason not to *try.*"

"I wouldn't expect anything less from you," Rupert said without rancor. They were passing a tej bar and he pulled her inside the entranceway. The glass in the door of the establishment was opaque so they would not be seen by the patrons when he kissed her soundly, which he did with slow deliberation.

When they came up for air, Solange said, "We should argue like that more often."

Rupert smiled. "It definitely gets my fire stoked." He pulled her close to his side. "Come on, we've only a few blocks to go. I'll treat you to dinner anyplace in the city after we get some of this grime off us, and perhaps later we can discuss sinning some more."

They stepped back into the pedestrian traffic on the busy street. Behind them Danyael moved out of the shadows and followed at a distance. He hoped they were headed back to the Sheraton. His feet hurt, and his cell phone had run out of juice. He couldn't phone for the hired car Theophilus Gault had put at his disposal.

"Wouldn't it do more for morale if you were there?" Samantha asked her father over dinner. She speared a stalk of asparagus and brought it to her mouth. Biting off the tender tip, she chewed thoughtfully. Her father was up to something and he wanted her safely in the States. It hadn't escaped Samantha over the years that her father could be ruthless when he wanted to be. He was in the middle of a deal that could cross the line between legal and illegal, she knew it! And he didn't want her anywhere near the crime. She bit off another piece of the asparagus.

"Must you challenge me at every turn?" Theophilus asked, sounding put upon. "My doctor made me promise to take a month-long vacation for my health . . ."

And she didn't believe that either. Not even when he'd said it two weeks ago when he'd announced he was going to Ethiopia. *Ethiopia!* He'd never invited Samantha on any of his trips to Africa. She knew he'd only done it to make his stay appear more kosher. Vacation indeed. Theophilus Gault didn't take vacations. He hadn't taken a trip just to relax since her mother passed away. He wasn't fooling her!

Out of respect for him, she said, "Oh, all right. I'll go to Colorado for the grand opening of your new plant. I'll

cut ribbons and drink a toast to prosperity. I'll even grin
for the camera. Then I'll hop the next plane right back
to Addis."

"No, you should go to D.C., settle things with Julian."

Things *were* settled with Julian. She hadn't given him
blow-by-blow details of her conversation with Julian the
previous night, but she had told him it was definitely over
between them. Wasn't that clear enough? Undoubtedly
her father was up to something wicked.

She perused him from across the long table. He'd never
looked in better health. A vacation at the insistence of
his physician? That was a bunch of hooey, and he knew
it! Okay, but where did that realization get her? Nowhere.
She would have to play the dutiful daughter, go to Boulder, Colorado, and represent him at the plant opening.

She would find a way to slip back into Addis, though.
The dutiful daughter part was her mother in her. The du-
plicitous sneak thief was her father's genes rearing their
ugly heads.

"Sure, why not?" she said at last. "You'll be home in
time for Thanksgiving, though, right? I'm going to make
Mom's recipes from scratch on my own this year."

"I'll be home. Lay in a big supply of Alka-Seltzer,"
her father quipped.

On the seventh day, she rested, Solange thought as she
absentmindedly tried to fit her big toe into the bathtub's
faucet. Wouldn't it be her luck to get it stuck? She'd been
soaking in the tub for the past twenty minutes or so. Sulk-
ing, really.

Today was the seventh day she'd spent with Rupert in
Addis. That wasn't why she was having a good pout. She
was thoroughly enjoying being in Rupert's company. And
Tesfaye had been on his best behavior all week.

The reason for the funk she was in was a conversation

with her mother less than thirty minutes before. She'd
finally followed Gaea's advice and phoned her mother to
tell her where she was. What she got for her trouble was
an earful from Marie DuPree.

"I've been trying to get you since Sunday," Marie
nearly screamed, starting in on her at once. Her mother
enjoyed having the upper hand in conversations. "I
phoned your office on campus and was told you were on
sabbatical. I know you're on sabbatical. What I don't
know is *where* you are!"

"I'll tell you if you'll only be quiet for a moment,"
Solange testily put in.

"Don't use that tone with me. I've been sick with
worry," Marie said, utilizing her right as a mother to lay
a guilt trip on her only child.

Solange had been sitting on the balcony with the cordless phone at her ear. It was dusk in Addis, the western
sky was tinged with orange and there was a hint of spice
in the air. It reminded Solange of their trip to Merkato,
the largest market in eastern Africa, a couple of days ago.
The spice market had been an experience for her olfac-
tory senses. Never had she smelled such a myriad array
of spices. Henceforth, whenever she thought of Addis,
she would remember the spice market.

The memory of it now served to calm her down after
her blood pressure had shot up at the sound of her
mother's unspoken accusations. "I'm sorry if you worried
needlessly, Mother," she'd said. "I had no plans to come
to Addis Ababa without giving you advance notice, but
I was presented with the opportunity and took it. I've told
you I'm doing research on the ancient African kingdom
of Kush." She waited for her mother's response. Sometimes her mother would make her wait simply to test her
patience. She knew she might be stretching the bounds
of sanity with this reasoning, but she believed her mother
took pleasure from making her prove her loyalty. Years

ago Solange had assumed her mother did this because she was feeling insecure after her divorce. Any hint of favoritism shown to her father was met with histrionics from her mother, who felt she was the wronged spouse in the divorce. Solange could not discuss her weekends with her father for fear she'd express more joy at spending time with him than she had when spending time with her mother. Marie seemed to feed on the negative reports. So at age fourteen, Solange started making up stories about her weekends with her father: His present girlfriend was young but dumb as a post. His apartment was small and cramped. His girlfriend couldn't cook and had given him ptomaine poisoning.

"Why did you phone me?" Solange asked. "Nothing's the matter, is it? Dad's all right, isn't he?"

"Why would I phone you about your father?" Marie always referred to her ex-husband in formal terms. "Believe me, the only reason I'd phone you with news of your father would be to tell you he'd died."

"That's a horrible thing to say," Solange said, sighing. Her parents had been divorced for twenty-one years, it was time her mother got over it and stopped spouting vitriol about her ex, who never returned the favor. Georges DuPree had gone on with his life. He was remarried now and as far as Solange could see, he was happy. "He never talks about you in that manner."

"He doesn't have the right to," was her mother's cryptic rejoinder. "And I phoned you because they found a lump in my breast. I'm going to have an operation in early December and I want you to take care of Clytemnestra for me. If it wouldn't be too much of an imposition." Her mother's French-accented voice was detached.

Solange thought she sounded as though she were asking her neighbor to feed her cat in her absence, instead of her daughter. Solange's mind had not yet recovered from the cancer disclosure. Her mother continued, unaware that her daughter was in a mild state of shock. "The plants should be all right for a few days, but Clymie needs to be taken care of."

The damn cat got a nickname, but her mother had never thought of some endearing appellation for *her*. Marie loved the cat more than she loved her own daughter. Solange's mind was running along a morbid track. Cancer. Her mother had cancer. And Marie DuPree was treating it as matter-of-factly as she treated everything else in her life. If the floor was dirty, clean it. If your husband cheats on you, get rid of him. If you find a lump in your breast, excise it. Don't waste emotions on it because that would be a sign of weakness. Simply handle it. Stay in control at all costs.

Solange couldn't be like that, though. In spite of the fact that her relationship with her mother had never been as close as it could have been, she loved her. She was the only mother she would ever have. It wasn't as if she could go down to the used-mother lot and trade her in for a newer, more daughter-friendly model.

Tears formed in her eyes as she sat on the balcony, frozen with fear. What if her mother died without ever having told her anything about her life in Haiti? So much history would be lost forever. The thought made her angry. Angry at all the time they'd wasted. And now her mother could be dying at fifty-two. Fifty-two was too young to die.

"How bad is it?" Solange asked, her voice breaking.

"The cat?" Marie asked, for she'd left the subject of her cancer in the dust in her headlong rush to secure a nanny for her precious tabby.

"No, mother, the cancer!" Solange's voice was too sharp. She instantly regretted her tone. It was possible her mother was in denial about her illness. That was often a symptom in the early stages of breast cancer. Not wanting to face reality. That could account for the cat's placement on her mother's list of priorities.

"I'm sorry for yelling," Solange said more quietly. "I'm a little upset to hear about the lump in your breast, that's all. I know we haven't had the best relationship. But you know I'll be there for you . . . Mama."

"It hasn't spread to the surrounding tissue, so I won't need a mastectomy, but it has to be removed. Then they'll decide whether I'll require chemo, or not. We're hoping the surgery will be effective. You'll really be here for me?" There was a catch in her voice. "I never thought I'd say this, but I'm scared. I've never been afraid of anything."

"Yes, I'll be there with you," Solange softly said. She wiped away tears with the back of her hand. "I'll be home before December. And when I get there, we've got to have that talk you've been putting off for way too long."

Marie sighed heavily on her end of the wire. "Why do you want to hear about my life before you were born? It was boring. We were poor. End of story."

"Does being poor mean you didn't have a life? No. Does being poor mean you didn't have people in your life you cared about? Like your parents, and your grandparents? No. Let down your guard, Marie Etienne, and invite me into your world. Help me to understand you better by telling me your life's story."

"It's the mother's duty to protect her child from the ugliness in this world."

Solange sat forward on her chair, instantly alert. This was the first time Marie had ever given her an inkling as to the nature of her life in Haiti. Good, bad, indifferent?

Solange had been given no clues. Maybe Rupert was right—her parents hadn't told her about their lives in Haiti because they wanted to forget it themselves.

"I don't want to make you dredge up bad memories.

You could tell me the good things. Like how your mother cooked. Was she a good cook like you are?"

"She was a very good cook," Marie said. "And she was a tiny woman. Even smaller than I am." Marie was five-foot-one. Solange had gotten her extra three inches from her father, who was six feet tall.

"Tell me all about her," Solange insisted. Happiness flooded her heart. Her mother was finally going to illuminate all the dark corners of her past. Open the blinds and let the sun shine in.

"Certainement," Marie said, converting to French, as she often did. "When you get home we will sit down and talk about Maman. I will bring her back to life for you."

"Tell me now!" Solange sounded like a petulant two-year-old.

Marie laughed delightedly. "At these rates? No, my dear one. The thought of your astronomical phone bill will surely kill me before the cancer has a chance to. Come home. This needs to be a face-to-face conversation."

Solange growled in frustration. She knew her mother would not budge, though. Marie was the most fervent penny pincher she'd ever encountered. She could stretch a dollar until the eagle screamed.

Solange let out a long strangled sigh. "Okay, you win. I'll ring off. But I'm really looking forward to our talk, Mama. Take care of yourself. I love you."

"I love you, too, mon coeur. Au revoir," Marie said softly, and hung up.

So—now she sat in a tub full of lukewarm water, fuming because she'd been within a hair's breath of her mother disclosing her past when Marie Etienne DuPree had backed off due to a frugal mindset.

So close, and yet so far!

Today was Sunday. She and Rupert had decided not to do any sightseeing today. This day was meant for relaxa-

tion alone. Solange held up her right leg and peered at
her foot. Her feet could use the down time. They must
have walked forty miles in and around the city the past
six days.

Tomorrow would begin their trip outside of Addis
Ababa. Their first destination was the monastery of Debre Libanos and after that it was on to Blue Nile Falls,
the second largest falls in Africa, the largest being Vic-
toria Falls in South Africa.

Solange carefully got to her feet and reached for the
fluffy white towel she'd left rolled up on the tub's edge.
She wrapped it around her torso and stepped out of the
tub onto a thick terrycloth rug. She wondered where Tesfaye had gone when he left them at the end of the day.
She thought he'd looked disappointed when she'd told
him yesterday that they would not be needing his services
next week. She and Rupert would be doing the final leg
of their trip as a duo. Plus, she didn't want Tesfaye around
when she went to the social services office to find out if
he had family anywhere in the country. He'd finally told
them his surname, Roba. Surely she'd be able to find out
if he had a long lost aunt or uncle, or perhaps grandparents, who could take him in. She realized Ethiopia's social services system must be overtaxed, what with all the
internal problems the country had, but maybe she'd meet
a friendly caseworker who wouldn't mind going the extra
mile for a lost child. Miracles happened on a daily basis.

Solange finished drying off in the bathroom and hung
the towel on a nearby rack, then walked naked into the
outer room where she'd laid out her clothing before going
into the bathroom.

Rupert was taking her to Addis Ababa Restaurant. It
was reputed to be one of the finest restaurants in the city.
The food was excellent and the tej was not to be missed.
The restaurant had its own brewery on the premises.

She was wearing the red dress again. If she had known

she was going to be staying in Addis, she would have brought more clothes. But since she hadn't anticipated staying longer than a day or two, she'd brought only the bare minimum. The hotel had a dress shop downstairs with lovely cocktail dresses and gowns in its display window. She'd stopped to window-shop once or twice, but the prices were beyond her budget. She believed she'd inherited a touch of Marie's frugality. Paying five hundred dollars for a frock didn't sit well with her. Maybe she could afford something like that when she became a tenured professor, but that was years away.

She slipped into a pair of champagne-colored bikini panties and then put on the matching lacy bra. Moving over to the vanity, she sat and removed the towel from her head. Running a hand through her thick black hair, she decided a slanting part would convey the sultry feeling which was slowly enveloping her.

Rupert. She smiled at her reflection. Meeting him had been propitious. Staying here in Addis with him had been inspired. Kissing him was a revelation. And when they made love she was sure the experience would be transcendent.

She laughed out loud. Was she comparing Rupert to a religious experience? Father Demetrius would be aghast! She laughed at that, too. Peering straight into her eyes in the mirror, she knew her elation was due to her budding friendship with her mother. Her mother's attitude had weighed heavily on her mind. Now that it appeared things were going to be better between them, she felt light and happy. Could it be that her mother's fight with cancer had served to soften her hard shell when years of pleading from Solange had barely made a crack in the surface?

There was a knock on her door. She rose and went to the closet to get her bathrobe. She tied it as she crossed the room to the door. "Who's there?"

"It's Rupert, may I come in?"

Solange laughed shortly, unlocked the door and pulled it open.

Rupert stood there with a large elongated box with a huge red ribbon tied around it. He handed it to her. "For you. It's an anniversary gift."

Solange immediately accepted the box in her right hand, balancing it on her hip while pulling Rupert into the room with her left. "For me?" she asked excitedly.

Her grin did things to Rupert's heart and his libido. Did she know she looked sexy as all get out when she was barefoot, wearing nothing but a bathrobe? His eyes devoured her face. Her eyes, like black pearls in her creamy brown face, were lit from within.

He closed the door and followed her across the room. She threw herself, bottom first, onto the bed. He smiled when she bounced a bit before settling down. Then she carefully removed the ribbon. He could not pull his eyes from her glowing face.

The tissue paper was drawn aside. She paused to look at him again before lowering her eyes to the surprise lying within. When she saw the deep green cocktail dress, the very one she'd been salivating over this afternoon, she let out a small scream and leaped to her feet, the dress clutched to her chest. The next thing she leaped for was Rupert, who grabbed her about the waist in a tight embrace.

"I guessed at your size," he said next to her ear. "But the lady in the shop said that if it doesn't fit, you can phone down and they'll bring up the right size right away. They don't close until eight. So if you'd try it on to see if it fits, we'll get this night started."

Seven

Solange walked into the dimly lit bar of the hotel and glanced around. She didn't see Rupert anywhere. He'd promised to meet her here at half past eight. She'd arrived exactly on the dot. After surprising her with the dress he'd kept an appointment with a Addis police detective. The detective had assured him their business wouldn't take long.

The bar was half full. Ethiopian instrumental music floated in the air. Turning, Solange was preparing to walk across the room and have a seat at the bar to await Rupert's arrival when Danyael strolled in, spotted her, and made straight for her.

Solange smiled warmly. He seemed like a nice man. She'd run into him twice since they'd met at the singing fountain in front of the Sheraton, the last time with Rupert in tow. When they were alone, Rupert had joked that Danyael had a crush on her.

Tonight he looked as if he were dressed for the opera: a black tuxedo, loafers polished to a high shine, a red rosebud in his lapel.

"Bonjour," he said pleasantly. His brown eyes danced.

"Bonjour," Solange responded in kind.

"May I say you look lovely in that dress? The color accentuates your complexion beautifully." He looked around them. "Mr. Giles can't be too far away."

"Thank you and, no, Rupert isn't far. He'll be here shortly."

"Ah," Danyael said, as he indicated with a tilt of his head that they should find a table and sit down. "I'm waiting to meet a business associate. Shall we wait together?"

Solange saw no harm in his suggestion, so she allowed him to direct her with a hand placed beneath her elbow, and they sat at a window table. She was curious as to what kind of business Danyael was in. She saw him around the hotel at all times of the day. She'd even seen him on the street a couple of times, ambling along as if he had no particular place to go.

"How are you finding our city?" Danyael asked.

A hawk-eyed waiter interrupted. "May I be of service?"

Danyael turned his golden gaze on Solange. "Would you care for something?"

"A mineral water with a twist of lemon, please," Solange said.

"I'll have an American beer," Danyael told the waiter, and he left to get their orders.

"Where did you acquire a taste for American beer?" Solange asked. "If I'm not being too forward." She smiled.

"I live in the United States, where I work for an American company. I still have family and friends here. I try to visit at least once a year. On this trip I'm obliged to work. The company wants me to interview several men they're interested in hiring."

"What's the nature of your business?" Solange inquired.

"We make electronics," Danyael told her. He smiled, embarrassed. "Our biggest sellers are the handheld computer games. People go wild over them. My own grandmother is hooked on them."

Solange laughed. "They are fun. And relaxing. You'd be surprised at how stress-relieving those games can be. I own one, or is it two?"

"Exactly," Danyael said. "What's more, you can take them anywhere. Waiting to see the dentist? Play a game or two. Stranded at the airport? Pull out your handheld video game. I've seen people playing them in any number of places. But that's enough about my business. Tell me about your work. I've always found archaeology to be a fascinating field of study."

"I don't know about fascinating," Solange said with a smile. "There's a lot of research involved. The work can be tedious at times. However, you've always got your eyes on the prize, so to speak, when all of your hard work will pay off. That notion has kept me digging for information many times."

"It's nothing like Indiana Jones makes it look, huh?" His keen eyes swept over her face. "The movies make it look very exciting."

The waiter returned with their drinks and served them. After the waiter had left, Danyael took a sip of his drink, his eyes never leaving Solange's face. "May I ask you a personal question, Solange?"

"You can ask, but I may not answer," Solange joked.

Danyael smiled. "Are you and Mr. Giles a couple? I only ask because you are so physically disparate. He is quite a huge fellow and you are . . ." He paused for effect, ". . . perfectly petite." His gaze lowered to her cleavage but quickly returned to her eyes.

Solange adjusted her shawl so that it covered her chest. She saw now that his actions had been calculated. He appeared polite on the surface, but underneath he was a snake. He had hoodwinked her each time she'd been in his presence. The question was, why was he allowing his baser instincts to show? What kind of game was he playing?

"That was undoubtedly the most subtle come-on I've ever heard," she told him. "And, to be honest, I'm disappointed in you, Danyael. I was beginning to like you." She pushed her chair back and rose.

Danyael quickly rose to help her with her chair. "I am a businessman, Solange. I was only presenting you with a better option. A trade-up, if you will. Ditch the Brit. You and I could be good together. I'd do things to you he could never imagine doing."

He had the unmitigated gall to rub the back of his hand across Solange's right breast. Solange slapped him so quickly, his head spun. She vaguely recalled Gaea's admonition about rude Ethiopian men and slapped him again. Danyael staggered back.

She waited a few seconds for his eyes to focus. "Danyael?"

"Mmm?" He looked dreamily at her, as if a woman's slap were an aphrodisiac.

She slapped him a third time for good measure. "That's just to make sure you got the message. Fichez moi la paix!" *Leave me alone!*

She said it in French, since he was so inordinately fond of the language.

Rupert walked into the room as she neared the exit. Seeing the angry expression on her face he assumed it was directed at him for being a few minutes late. "Darling, forgive me, Detective Bedele had a lot of questions about Makonnen. It seems that after he was bailed out of jail by his lawyers, he and his wife left the country. He's now an international fugitive."

Solange stopped short. She wasn't going to let the comments of an oily handheld-video-game salesman rob her of an enjoyable evening with Rupert. "Another rich man escapes justice," she complained. She went and put her arm around Rupert's waist as they turned to leave the bar. "I hope they held our table at the restaurant."

"If not, we'll find another more splendid place to dine," Rupert said, pleased she was not upset. Her cologne wafted over him. The detective's bad news was soon forgotten. All he wanted to do was to hold Solange in his arms and forget Yusef Makonnen had ever existed. Let the Ethiopian authorities worry about him.

"Why did you look so upset? Did you think I'd forgotten our date?" he asked when they were outside descending the hotel's steps.

"No," Solange said. The night air was bracing. She'd brought her coat this time, and slipped into it with Rupert's help. "While I was waiting for you, Danyael came into the bar and we sat down together. We started talking about our jobs, and before I knew it he'd made advances. Just like that, he turned into a slime in an expensive suit."

The muscles worked in Rupert's strong jaw. He glanced back at the hotel's entrance. "I'll break him in half," he said through clenched teeth. He turned purposefully toward the hotel. "I'll stomp his face until it's more pockmarked than it already is."

Solange had hold of the hem of his leather jacket. "Rupert, don't!"

Rupert, however, was in the throes of another kind of passion: Someone had insulted his lady and he would have satisfaction. *Tonight.*

Solange held onto his jacket but her slight weight was no deterrent when his two hundred pounds were in forward motion. He dragged her along after him.

"I've already slapped him three times. His ears will be ringing for hours," she said, hoping the knowledge would appease him.

It did not.

Trying another tack, Solange released the hem of his jacket to go around and block his path. They were standing in the middle of the lobby. The high-ceilinged room made the acoustics more effective so she had to nearly whisper in order not to be overheard by those milling about them.

Her hand was on his chest. "Rupert, he's just a tiny worm of a man. He isn't worth going to jail over. I'm asking you not to pursue this." Angry golden-brown eyes pierced pleading dark brown ones. She could tell by the determined expression in his gaze that he wasn't buying her entreaty.

She tiptoed and grabbed him by his lapels, bringing his face down close to hers. Their mouths were mere inches apart. Rupert's breathing was labored. Solange knew it was because he wanted to pound Danyael into the dirt. But she was not going to allow him to do something as foolish as assault a man half his size. No one looking on would believe Danyael was in the wrong. Plus, Danyael was an Ethiopian and Rupert was a foreigner. It wouldn't go well for him.

"I handled it, Rupert. Don't go caveman on me and try to defend my honor. We're living in the twenty-first century, not the nineteenth. If you insist on punching Danyael in the face, know this: I will not sit idly by while they cart you off to jail. I will yell bloody murder until they take me right along with you. So if you don't want both of us to go to jail tonight, let's go to dinner as we'd planned. Please!"

Rupert calmly removed her hands from his lapels, grasped Solange by the shoulders and gently set her aside. Peering down at her he said, "I won't hit him hard. I'll just give him a love tap."

He turned and continued walking across the lobby toward the bar they'd left only moments ago. Solange followed, talking all the way. "Whatever happened to honesty? Huh? You said we should be truthful about everything. I told you the truth about what happened with Danyael and now your actions are going to bring about dire consequences. We'll end up in an Ethiopian jail. And

for what? Because you had to prove you're a man! I know
you're a man, Rupert. I wish you'd go ahead and take me
to bed and get rid of your frustration that way. At least
then we wouldn't be eating gruel for breakfast in the local
jail in the morning."

Rupert stopped. They were standing adjacent to the
bank of elevators off the lobby. Around the corner was
the bar. In front of them the doors of an empty elevator
were sliding open. He quickly pulled Solange into the
empty conveyance and pressed the button for their floor.
"Offer accepted. I can pound Danyael tomorrow."

He lowered his head to kiss her and Solange gave a
relieved sigh against his mouth. "Thank you." She clung
to him as his mouth devoured hers. Her handbag fell to
the floor with a thud. Rupert's hands lowered to her bottom. They pressed closer and soon the hem of the dress
he'd gifted her with was up around her hips. Rupert raised
his head to look deeply into her eyes. "He didn't touch
you, did he?"

"No, no," she lied. If she told him Danyael had put
his hand on her that would be the end of this delicious
interlude. She didn't want it to end, it was just beginning.

"I care about you, Solange," Rupert said softly. "I
want to protect you, keep you safe. If anything happened
to you I would never forgive myself. From the first moment I saw you standing on the lawn of that building at
the University of Miami, I knew getting to know you
better would affect me this way." He gently ran the pad
of his thumb across her lower lip. "I sensed you had a
tender heart. Your concern for that guard told me that.
Plus you had an air of innocence about you. And there
was something else."

In this light the striations in his topaz-like eyes looked
emerald. His eyes glittered. Solange had been holding her
breath in her excitement. She released it and asked,
"What was it?"

"Vulnerability," Rupert told her. "You looked very vulnerable. I wanted to be your hero from that day forward."

Solange felt full. As if her emotions would spill over and not stop flowing until both she and Rupert were limp with satisfaction. The elevator could not move swiftly enough for her. "Rupert, no one has ever said anything more beautiful to me."

Solange heard the ding of the bell a millisecond before the elevator came to a stop on their floor. She and Rupert hastily parted and she smoothed her dress about her legs, lowering the hem back to just above her knees. Rupert had picked up her purse for her and, now, he handed it to her. They'd completed their ministrations by the time the doors slid open. Good thing, because several guests were waiting for the elevator's arrival.

She and Rupert quickly stepped from the conveyance and clasped hands as they turned left to head for their suites.

"My room?" she asked.

"You've got condoms?" Rupert wanted to know.

"No."

"My room, then."

At his door, Solange leaned against the wall, watching him fumble with the key. She smiled. He was as nervous as she was. Was it too soon? Was that what was running through his mind as he unlocked his room door?

They went inside and Rupert closed and locked the door behind them. He helped Solange off with her coat and took it with him as he crossed the room to the closet. He entered the closet, removed his leather coat, and hung his and Solange's coats side-by-side. "Make yourself comfortable," he called, as he completed his task.

Solange was doing just that. She'd already removed her pumps and tucked them out of the way beneath a chair near the bed. She worked her toes in the plush carpeting. Maybe she'd let him give her a foot massage before the night was over.

Rupert came back out into the outer room. He'd removed his shoes. He smiled when he saw Solange standing next to the bed wiggling her toes.

"One day soon you'll lose your vanity and get rid of those shoes."

She looked up and smiled at him. "Yes, when I'm eighty-five and have to get around with a walker."

Rupert crossed the room and slowly circled her. "Forest green suits you." He stopped behind her and bent to place a kiss on the side of her neck. "Although I'd be willing to bet you'd look good in absolutely nothing."

Solange closed her eyes, exulting in the feel of his lips on her skin. "Nothing is what I look best in."

Rupert undid the zipper on her dress. The dress was linen covered with lace. It had a scoop neck and cap sleeves and fit her hourglass figure like a glove. Rupert had been taken with the voluptuousness of her body from the beginning. Feminine curves were more desirable than sharp bones and angles, no matter what the fashion moguls had to say about it. He loved holding Solange against him.

He kissed the warm skin on her back after the zipper was down. He stopped when he saw a tiny tattoo of a butterfly, a monarch. He had a few tattoos himself. Most of which he'd gotten in Hong Kong when he'd been assigned there.

"Love your butterfly," he murmured.

Solange was in a mellow place. Her body was awakening to his touch. "I got it on a dare when I was sixteen," she said, her voice low. "Wait until you see its twin."

She worked one shoulder out of the dress, then the other. She stepped out of it. Underneath she wore a beige silk teddy and stockings. "I'm going to hang this in your closet." She turned away.

"Help yourself," Rupert said. He helped himself to an eyeful as she made her way across the room to the closet. He liked the motion of her hips.

Returning, Solange went straight to him and began unbuttoning his long-sleeve black raw silk shirt. His cologne, an oriental blend, combined with the warmth of his skin, did crazy things to her senses. She breathed in deeply. "Damn, you smell good."

"It's my aim to please," he said, twisting his sensual mouth into a grin. "I love the smell of your skin first thing in the morning. I wait for that smell every morning. It's like a drug to me, I've got to have it."

Solange had succeeded in getting all of the buttons on Rupert's shirt undone. She massaged his shoulders. "What do you do to get shoulders like these? You must work out every day to be as fine as you are."

"I'm a lazy bum," Rupert disavowed. "Jogging three times a week when I can work it in. Tae kwon do five days a week. Weightlifting two or three times a week. I love to swim when I get the chance."

"Whew!" Solange said. "I'm worn out just hearing about your schedule."

"What do you do to stay in such great shape?"

"I stopped eating fried foods," Solange quipped. "I'm a college professor, baby, not an Olympic athlete. I was a gymnast in high school and college. I went to college on an athletic scholarship. But by the time I received my doctorate, I'd decided being a couch potato was the life for me!"

Rupert laughed. "Well, it's working for you, because you have the nicest bottom I've ever seen, and your stomach muscles are nothing to sniff at. Admit it, you do sit-ups."

"Okay, a few sit-ups while watching TV. But that's all."

"And you live in Florida. You must swim."

Solange sighed. "I've been known to hit the pool at the women's gym a few times a month, but not on a regular basis."

"Think you could beat me?"

Solange cocked an eyebrow at him as she ran her hands over his washboard stomach. "You're very competitive, aren't you?"

"Guilty," Rupert said with a smile. "It comes from always being expected to be the best athlete at school. They figured since I was black I should be like Mike."

"Plus you were so big and strong." She pressed her upper body against his chest.

"That's true. I was the big, square-headed dope who couldn't get a date to save his life. Girls would look but would not touch."

Solange's brows knitted in mock concern. "Poor baby." Throwing her arms around his neck, she pulled him down. Rupert grabbed her bottom with both hands and lifted her off her feet. Solange wrapped her legs around his torso. "Well, I'm going to look and touch." She kissed him then, drawing his tongue into her mouth with the enticement of her own. Rupert moaned and moved backward, carrying the both of them to the bed. He fell onto the king-size bed with Solange on top of him. She straddled him and while he lifted his upper body from the mattress, she finished removing his shirt. She felt his erection on her thigh and was reminded that his slacks were still on. They were dress slacks with a clasp on the waistband and a zipper. No belt. She was thankful for that. Less time wasted. Her hand was on the fastener.

Rupert reached up and stayed her movements. "Be careful of the goods, sweetness."

Solange placed a hand atop his erection. She gave him a smoldering look. "I'll try my best." Then she smiled mischievously and undid the clasp. Rupert inhaled and slowly exhaled as she unzipped the slacks. Then she had him in her hands. She wrapped both hands around his fully erect penis. "My, my, my. Perhaps I should amend my statement: I'm not only going to look at you and touch you, I'm going to taste you."

She lowered her head, but Rupert protested, saying, "Don't, sweetness, because if you do, I will undoubtedly orgasm. It's been a while and I'm not at all certain about my level of control what with wanting you as badly as I want you now. Then that would leave you unsatisfied, and I can't have that on my conscience."

Solange kissed him there instead, then licked her lips.

Rupert smiled and pulled her close to his chest. "You're so bad. But that's good."

He rolled her over onto her back, then got to his feet and got out of both his slacks and boxers. His erection bobbed as he walked over to the nightstand to retrieve a foil-wrapped condom. He quickly opened it and slid it onto his penis.

Solange watched all this from the bed. He made these awkward moments look almost graceful. She lay curled on her side, her breasts spilling out of the teddy's bodice.

His dark brown body was one color all over except for the various wounds he'd shown her the other night. How could any man have a body like that and not be vain, she wondered. Yet she knew he wasn't. He seemed to consider his body an instrument that he had to keep tuned or else it would not play as beautifully as it should.

Rupert came to her, pulled her to a sitting position on the edge of the bed, then knelt before her. Their eyes met. In his eyes she saw the desire he felt at that moment, but also a great deal of tenderness. He reached up and pulled the straps of the teddy off of each shoulder. The result was the teddy lay about her waist and her full breasts were captured in his big, rough hands. He pulled her closer to him as he knelt there and manipulated both hardened nubs with his tongue. Solange resisted doing something foolish like swooning. Rupert's tongue should be registered as a deadly weapon. Her nipples were tight and swollen. Her female center throbbed and grew moist and slick. She'd never had an orgasm solely by having her breasts suckled, but felt she just might tonight. Rupert abruptly withdrew his mouth, precisely at the point when she was about to shout. She lay back on her elbows. Rupert busied himself by pulling the teddy past her hips, coaxing her to raise them a bit to make his efforts less taxing. He had to save his energy for what was to come next. His nostrils flared when the unique odor that was a woman's assailed them. His mouth watered too, for he longed to taste her honey. But not now. Later.

He ran both hands along the insides of her thighs. How silky and smooth they were. Her skin was the color of milk chocolate, and tanned. He knew a tan when he saw one. She liked being outside. And from her tan lines it was apparent she wore a two-piece bathing suit to the beach. The thought of seeing her lying wet and inviting atop a towel at the beach made his penis sit up and take notice. To say nothing of the appeal of the triangle of delight awaiting him between her thighs.

He was a man who ate one course at a time, though, and would not be rushed.

Solange tensed when she felt his mouth on her inner thigh. Oh, no, she was ticklish there. Didn't he remember she suffered from that malady? And a malady it was, when the slightest giggle at a critical juncture in lovemaking could make a man's nature fall flat on its face. It had happened with Nick. Once he'd gotten so upset, he'd gotten up and gone home. That was one of the good times. The bad times were when he'd accuse her of sabotaging their love life. How could a man concentrate and maintain an erection when she was braying like a jackass every time he accidentally touched a sensitive area on her body. It was demoralizing.

Rupert kissed the inside of her other thigh and Solange couldn't help it, she laughed. She peered at him. Rupert smiled. "Wonderful. I thought you'd gone to sleep." He licked her thigh this time. Solange let out a guffaw.

"I'm sorry, I'm ticklish there," she apologized, tears running down her cheeks.

Rupert bent his head and thrust his tongue in her warm, wet female center. Solange stopped laughing and sighed deeply instead. He grinned at her. "I found a spot where you're not ticklish."

Solange responded by lying flat on the bed and opening her thighs a tad wider for easier access. And they say the British don't know how to make love! This one could teach the French a thing or two.

Rupert went deeper, his tongue gently laving her clitoris. He felt it swell against his tongue. Felt her quivers. Heard the moans she was trying to muffle with an arm thrown across her mouth. He was not rough, though when she bucked he sometimes got the impulse to be. He knew, though, that her pleasure would be more intense if he did not rush. She would let him know when to increase the pressure.

Solange was going crazy trying not to climb to the top of the precipice and shout out loud. She wished she could make this last for hours, but her body wasn't having it. It had gone too long without loving. And she was too grateful for it. Yes, grateful. A body should not go for nearly three years without being fully appreciated. Rupert was showing his appreciation to the max.

Long strokes along her labia. Short back and forth strokes concentrated on her clitoris. Ah, it was sweet heaven. Every pleasure point on her body was ready to shout hallelujah.

Then it happened. She exploded with what felt like a fluid fire spreading to every nerve ending of her body, igniting pure bliss. She jumped from the precipice and floated downward like a feather caught on a summer breeze. That was how easy she felt her descent was in Rupert's hands.

"Oh my God," she breathed.

Rupert rose and lay beside her on the bed. He nuzzled her neck and enfolded her in his arms. "You looked so beautiful when you cried out just then." He kissed her lips.

Solange turned toward him. Her big brown eyes were understandably dreamy. "I could die in your arms right now and go without a complaint."

Rupert smiled his pleasure at the compliment. "You can't die now, the night has just begun."

"Did you do what I asked you to do?" Theophilus asked the simpleton.

"Indeed," Danyael spoke clearly into the cell phone. He was taking a stroll on the grounds of the Sheraton as he talked. "I propositioned her."

"How did she respond?"

"She slapped me twice, undoubtedly after hearing the myth that it's the only way to dampen an Ethiopian man's ardor. Then she slapped me again just in case it was three times instead of two. I think I upset her when I touched her breast."

"You touched her breast? I didn't tell you to touch her breast, you fool."

"I threw that in as a bonus."

"Idiot. She'll never let you within ten feet of her now. I wanted you to get her out here for a talk, but I didn't want you to have to kidnap her. Is she ever without Giles?"

"Never. They go everywhere together. I know I've seen him somewhere before," Danyael said, thinking out loud.

"Well, you're going to have to keep a sharp eye out.

Samantha will be going back to the States in five days' time. After that we have to act fast. I want Dr. DuPree here at the villa as soon after Samantha leaves as possible."

Danyael sighed. "This could be dangerous. I heard from one of my spies that Dr. DuPree told Giles I had come on to her and he wanted to cause me bodily harm, but she convinced him not to. I will have to stay out of sight from now on. If he catches up with me, he'll cripple me."

Theophilus was silent a moment. "I should have known not to send a fox to guard the hen house."

Danyael was not familiar with his employer's Americanisms. But he got the gist of it. "If you mean I should not have touched her, I agree. My ears are still ringing. If you don't mind my saying so, Mr. Gault, you should simply come to the hotel and ask her for her help. All of this sneaking around, it doesn't sit well with me. I'm a butler, not a spy."

"You're my most trusted employee and that's why you got the assignment. I know you would never inform on me. I know where all your skeletons are buried. The world must never know upon what potential foolishness I'm about to embark. I would be the laughingstock of Wall Street if they learned what I'm planning. Now get back inside before Rupert Giles sees you and gives you the beating you so richly deserve, you wolf in sheep's clothing." He laughed uproariously. "And keep your hands to yourself from now on."

Danyael hung up to the sound of his employer's laughter. First he had been forced to venture out from the relative safety of his normal environment. Now he had to put up with Theophilus Gault's teasing. Life was not fair. Though, in all honesty, he had enjoyed getting slapped by Dr. Solange DuPree. He smiled, remembering. Perhaps if he could catch her alone he would be able to

persuade her to accept his apology. He worked his jaw.
It was still a little sore.

"I forgot to tell you, I always nap after an orgasm.
Wake me in about twenty minutes and I'll be ready to go
again," Solange said, after confessing to Rupert that she
could die now and have no complaints. On her side of
the bed, she placed folded hands beneath her head and
closed her eyes, smiling all the while. "Get the lights,
would you?"

Rupert laughed. "You'd have to be a truly heavy
sleeper to snooze while I'm inside of you. Come here,
girl."

He gathered her to his chest. Her eyes sprang open.
Hard muscles strained as he moved backward off the bed,
holding her in his arms. Standing, he carried her to the
bathroom and into the large shower stall. Solange
shrieked when he turned on the cold water, and it rained
down on both their heads. "Are you awake now?" he
asked.

"I was only joking, you big bully." Solange laughed,
adjusting the water's temperature.

She glanced down. Cold water tended to do negative
things to a certain part of a man's anatomy. Rupert wasn't
affected at all, his member was stiff and hard. The condom was stretched to its limit. She reached down and
grabbed him, her hand unable to close around the cir-
cumference. "I don't know if I can take you."

"I think you can accommodate me. Let's give it a go,
shall we?" Then he reached behind her, turned off the
water and lowered his head to kiss her mouth.

The tub's surface was nonskid. Rupert tested the feature before lifting Solange by the waist. A fast learner,
she knew where he was going with his actions, and
guided him inside of her as he slowly lowered her. Then

she wrapped her legs around him and got closer. She was still wet and slick from her recent orgasm and his entrance caused her no discomfort.

"Perfect fit," Rupert said. "Now, hold on tightly."

He stepped out of the stall and carried her back to the bed with his shaft inside of her. Solange had never done anything so kinky. She was simultaneously turned on and afraid they were going to tear, strain, or pull something. She didn't want to imagine how many women Rupert had carried to his bed in this manner.

She continued to cling to him when they got to the bed. He placed both hands beneath her bottom, holding her in place and then gently lowered her to the bed. Solange eagerly spread her legs. On his knees now, Rupert thrust deeper, coming nearly completely out again with each thrust. Solange felt the warmth of him inside of her; then he'd pull out, and he'd feel slightly cooler going back in. All the while he was expanding until his penis was so engorged it rubbed against her clitoris with every thrust. She was nearing another colossal orgasm.

Rupert watched her face. She'd closed her eyes, her lips were slightly parted, her skin was flushed. Her breath was coming in short, raspy intervals. He had to close his eyes because the sight of her in the throes of another orgasm was heightening his own pleasure and he didn't want to come just yet. "Get on your knees for me, sweetness."

Solange complied though a bit grudgingly. She could feel her heartbeat down there, she had been so close to coming. Her willingness to learn overrode that momentary selfishness and she got on her knees.

Rupert squeezed her lovely round buttocks. He kissed each cheek and then entered her female center from behind. Solange quivered. Her vaginal muscles tightened around his shaft. Rupert groaned. He felt each minute movement. He went deeper, bent over her and grasped both plump breasts in his hands. He rubbed the nipples gently with the palms of those hands. Then he rubbed both nipples between twin forefingers and thumbs.

Solange threw her head back and moaned loudly in orgasmic release.

Rupert let go of her nipples and kissed the hollow of her back. His moist lips began at her neck and worked their way down to her buttocks. He felt her vaginal muscles relax and that was his cue to increase the intensity and rapidity of his thrusts.

He was so hard he was in pain. Groaning, he gave one last series of deep, deep thrusts. Solange sighed as ripples of pleasure coursed through her body. It was this that pushed Rupert over the edge. His seed spilled into the condom and he contracted inside of her. Over too soon in his opinion. But he had expected as much. His eagerness had been his downfall.

As he pulled out of Solange he saw, to his horror, that the condom had broken. "Dammit," he said, holding himself.

He hurried to the bathroom.

Solange got to her feet in time to see Rupert entering the bathroom. Her first thought was that his climax had been somewhat of an anticlimax. She had pegged him for a cuddler, not one of those who immediately ran off to the bathroom to wash away the bodily fluids as if they were poison. "What's wrong?" she called after him, walking toward the bathroom.

"The condom broke," Rupert said.

By the time she got to the bathroom's doorway, he'd disposed of it and was busy soaping a washcloth, probably to wash himself with. He turned an apologetic smile on her. "I'm sorry, Solange. They were brand new. I thought they were a good, sturdy brand."

He ran hot water over the washcloth, rinsed it, and wrung it out. Wiping his hands, he said, "If you get pregnant, I promise to be a stand-up type. I've never reneged on a responsibility in my life."

"I'm not worried about that," Solange said. "There's no chance of a STD, is there?" *Perfect time to be asking,* she thought.

"Oh no," Rupert assured her. "I've been having AIDS tests done for the past ten years. It was required in the military due to the fact that we were often exposed to other people's blood in hand-to-hand combat from biting, clawing, scratching, or stabbing. I'm healthy. You?"

"Just to be on the safe side, I got tested after leaving Nick more than two years ago. I'm healthy. It's a good time to be asking all of these questions, isn't it?"

Rupert smiled at her. "Sex can be scary nowadays. That's why I'm selective about my partners." He placed the washcloth on the sink and walked over to her. Pulling her into his arms, he held her a few seconds before peering down into her eyes. "I meant it: If you should be pregnant, I will support you in whatever you decide to do."

Solange felt a sadness come over her. It was as if the joy she'd experienced a few minutes ago had instantly been obliterated. He looked so earnest when he'd promised to stand by her. She didn't doubt his sincerity.

She had to break up this tender moment right away. She didn't need him getting sappy on her. They'd both gone into this with their eyes wide open. He'd known it was sexual between them. She'd known she should take what she could and walk away at the first opportunity. It was either that or watch him leave her sometime down the road. Hadn't he told her he wanted a house full of children someday? He hadn't implicitly stated it, but she knew he meant children who were conceived the old-fashioned way, not adopted or brought about with the aid of a fertility specialist. No, he wanted to see himself reflected in the faces of his children.

She was not the woman to give him that.

Looking at him now, mellow after sex, feeling all was right with his world, she couldn't bear to tell him.

"I'm not pregnant," she said, laughing. "What I am is ravenous. Let's order dinner from room service, then jump in the shower."

Rupert let go of her. Something had changed between them. But things always changed after you made love. The next few days would determine whether or not they continued seeing each other once they returned to their respective countries or not. He knew he wanted to try with every fiber of his being. But did she? He'd made a promise to himself, after Lauren: He would never beg a woman not to leave him again. He hadn't told Solange, but he'd loved Lauren so much he had thought he'd die without her. But no amount of pleading on his part could break her parents' influence over her. He was done with that. He'd rather be alone and have his pride intact than get down on his knees to another woman.

On the other hand, he was tired of playing the field and wanted to make a life with a woman who would stand by him, no matter what. He was looking for fierce loyalty and an independent spirit. He sensed Solange possessed both. But there was something else about her that warned him off: her vulnerability, the same vulnerability he'd seen in her that day in Miami. What had caused it? She had yet to reveal that part of herself.

Part Two

Shadows fall on the desert where
my ancestors used to roam.
Much like me: I'm a nomad,
there's no place I can call home.

The wind cuts sharp, like a knife,
as indigo night falls.
I'm a warrior. I don my sword
when my savage past I recall.

The earth is covered with bodies
of the innocent.
Weary warriors who took orders,
where do they go to repent?

God in his sky looks down upon
us, His children, His own.
Does He ever wonder, like all parents,
"Where has the time gone?"

Still we search for answers, for
some hidden clue.
To the reason we're put here.
Why I'm me, why you're you.

Can it be that our present lives
are as a result of the past?
And we go around in circles
living lives that don't last?

If so you must fight for those you love,
and hold them close to your heart.
Covet them as a miser does gold.
Keep to a minimum the times you're apart.

I'm an old warrior. I know whereof I speak.
Listen to these words, take heed:
Unless your fight in life was for love,
your life has been in vain, indeed!

—The Book of Counted Joys

Eight

"You told him we wouldn't be needing him this week," Rupert reminded Solange the next morning as they left the hotel. Solange took in the clear, blue sky above them. Gorgeous. No wonder so many countries had attempted to colonize Africa, it was beautiful. "I know," she said, as they headed south toward the nearest bus station. "I'm so used to seeing his face first thing in the morning that I guess I was looking for him out of habit. I'm going to miss him when we leave."

They were both dressed for travel. Sturdy slacks, shirts, and boots. Knapsacks thrown across their shoulders. Down jackets stuffed in them in case they got caught outside at night when the temperature plummeted. Since it was too cold at night to camp outside, Rupert had planned their sojourn north of Addis Ababa so that they would be near suitable accommodations by sundown each day, so he was in a military frame of mind when it came to keeping schedules. He'd written down the departure times for all of the buses they would be passengers on. He intended to make each departure time or die trying.

Their destination today: Debre Libanos, 115 kilometers or just over 72 miles north of Addis. They would have to take one bus to a nearby town called Fiche, then get a minibus from there that would take them on to the Debre Libanos site.

Solange matched her pace with his. "Rupert, do you think it would be a good idea to try to see if we can find Tesfaye's relatives?" She hastened to add, "He must have *somebody* who can be responsible for him. It doesn't make sense that he doesn't have one living relative."

"Do you know how many children are living on the streets here in Ethiopia? Hundreds of thousands, made orphans by war, famine, or disease. He probably slipped through the cracks years ago. They've stopped looking for him because they don't have the funds nor the manpower to continue their search. Millions of their people are living hand-to-mouth. What makes one boy so special?"

Solange didn't answer, because she knew it wasn't a question but a declarative sentence. Nothing made Tesfaye more special than the other children on the streets. Except that she had met him. She'd met him and found him infinitely important.

"When we get back to Addis in a few days, I'm going to try anyway," she said, her tone determined but not combative. She didn't want to argue with Rupert. He could help or not. She would see what could be done. What would she do if Rupert were right and her inquiries got no results? *Keep trying.*

"I knew you were going to say that," Rupert said, pulling her close to his side. "I'll help in any way I can."

Solange smiled and put her free arm around his waist.

On the filled to capacity bus to Fiche, they talked about the atrocity that had occurred at Debre Libanos. The site was one of Ethiopia's most holy because the founder of the thirteenth century monastery that had sat on the site many years ago, Tekla Haimonot, was said to have been the one who helped spread Christianity in the highlands of Ethiopia. He was considered a saint today. In more recent history, Debre Libanos was the site of a massacre brought about by Mussolini's viceroy, Graziani. In May of 1937, Graziani ordered soldiers to execute 267 monks who resided at Debre Libanos. He accused the monks of encouraging the rebels in their fight against Italian occupation.

Graziani hoped that if the monks were killed, the people's spirit would be deflated and the rebels would give up. A week after having the 267 monks executed, he ordered the deaths of the remaining 129 young deacons.

"War is hell," Solange said. "The innocent die and so-called great men, the ones who send their soldiers to fight, remain safe and have a guaranteed place in history books. Men like Hitler and Mussolini, Saddam Hussein and Idi Amin."

"Amen," Rupert concurred. That's why he'd gotten out of the soldiering game. He couldn't stand to go into another Third World country under the cover of darkness and do the bidding of those who were so far removed from the carnage they had not the slightest idea of the degradation. Rupert felt his superiors sometimes thought of themselves as giants who manipulated their soldiers like pawns on a chessboard.

Solange sat next to the window. She tried to guess at what speed the bus was traveling. It felt like they were creeping along. The driver would stop whenever he was flagged down by a potential rider. It didn't matter whether they were standing at a designated bus stop or not. Obviously the locals greatly depended on the buses to get them from one town to the next, but Solange observed that most people still walked everywhere. The bus fare was probably beyond their means.

The other passengers were men, women, and children dressed in myriad ways. Some were in western attire, some in traditional Ethiopian garb. The tourists were easy to spot—they were busy peering out windows, snapping photos, wearing amazed expressions whenever their eyes took in an unusual sight. The locals, in contrast, talked amongst themselves, read the paper or, in one case, knitted. There was nothing astonishing about their surroundings to them.

Two hours into their trip, Rupert checked his watch. "Three hours from Addis to Debre Libanos, the guidebook said. I don't think we're going to make it in that time."

Solange smiled and lay her head on his shoulder. "Relax. We'll make it in plenty of time to look around the site and get a ride to Bahar Dar. We should be able to find a place there to stay for the night."

Rupert cocked his head to the side, making a connection with hers. "You're good for me. I'd forgotten we're in no rush."

That was oftentimes hard for visitors to Africa to fathom, Solange reflected—that everything didn't run on time. The pace was slower. But when you fell into the flow of the life there, allowing yourself to go with it, you found that being on time for everything was not all it was cracked up to be. There was another way to live. Returning to the fast pace of your normal everyday life could be a shock to the system.

Solange was soon fast asleep.

Rupert sat gazing into her face. She was even lovelier in repose. Her black lashes lay against the coppery brown skin of her cheekbones. Red lips parted slightly forming a tiny 'o'. Remembering their lovemaking last night, he could practically feel them on him. Last night. He didn't want to start analyzing everything that had transpired between them, but he had to wonder why she had laughed when he'd said he'd stand by her should she be pregnant as a result of their coupling. It wasn't unheard of for a woman to conceive the first time a couple made love. Perhaps she had been trying to make light of the situation in order not to spoil the high they were on.

He had to admit, learning the condom had broken had

put a damper on his mood. Ah, but prior to that everything had gone better than he'd imagined. She was an enthusiastic, inventive lover who gave as good as she got. He had not expected anything less. He'd learned a long time ago that when a woman was generous and caring in her dealings with others, she was usually that way in bed, too. Solange had a heart so big it could encompass the world.

Thinking of her capacity to love, his mind went to the boy, Tesfaye. He feared Solange was heading for heartbreak in that direction. For one thing, it was highly unlikely Tesfaye was even his name. If Rupert's instincts were correct, Tesfaye had many reasons to conceal his identity. Among them, his need to remain a lost child. If the home he'd been assigned to had been such a wonderful place to live, he wouldn't have run away. He could also have made enemies on the street. At any rate, it was to his advantage to be invisible.

The bus came to a stop along the road to Fiche. The cheery bus driver welcomed aboard a middle-aged Ethiopian man and a young woman who appeared half his age. He preceded her onto the bus and when they came to the sole empty seat, he gave it to her. When she turned sideways, Rupert saw that she was expecting.

Rupert bent and softly kissed Solange's forehead. Why was the thought of her carrying his child not sending him into a major panic?

Solange awoke when the bus came to a halt in Fiche. She smiled at Rupert who was smiling at her. "Thanks for the use of your shoulder."

"You're welcome. We're in Fiche."

"Lovely, I hope there's a restroom nearby."

Tesfaye was bored. He'd left his makeshift home behind a bakery, whose owner knew of his presence there and sometimes left him day-old bread, and walked the ten blocks to the Sheraton in hopes of catching the strange pothole-faced man who was always following Solange. Tesfaye's antennae for miscreants was working overtime with that one. What was his interest in Solange? He saw the way he looked at her. Not that he cared what happened to Solange. She was a pest. She was a mosquito sent by the Devil to trick him into believing in adults once more. He would not fall for her charms, not even a little. He naturally had an inquisitive mind. It was what got him out of tight spots, and oftentimes what got him into them.

After waiting more than an hour on a bench across the street, his patience was rewarded when the pothole-faced man strode out of the Sheraton's entrance and hurried down the steps to a waiting luxury car. Tesfaye did not move an inch. He committed the license plate number to memory, however. He had a talent for numbers, and once he saw one it was in his mind forever. Old Mitke, from whom he'd learned his trade, told him his ability to recall everything he read was called a photographic memory. The eyes take a picture that the mind develops and commits to memory.

As for his proficiency with numbers, Old Mitke was not pleased with it—especially when he learned he could not cheat him out of his fair share of the day's take.

Samantha was in the library when the doorbell rang. Since she was closer to the door than Mary, their housekeeper, she went to answer it.

Danyael stood on the other side of the door, a frown marring his normally smiling face. Samantha had known Danyael all her life. He'd been employed by her parents when she was a year old. That meant she'd known him nearly as long as she'd known her own father. She fancied that she knew them equally well.

"Danyael, I didn't know you'd be back from visiting your family in the north this soon. Come in. Daddy's upstairs in his office on the phone with D.C."

"I hate that driver," Danyael complained. "He takes corners like he's in the Indianapolis 500. And he brakes in a panic. One time I got in the back and forgot to fasten my seat belt. He stopped at a red light and threw me across the front seat."

He came inside. "Samantha you look as fresh as a summer day. Your father tells me you're off to Colorado in a few days."

Samantha closed the door and turned to face Danyael. "To take his place at a plant opening. I think it's just his way of getting rid of me. He's up to his old tricks."

Danyael cleared his throat. "Well, let's hope not."

"Mom isn't here to be his conscience," Samantha theorized. She always assumed that if not for her mother's gentle influence on him, her father would be more of a corporate pirate than he already was. Theophilus Gault had the reputation of mowing down the competition and turning them into mulch for his vast garden of financial holdings. In other words, he kept his eye open for businesses that were crippled financially, swooped in and purchased them at ridiculously low prices, and fed them to the huge machine that was Gault Electronics. A plant in Boulder, Colorado, was his most recent acquisition.

Samantha looked straight into Danyael's eyes. "Then you don't know what he's up to?" she asked. From an early age she'd figured out how to tell when Danyael was lying—he blinked incessantly when he was being dishonest. "Because I am loath to leave him if he's bound to get into trouble in my absence. Somebody has to bail him out of jail."

At the mention of the word "jail," Danyael started

blinking. He rubbed his eyes to try to conceal the afflic-
tion, to no avail. Samantha turned away, her heels clicking
smartly on the marble floor. "I thought so."

Danyael caught up with her some distance down the
hall. He grabbed her by the arm. "Please don't say anything, Samantha. You know your father, he'd be furious
if he thought I'd spilled the beans. He'll fire me. Besides
it's nothing he could go to jail for." He stretched his eyes
in an attempt to ward off the blinking. He blinked anyway.

"Listen to me, Danyael," Samantha said. "Whatever
my father is up to, you have to stay by his side and
keep him out of trouble. I'm going to Boulder. If I
didn't, he'd know I suspected something and then he'd
have his guard up. But I'll be back within three days.
Three days, Danyael. Do you think you can prevent
whatever he has planned from happening for three days?
Because when I return, he will have to abandon whatever madness he has set in motion. If there's one thing
I know about my father, it's that he doesn't want to be
seen in a bad light by me."

"That's true," Danyael said, his blinking under control.
"I'll try my best."

"That's good enough," Samantha said confidently.

She left Danyael standing in the foyer, his hand on his
stomach. Darned if his ulcer wasn't acting up. Theophilus
Gault and his harebrained schemes would be the death
of him yet!

Solange's thigh muscles burned but she was determined to reach the top of the cliff so she could look down
on the site where the original monastery at Debre Libanos
had stood centuries ago. Rupert was behind her, not
nearly as winded.

At last they were far enough up to gaze down on Debre
Libanos. It sat on the edge of a gorge and though the

terrain was rocky in spots, in some directions the rolling green hills undulated toward the blue sky and the horizon. The largest building was the church Emperor Haile Selassie had ordered built in 1961. It was made of white stone and had the distinction of being constructed in various architectural designs. The tomb of Tekla Haimonot was housed in the church.

"What are all those people doing down there in white robes?" Solange asked.

"It says in the guidebook that there are several religious schools on the property," Rupert replied. "They're probably novices."

Solange took photographs from her vantage point. "Shall we go down and visit the cave where the holy water is supposed to come from?"

"Can't miss that," Rupert said.

"They say it's good for chasing away evil spirits and an upset stomach. Are you plagued with either of those?"

"Unfortunately, no. I guess we can't test the water's restorative powers after all," Rupert joked. They started down the precipice, going slowly so as not to stumble and fall. Since they had started out early, it was only half past one. It didn't start getting dark until after six P.M. They had plenty of daylight left.

"Bahar Dar is too far to travel tonight without the assurance of a place to stay once we get there. Why don't we spend the night in Debre Markos instead, and get up early and make for Bahar Dar. From there, Blue Nile Falls isn't very far at all."

"Sounds like a plan," Solange agreed, as she paused to click off one final photo of the church from this height.

The cave where Tekla Haimonot was said to have done his praying was roped off for the tourists' safety. A walk-through took a mere ten minutes, and neither of them was brave enough to wait in line, for there were several people waiting to try the restorative waters.

Instead, they walked through the church, admiring the stained glass windows and the murals on the walls. Then they visited the tomb. The mood in the church was somber, and the air chilly, due to the stone walls.

As they stepped outside in the bright sunlight again, Solange and Rupert clasped hands and began walking to the car park where they were to meet the minibus that had brought them here. Rupert had been ruminating on something the entire day, and now found the courage to ask, "Why did you and Nick break up? You told me it was not an amiable parting. Did he hurt you in some way?"

Solange inwardly cringed. What would he do if she told him the truth? Run for the hills, that's what. Oh, he'd try to be magnanimous, but that wouldn't last long. She peered into his eyes. Was it so wrong to want to spend a little more time with him? Was it wrong to seek the pleasure of his arms for as long as she could?

"Do you remember I told you he had a cruel streak?"

"Yes," Rupert said quietly. He watched her face intently.

"He asked me to marry him, and from that day forward I could not do anything to please him. He wanted me to give up my position at the University of Miami and move with him to West Virginia where he'd been offered a position with a prestigious college. I told him I didn't want to give up ten years of an ideal career at U of M where I was working toward tenure. He thought I should be willing to give it up for him. I balked. He tried to bully me into doing his will. I told him it was over, and he wouldn't have it. He followed me around town. Left nasty notes on my door. Sent me dead flowers."

"He became obsessed with you," Rupert put in. "I've seen it happen. He could not believe you didn't want him anymore. Did you love him?"

"Yes, I loved him. But I came to fear him."

Rupert placed a comforting arm around her shoulders. Solange sighed with relief. She hadn't lied to him. She just hadn't told him the whole truth.

The minibus was waiting with its motor idling when they got to the car park. Rupert allowed Solange to get on before him. The driver was a gregarious Ethiopian man who was tall and lanky. "How are you finding our country?" he asked Rupert.

"I hung a right at Cairo, and here I am," Rupert joked. The man laughed heartily. "Ah, I get you."

"Your country is beautiful," Rupert said seriously, then went to sit down next to Solange, who had already claimed their seat in the back of the bus.

Debre Markos, the capital of the Gojam province, had several hotels and restaurants from which to choose. Solange and Rupert settled on the Menkorer Hotel, where they reserved a room with a double bed for the night. It was all that was available; the hotel was booked up, or they would've gotten a bigger bed. Then they hired a car to take them to a restaurant. They were famished.

The restaurant served basic Ethiopian fare. The wat, or stew, was delicious, and the injera was the best kind, thin and freshly made. Solange was beginning to like the pancake-like bread.

She tried tej, a mead—or beer—made from honey. It was also delicious. Its sweetness was deceptive, however, because it packed quite a punch. She looked across the table at Rupert after she'd half finished her second glass and swore she was seeing two of him.

"I think I'm stoned," she said, holding the glass aloft. Rupert smiled and gently removed her fingers from around the glass of tej and placed the glass out of her reach. "This stuff should come with a warning label. No more for you, sweetness." He brought her fingers to his mouth and kissed them individually.

Solange gave him a crooked grin. She rested one elbow on the table and sat with her chin in the palm of her hand, looking at him. "I wish I could give you *ten* babies."

Rupert laughed softly. "One would be sufficient."

"Nah," said Solange. "You said you wanted a houseful."

"We'd live in a small house."

"You're a big man, you need a big house," Solange countered.

Rupert smiled at her. She was apparently a loquacious drunk. The kind whose mood elevated, the kind who derived the utmost pleasure from word games.

She was still staring at him intently. "Let's go practice making babies. Practice makes perfect."

Rupert motioned for the waiter. When the short, squat man arrived Rupert handed him several Birr notes and a generous tip. "You enjoy?" asked the man.

"Very much," Solange told him. "Anten foto mansat yichalal?" *May I take your photo?*

He looked pleased at the notion and vigorously nodded his acquiescence. Solange, who took her camera with her everywhere, quickly took his photograph.

"I want a complete record of this trip," she told Rupert as they were exiting the restaurant. "Because when I return to Miami it may be hard to believe I was actually here with you."

"Be careful what you say while you're drunk. You know what they say about booze. It loosens the lips as well as one's inhibitions."

Solange was, indeed, feeling no pain. "Ask me anything!" she boldly cried.

They had to walk a couple of blocks before Rupert was able to hail a passing cab. More than once, he had to catch Solange when she stepped off the curb. "You can't even walk straight. I'm not going to ask you questions you may not want to answer."

Solange stopped in her tracks suddenly and inhaled deeply. "Smell those spices? God, this is a sensual country. So much to touch, taste, see, smell. It's not antiseptic. Do you like that word, *antiseptic?* If you break it down into its root meanings, you have *anti,* which means against, and *septic,* which means poisoned or full of pus. But in that case, my description of Ethiopia not being antiseptic doesn't make any sense at all, does it? What I meant was, it's not dull or unimaginative. It's rich, and warm, and full of life!"

"Like you," Rupert said.

At last, a taxi stopped at the curb and he helped Solange inside and slid onto the seat beside her. "The Menkorer Hotel, please."

Their room was on the second floor, so they took the stairs—Rupert felt the exercise might do Solange some good. She leaned heavily against him the entire walk up.

"I'm never going to touch tej again," she vowed.

"That's what they all say," Rupert said with a short laugh. On the second-floor landing he swept her into his arms and carried her the rest of the way to their room.

"I'm not that drunk, I can walk," Solange half-heartedly protested. "I've never been drunk before. It's not fair that that devil brew should taste so sweet and be so mean once it gets in your stomach."

Rupert leaned her against the wall next to the door while he put the key in the lock. "Yeah, yeah, yeah. I know, I know," he sympathized.

"You should've warned me it was so powerful."

"I was wondering when this would fall into my lap," Rupert groused good-naturedly.

He had the door open now. He slung her over his left shoulder fireman style and entered the room. After kicking the door closed, he carried Solange over to the bed and gently lay her on it. Then he went back and secured the door. He should have warned her not to drink more than one glass of the tej, but he hadn't been aware of its potency. He did know, however, that men had a higher tolerance for alcohol than women did. Men usually weighed more than women and size had something to do with how alcohol metabolized once it was in the system. Plus, men had more of a certain enzyme that broke down sugars in alcohol more effectively.

He went to her and said "Come, sweetness, it's a bath for you, then bed. You've had a long, tiring day."

Solange had curled up on the bed and gotten comfortable. She felt perfectly capable of sleeping in that spot all night. "Later. Sleep now, bathe later."

"All right," Rupert said. "But what about that tartar building up on your teeth?"

He knew she was a maniac for flossing each night.

"I dare say it'll be an inch thick by morning."

Solange stirred. "Oh, okay. I'll floss and brush." She pulled herself to a sitting position on the edge of the bed. While she was sitting up, Rupert took the opportunity to remove her jacket. "Thank you," said Solange.

"You're welcome. Do you want me to help you with the rest of your clothes?"

She primly rose. "I can do it."

She was successful at getting the blouse unbuttoned and removed, but the khaki slacks were more difficult. She unzipped them and pulled them down past her hips but when she tried to pull her right foot out of the pants leg, she lost her balance and would have toppled over if Rupert hadn't caught her in time. He firmly guided her bottom to the bed. "Sit. I'll remove your boots and slacks. That was the problem. You should have removed your boots first."

"Forgot I was wearing them." She smiled affectionately at him. "You're so good to me, Rupert. I still can't believe that's your name. Did you know you have the same name as—"

"A character on a popular TV show," Rupert finished for her, amused. "Yes, I finally get the cosmic joke my parents inadvertently played on me. Though in their defense, I was the first Rupert Giles. Some writer created the other one."

"I love your name," Solange sincerely told him. "It's a strong name. It's the name of a medieval knight. It suits you perfectly."

"I *know* you're drunk now," Rupert quipped. He'd removed her boots and socks and placed them out of the way underneath the bed for fear she might trip over them. Pulling her to her feet, he said, "Let's try this again, shall we? To the bathroom, sweetness. I'll paste your brush for you."

Wearing only a bra and bikini panties, Solange took a step toward the bathroom and found the urge to topple did not recur. Must have been those darn boots after all. She was in full possession of her faculties. A little honey mead wasn't going to get the best of her!

She had to concentrate harder than she usually did in order to floss and brush, though. The floss wouldn't remain wound around her forefingers. But after a couple of tries she found that if she cocked her head at an angle, she could get in there better with the floss. Rupert was flossing beside her at the sink. He finished in half the time, but waited until she'd finished to put the toothpaste on her toothbrush for her. "Here you are."

Solange sighed. "I never knew how tiring this was. My arms are heavy, for some reason."

"Give it your best try," Rupert coaxed her. "Then perhaps you'll feel up to a quick shower. I'll help you into the tub."

It took some effort, but Rupert got her into the shower, where he soaped her entire body and rinsed her off. Then he toweled her dry, slipped one of those diaphanous nighties she preferred over her head, and led her to the bed. He tucked her in before returning to the bathroom and showering himself. When he returned to the outer room, Solange was sound asleep.

The room's temperature was sixty-five. Neither of them cared for too much warmth while sleeping, it impeded a good night's rest. It was warm enough for him to sleep in the buff, his favorite state to sleep in. So he doused the lights and climbed into bed where he pulled Solange's warm body close to his and fell asleep almost as swiftly as she had done.

In the early morning hours Solange awoke, her head clear of the effects of the tej. Rupert's arm lay across her waist and his breath caressed the back of her neck. She relished the feel of his body against hers. She wondered if she could capture the moment on film, as she'd captured all the places and the people she'd seen that day. If only she could. For it was worth keeping. So was Rupert. She'd give anything if she could keep him. For now, he was hers. But in a matter of days she would have to do the right thing and give him back to the world. Give him back, so he could find real happiness with a woman who would be able to give him everything he so richly deserved.

She could indulge in fantasy for a while though. There was no rush. This was, after all, an experiment, a chance to see if they were compatible. No, they didn't share the same political ideologies. But they respected each other and didn't allow that to come between them. Emotional compatibility was also evident. Neither of them were afraid to express their opinions. But kindness smoothed ruffled feathers, and Rupert was innately kind. In spite of his seeming irritation with Tesfaye, he was never mean to the boy.

Solange felt warm lips on the back of her neck. "The

sound of your breathing changed and it woke me. Are you all right?"

"I'm fine, thanks to you," Solange said, turning to face him.

"You don't have to thank me for something I take such pleasure in. Besides, you're not very high-maintenance. You're not demanding in the least and you are appalled at the notion of a man supporting you. Though I still insist on taking care of all of our expenses."

"Are you made of money?" Solange joked.

"I'm paid very well for what I do. I get a percentage of the claim each time. I'm not hurting. Forgive me, but I know what college professors earn and it's not nearly as much as they're worth."

"I won't argue with you on that point," Solange said. "I still don't want to be—"

"Beholden to me?" Rupert asked with a soft laugh. "Is that word still used in modern English? You were so funny tonight when you tried to explain what you meant by Ethiopia not being antiseptic." He gently kissed her forehead. "Consider it a bribe, then. For spending time with a man who is not worthy of you."

Solange laughed softly at his assertion. She recognized it as nervous laughter, but Rupert simply found it endearing. "Solange, I need to tell you something that could drastically change how you feel about me. However, I have to bite the bullet and tell you anyway. It's the only way I know how to proceed with this relationship, and I want to continue seeing you. Remember when I told you Lauren was not honest with me from the beginning? Well, I haven't been honest with you either. I lied about my years in the Special Air Services. I was recruited into the group, but after three years of distinguished service, I was asked to join another group. A specialized, elite agency that answered only to the Prime Minister. In other words, I was a spy just as Toni suspected."

Solange held in a gasp. She didn't want to deter him from continuing when he'd gotten this far. Breathing in slowly and exhaling even slower, she asked, "Was? Then you no longer work for them?"

"No, I voluntarily left the agency more than four years ago. Our ideologies didn't jibe, and the agency considers those who are not 100 percent pro-agency a liability. I signed a nondisclosure agreement and it was understood that if I ever revealed any pertinent information about the agency I'd be killed. So, don't ask me any specific questions. I had to tell you, though, because you should know who and what you're getting involved with. I've done things I'm not proud of. Even though they were done in the service of my country. Many of these acts haunt me. I feel as though they're a taint on my soul, have made me unclean—as though I can never again know what it feels like to be a whole man." His voice broke and Solange immediately pressed her body closer and touched her cheek to his.

"Don't tell me anymore," she pleaded.

"I have to tell you, sweetness, because my heart has chosen you. And if you're going to leave me because of this, I'd rather it be now than later. Therefore, I'm sharing the worst of me with you so I'll be free to give you the best of me, if you want it."

She heard the need in his voice and wanted to tell him yes, she wanted him desperately. But knowing what she had to do in a few days silenced her tongue. What she should do was tell him about her condition right now.

"And another thing," Rupert continued. "I was standoffish with Tesfaye because I didn't want to care about him. His situation is too close to my own experience. He's an orphan. I was an orphan. However, I realize now that what you said is true, we can't save the world but perhaps we can save one child. I know some people. Between you, me, and them, we'll get him the help he needs.

I like kids, Solange. I don't want you to think I don't like them. Since I was adopted myself, I'd like to adopt one day. Give a kid a good home."

Solange sighed. She would tell him now, before she lost her nerve.

But Rupert was not finished. He laughed shortly before going on. "But most of all I'd like a child of my own. The one thing I've never had in my life is someone who looks like me. Growing up, I felt like an outsider on family visiting day at school. Fathers and sons, mothers and daughters. They all resembled one another. Sometimes sons would be the spitting image of their fathers. I tortured myself thinking I was being ungrateful for everything my parents had done for me, wishing my father and I actually looked alike."

Solange felt deflated. There was no way she could tell him now. Not after hearing his deepest wish. What could she say after that disclosure?

As anyone who is caught up in his own narrative eventually realizes, it dawned on Rupert that Solange had not said anything for some time. He squeezed her in a tight embrace. "I'm sorry for laying all of this on you. Have I frightened you off? Are you repulsed by my past? Tell me how you feel."

"Relieved you're not a child-hater," Solange managed, her tone surprisingly clear since tears were in her eyes and threatening to wet her cheeks very soon. "And as for your past, you were a soldier who took orders. If I were to consider *you* a killer, I'd be condemning hundreds of millions of veterans worldwide. We fight for our countries, and when the fighting's over we go home to those we care about and try to live as normal a life as possible. You've earned the right to happiness."

Once again the selfish little devil perched on her shoulder spoke up: *And so have you!*

Now that she knew her only course of action was to

leave him, she wanted to make enough memories with him to last her the rest of her life. When she was a doddering old woman, she would look back on her time in Ethiopia with Rupert Giles and smile. She would have no regrets for what she was about to do.

"Nothing would please me more than to get to know you better," she told him, her voice rife with passion. Rupert's mouth rested high on her cheek. He felt the dampness the tears had left behind. His stomach muscles constricted painfully. His groin grew tight. He hadn't wanted to hurt her. Those tears were for him, though.

Her pain was a palpable thing to him. "Solange . . ."

Their mouths met with intense need and pent-up desire that felt combustible in nature. Fierce emotions commanded immediate physical release.

Solange felt his manhood swelling against her stomach. "Stay there," Rupert said as he climbed out of bed, walked across the room, and picked up his knapsack. He rummaged inside a moment and came out with two condoms. This time if one broke there would be a backup. Only the moonshine coming in through the single window illuminated the small room.

Coming back to the bed he handed one of the foil packages to Solange. She quickly sat up and tore it open. "Come here," she said softly. She adeptly placed the latex condom on the tip of his penis and rolled it toward his stomach. Rupert slipped on the second one. Solange moved over in bed, raising the covers for him.

Rupert got into bed and pulled the covers up over them both. Solange turned toward him. He grabbed handfuls of her bottom and they rolled over so he was on top. Solange spread her legs. Rupert's manhood lay hard, hot, and heavy between them. He lowered his head and kissed her, the momentum building. Solange craved him inside of her, but he was not ready for that. He lazily broke off the kiss and began working his way downward, leaving wet kisses in his wake. Her nipples were sweet on his tongue. He could have spent hours suckling at both plump treasures. But there were other areas to enjoy. He impatiently pulled the nightie over her head and dropped it somewhere behind him on the bed. He ran his hands along both sides of her, sculpting her lush figure, pausing at her waist a moment, then going down to her hips. How silky her skin felt beneath his hands. Hot and smooth. He kissed her belly, ran his tongue around her navel. Solange arched her back, ready for him to enter her.

"Not yet, my love," he said. Instead he ran his hands inside her thighs, down her legs. Kissed the soles of both feet. She was a delectable feast and he was not one to get up from the table until he'd sampled every morsel.

Solange was panting softly, repeatedly saying his name. "Rupert, Rupert . . ."

Rupert sat back on his haunches and gently pulled her closer to him. Solange could not see what he was doing but she felt his hands when he gently touched the soft insides of her thighs again and then began rubbing her nub with the pad of his thumb. Rupert felt her vaginal muscles contract, release, contract, release. She was so wet he was tempted to go ahead and partake of the gift she offered. He wanted to feel her body rock when he had finished what he was doing, though. Her pleasure was worth the postponement of his own.

He did not penetrate her with his fingers, but kept up the pressure with the pads of his fingers. No nails inside, because nails, though neatly trimmed, could be a rude intrusion into a soft place that was used to warm skin only. Solange bucked against his fingers. She was not a shy, retiring type who just lay there. Rupert loved that about her.

At the moment when her bucking increased, Rupert held his manhood in his hand and slid inside of her. Solange moaned loudly and spread her legs wider. Rupert reached down, raised her hips off the bed with both hands and thrust deeper. She felt so good to him he could barely hold on. Solange returned thrust for thrust. She was torn between her guilt and her intense desire to be loved. How long could she go on before she was torn asunder? The orgasm caught her by surprise, she had not expected to be able to function normally with lies and guilt riding her. Still, it ripped through her body. Tears followed and Rupert kissed her slightly swollen lips and lay, spent, beside her in the dark. Momentarily, he got up and went to dispose of the condoms. Returning to the bed, he gathered her into the crook of his arms and pulled the forgotten covers up over them. A short while later, Solange heard his soft snores.

Solange lay with her eyes wide open. She hadn't known she would fall so hard for him. If she had, she wouldn't have agreed to stay in Ethiopia. She would have gone back to the States with Toni and the rest. She could be back at school now, continuing her research. Instead, she was falling down a hole so deep, she might never find her way out again. So much for her resolution to live life to the full and stop obsessing about her infertility. She had to face the facts: her infertility would always stand in the way of her happiness until she found a man who sincerely wanted to adopt a child instead of bringing his spitting image into the world. Tomorrow she would force herself to admit Rupert Giles was not that man. Tonight she would pretend he was.

Bahar Dar sits on the shores of Lake Tana, Ethiopia's largest lake. After checking in at the serene Abay Minch Hotel, Solange and Rupert took a stroll around the attractive, well-landscaped town. The wide avenues bordered by palm trees were very pleasant to walk through. The day was a bit chilly, though. The higher they got in the mountains, the lower the temperature became. They both wore light jackets.

Strolling through the markets in town, Solange was struck by the vibrant colors the people wore. Deep shades of gold, red, purple. The women especially. It seemed color played an important role in adornment. The wearing of flamboyant jewelry was also prevalent. Women wore colorful beaded necklaces, bracelets, and earrings. Some even wore golden hoops in the side of their noses. Nothing big and ostentatious, just a tiny gold ring. Some of the rings had tiny beads in them.

"They're less garish than those I've seen in London," Rupert joked. "You'd look lovely with one. The right nostril would be the ideal place."

"I would do it," Solange said, playing along. "But my mother would have a fit. She still doesn't know about my tattoos."

"Definitely not the one on your bum," Rupert said with a grin.

"Heaven forbid!" Solange returned.

She picked up a locally woven piece of cloth. It had horizontal stripes in earth tones and was edged in fringe. The weight of it was impressive. She assumed it was winter weight material, and regretted she couldn't buy it. One thing she'd learned in her travels was not to buy everything she came across, even if she could afford it. Finding room in her cases for all the extra goodies would be impossible. Plus, there was the hassle of determining what customs would allow her to carry on the plane on her trip home.

They moved on. When they'd arrived by bus that morning, Rupert had spotted a bicycle shop across from the bus station. He proposed they bicycle to places of interest just outside of Bahar Dar, like the Weyto village. The Weyto people were able canoe makers. Called tankwas, the canoes had been in use in the area for hundreds of years.

Solange stood aside while Rupert negotiated the price of two rental bikes for the day. He seemed to be picking up Amharic quite swiftly, whereas she relied on a few phrases to get her by.

After a minute or two, he turned and smiled at her. "We're set. We have to have them back by six tonight."

It was then a quarter past ten A.M.

The bikes were old but in good repair. The roads outside of the city were bumpy in places, but the ride was made pleasant by the scenery: acres of greenery, brightly colored houses made of local wood, and the stone churches they caught glimpses of as they passed.

At Weyto Village they watched men take large pieces of papyrus, wet them, and form them into the shape of canoes. The men used a kind of natural resin on the papyrus to make the canoes watertight. When they'd finished with the canoe it would be able to bear heavy loads across Lake Tana. Solange thought the Weyto people remarkably intelligent and inventive to fashion canoes out of papyrus, which was an aquatic plant. Of course their boats would be at home in the water!

Tesfaye waited across the street all day for the potholefaced man to return. When the man finally put in an appearance it was dusk. Tesfaye swiftly crossed the street.

Once he hit the walk in front of the Sheraton he slipped into his invisible mode. He was good at being nondescript. Tesfaye might be within two feet of a mark and not be noticed by him until he discovered his wallet was missing; then his cognitive mind would think back and recall how a small, brown-skinned boy in dingy clothes had gotten too close to him in the crowd. By that time Tesfaye would be long gone.

He blended right in to the pedestrian traffic moving past the hotel. The pothole-faced man was climbing out of the luxury car, muttering something derisive under his breath about what a fool the driver was. Tesfaye accidentally ran into the pothole-faced man. The man none too gently caught Tesfaye by the shoulders and glared down at him.

"Watch where you're going, young pup," he said testily.

"I'm sorry. Please forgive me," Tesfaye said, feigning remorse.

"Just don't do it again," Pothole-face said. "Now, off with you."

Tesfaye hurried away. When he was a block up the street he ducked into an alleyway to examine Pothole-face's wallet. Out of habit, he checked the money clip first. There was over a thousand in Birr notes, plus more than a hundred and fifty American dollars. After checking on his newfound wealth he perused the American driver's license that declared Pothole-face's name to be Danyael Abate, and noted that he was from Washington, D.C. Tesfaye didn't know exactly what he would do with this information, but he was certain he would find *something* to do with it.

He smiled broadly as he continued along the avenue. It had been a very good day.

"Hold still," Solange admonished as she sprayed the deet-laden bug spray on Rupert's arms. When she finished, she allowed him to return the favor.

They were on a boat chugging toward the monastery at Tana Cherkos, where Ethiopian history claimed the Ark of the Covenant had been hidden for over eight hundred years. It would take them more than two hours to get to the island; then there was a forty-five–minute walk up a steep hill.

There were about ten other travelers aboard, a couple of them from the U.S. Solange was sitting next to one of them, a tall, queen-size African-American woman with auburn braids down her back. "I guess you and I will make that trek up the hill just to see the monastery," she said to Solange. "You know they don't allow women inside their gates?"

Solange nodded, resigned. She dearly wanted to go inside. "But it isn't just human females they don't allow on the property, they don't allow nanny goats either." The woman threw her head back and laughed. She goodnaturedly elbowed Solange. "I wonder if they check the mice to see if any of them are female?"

Solange laughed along with her. "Or the cockroaches? They do have cockroaches in Africa, don't they?"

"Honey, they have cockroaches everywhere!" After she'd stopped laughing she looked at Solange. "I'm Ruthie Aronson from Detroit." She pointed to a tall, broad-shouldered man with salt-and-pepper hair standing on deck. "That's my husband, Harold. This is our second honeymoon. He asked me what I wanted to do to celebrate our twenty-fifth wedding anniversary and I told him I wanted to go to Ethiopia. After he picked his jaw up off the floor he said 'Okay, sweetie. Whatever you say.' Here we are! How about you and that fine-looking brother next to you?" She glanced down at Solange's left hand.

"Solange DuPree, from Miami," Solange told her. "And this is Rupert Giles, who is from London. We just decided to see Ethiopia together. No special occasion."

"That's the best reason to do anything," Ruthie said with a smile. "Don't save up what you want to do in life for a special occasion. Life will have passed you by before you get around to doing it."

"That's good advice," Solange said sincerely.

"Have you been to Tis Isat yet?" Ruthie wanted to know.

"Not yet, but we're planning to go."

"Don't miss it. It's one of God's greatest creations. I declare, I had a religious experience just being there. We don't know Africa. What we see on TV pales in comparison to the real place. And there's so much negative propaganda. Starving children with their bellies swollen. Tribal wars. Natural disasters that devastate entire countries and leave the nations more bereft than they already were. I'm not saying the news shouldn't report these events. It's important to know so we can offer aid. But they could also report some of the good things about Africa, like how damned beautiful it is. This is the most beautiful place I've ever seen, and I've been many places. Harold and I were in the military for twenty years each. So we've lived in Germany, Japan, Alaska—I even did a hitch in Paris, France. I was a communications officer. As you can tell, I love to communicate." She laughed softly at her own long-windedness. "There are only a few places I'd recommend people see before they die, and Ethiopia is one of those places."

As it happened, Ruthie and Solange were the only two women aboard. So when they disembarked at Tana Cherkos and walked for nearly an hour entirely uphill, they were left atop the rise looking after the men as they departed for the monastery.

Rupert looked back at Solange with a regretful expression before catching up with the rest of the males. Solange and Ruthie sat down on a patch of grass to await the return of the men.

"That man adores you," Ruthie observed. She looked wistful. "I remember that look. It's been quite a while since Harold has been able to muster it up to that magnitude, though. Don't get me wrong, Harold is a passionate man. Ours is an easy kind of love. When you get older you settle into something different. Something less heart-pounding, if you will. Love him? I'd die for him. Swing from the ceiling? Now that I would attempt but probably wouldn't be able to pull off. Arthritis, you know." She ended with a throaty laugh.

Solange was actually blushing. The tips of her ears had grown warm. Her mother had never discussed passion between a man and a woman with her as this stranger was doing. The thought of her mother made her heart ache. She would get home in plenty of time to be with her during her operation and recovery, but she also wanted to be with her for the days leading up to the operation. She would tell Rupert she had to go home a week earlier than they'd planned. She knew she was partly using her mother's illness as an excuse to leave Rupert. What good did spending even more time with him do either of them? He was going to be hurt no matter when she left. She was going to miss him the rest of her life.

"I would be very happy to have the kind of love you and Harold share in my life," she said to Ruthie. She stretched her legs out and crossed them at the ankles. "I haven't been lucky in love."

She wanted to talk to someone about her predicament and Ruthie Aronson seemed the trustworthy type. Plus, Ruthie had the advantage of being a stranger. It was highly unlikely anything she said would get back to anyone Solange knew.

"A pretty girl like you?" Ruthie asked with a note of incredulity. Her attractive face screwed up in a frown. "I can't believe that."

Solange met Ruthie's eyes. "I'm infertile. Most men want to have children with the women they fall in love with. I don't think it's going to last between me and Rupert for that reason. I'm going to leave before we take the relationship too far."

Ruthie had gone silent. Solange imagined there wasn't much that could quiet Ruthie Aronson. She felt she'd said too much and turned her gaze to the sky, her eyes shining with unshed tears. "I'm sorry. I shouldn't have told you that. We've just met."

"No, no, sweetheart," Ruthie said. She sighed heavily. "You've got a burden to bear. Do you tell him, or do you not? Will he accept it, or won't he? How long do you wait to tell a man something like that? It's hard to say. I feel for you! I wish I had an easy solution for you. God knows I'm known for handing out advice, left and right. But this is a difficult situation. All I can say is, pray about it. Ask God to guide you. My instincts say he'd want you over fatherhood. But I could be thinking that way because I like you both after knowing you only a couple of hours, and I wish you the best."

Nine

"What was it like?" Solange wanted to know all the details of Rupert's visit to the monastery at Tana Cherkos. She and Rupert were standing on the deck of the large boat. They'd found a private spot at the opposite end from where the seating area was.

"Old, very old," he said, teasingly. He wanted to talk about them, not some musty old monastery. "The church on the grounds today dates back to the nineteenth century. It resembles the other island monasteries, except for one thing: They have replicated the room that had been the Holy of Holies in the original church when the Ark of the Covenant was supposedly kept there. The murals on the walls were faded but quite beautiful. We were told they'd been originally painted by a monk who'd lived nearly five hundred years ago. He was called Abuna Mikael and he was the keeper of the Ark until his death at ninety-seven."

The sun was setting on the horizon and Solange was getting chilly. She leaned close to Rupert as they watched the glorious orange and purple-streaked sky. "I know you told me you think their claim of having the Ark is a myth," Solange said as Rupert put his arms around her. "But I think it's a lovely myth. I mean Ireland has fairies and brownies and all kinds of magical myths. Why can't Ethiopia have one about a box through which they can communicate with God and raise monoliths?"

"It'll take a few days to get to Aksum," Rupert said. "But if you want to see the Northern stelae field, we'll go."

"I can't," Solange told him. She met his eyes. "Rupert, I should go home next week instead of week after next. I need to be with my mother when she's going through this crisis. She'd never ask me to come back early, but I think I should. She needs someone there to offer encouragement. Our talk made me optimistic about our future together. Maybe things are going to be better between us from now on."

Rupert bent his head and kissed her forehead. Smoothing her wind-tossed hair away from her face, he said, "Of course you should be with your mother. I'll miss you, though." He hugged her tighter. "I'll go back home and pine for you."

"You'll go back home and another assignment will be waiting for you, taking you to some exotic locale. You'll be too busy to miss me."

"I don't care how far apart we are, I will always have you in my heart."

"Oh," Solange joked, "now you're getting poetic."

Rupert laughed. "That *was* pretty bad, wasn't it?"

Known locally by the name, Tis Isat—*smoking fire*—the Blue Nile Falls has a width of over 1,200 feet and a depth of over 135 feet. The sound of the falls can be heard nearly a mile away.

Solange and Rupert could hear it long before it came into view early the next morning. They had walked from the village of Tis Isat, down into a gorge, across an ancient bridge that spanned the Abay River, and up to the falls. The churning water below the bridge was rust-colored due to the red clay nearby.

Over the years a rainforest had grown up next to the

falls, deep green vegetation nourished by the underground system of the falls. The rainforest was home to various species of birds. Among them the parrots, whose song Solange and Rupert now could hear.

Solange took photo after photo, smiling all the while, her sensory mechanisms bathed with stimuli coming from all directions: The sound of the falls, the singing of the birds, the pearling of water on her face due to the spray from the falls. And another animal call that wasn't like the song of any bird she'd ever heard.

She was unaware of it, but while she was busy taking photos, Rupert was watching her reaction to Tis Isat. Solange wanted to capture what she saw on film, but he was seeking to store her every nuance in his memory.

He smiled at the curiosity and fear mirrored on her brown face. "It's probably just vervet monkeys. They live in the area. Don't worry, they're harmless."

Solange had a fear of monkeys. Sure, many people thought they were cute, but they were also exceptionally strong and had sharp teeth. She preferred to give them a wide berth. "I won't worry as long as they stay out there," she said, referring to the forest. "Smile!" She lined up a shot of Rupert with the falls serving as a backdrop.

"Your turn," Rupert said, reaching for the camera after she'd finished.

Solange smiled prettily for him. He took several shots of her from various angles.

"I wish there were someone here who could take our picture together," Solange said.

"No problem," Rupert said, pointing at a monkey on a lower branch of a tree not ten feet away from them. "You can ask him to do it."

Solange yelped and stumbled into Rupert, causing both of them to fall to the ground.

Rupert dropped the camera, and it rolled down a slight incline; the monkey leaped from the tree and went after it. Solange watched in horror as the monkey dragged the camera by its strap into the thick underbrush.

"Get back here," she yelled, clambering to her feet.

She took off after the monkey, her boots flattening vegetation on the forest floor that had never been trampled by human feet. Rupert followed.

"Be careful," he called after her. "We're close to the cliff."

"I can see him! He seems to be having a hard time figuring out how to hoist the camera into the trees."

Rupert got an idea. "You have a mango in your knapsack. Break it open and offer it to him, maybe he'll trade you." It was not easy to keep a straight face, what with the monkey looking back at Solange with a frightened expression on its face, and Solange in relentless pursuit of it with a furious expression on hers.

Solange paused long enough to take Rupert's advice. The monkey stopped, too, possibly tired from dragging the heavy weight of the camera. He was only a small monkey, and the camera was a technological wonder that felt substantial even when held in human hands.

Solange took the mango and split it down the middle with her Swiss Army knife. Then she pulled it apart and slowly approached the black-faced monkey. Its fur was dark at the base and lighter on top. It had a prehensile tail.

Darned if it didn't look at the mango, then look up into Solange's face several times. Solange was a little winded and grateful for the time out. "Here, boy. I bet you don't get one of these very often, do you?" She bit into the succulent mango. The juice dribbled down her chin, but she didn't attempt to wipe it off. She could worry about neatness when she got her camera back.

The monkey inched toward her. Solange placed both halves of the mango on the ground in front of her. She hoped that the creature would be as greedy as it was light-fingered and want both halves of the fruit. He would have to use both hands in order to snatch them up. To do that he'd have to let go of the camera.

Solange waited. The monkey was breathing hard. It sat on its haunches, thinking. In a split second, it let go of the camera's strap and swept up a piece of fruit in each hand, then high-tailed it for the nearest clump of bushes, screeching all the way.

Solange had her camera in her hand before the tip of the monkey's tail disappeared into the thicket. "Good riddance!" she said, laughing.

"Mission accomplished," Rupert said, laughing and shaking his head in astonishment. "I didn't think it would work, but you pulled it off."

Solange slung her camera across her shoulder and turned to face him. "This camera cost me six-hundred bucks. It was either the camera or his furry little butt!"

"Casting aspersions on a monkey's behind. I think that's a misdemeanor in these parts," Rupert joked. He went and put his arm about her shoulders. "Come on, I think we've seen enough of the falls for one day."

By the time they got back to the spot where they'd taken photographs, it had begun to rain. Though the day remained sunny and bright, a light drizzle settled in. Rupert quickly went into his knapsack and produced the umbrella he'd brought along just for this contingency. He pulled Solange close to his body with his right arm and held the umbrella over them with his left. "It won't last long," he said.

They stood huddled together for several minutes gazing at the wondrous sight the falls made in full flood. Listening to the thunderous sound. Rupert had been right, the shower didn't last long. It was over in under twenty minutes. Left behind, spanning the falls, was a rainbow.

"And God set his rainbow in the sky as a sign of his covenant with mankind never again to destroy the earth with a deluge," Solange quoted, looking at the rainbow. "Isn't it beautiful?"

But Rupert was looking only at her.

That night at dinner it was Solange who couldn't keep her eyes off him. Dressed entirely in black—the man looked *good* in black—he exuded strong, sexy masculinity. If she searched a million years she'd never find another man who affected her the way he did. If he searched a million years he'd never find a woman who could love him as deeply as she could—if she got the chance. Alas, she wasn't going to give either of them the chance to test her theory. It would be better for the both of them if the cut was swift, clean, and decisive. No explaining why. The "why" would take too long to explain. No hows. As in, how could she do this after what they'd said to each other? They had an agreement that they would try to make a go of this, didn't they? If she stayed around to enumerate how she could leave him, she would wind up staying. And staying would be a costly mistake they would end up paying for many years down the road when he figured out he'd married a woman who could not help him fulfill his fondest dream, a mini-Rupert with those gorgeous golden-hued eyes and rich dark brown skin and big hands and feet, long legs, and athletic build. A heart as big as Kilimanjaro beating in his chest. No, it was best not to explain why she was leaving him.

"What's got you in a pensive mood?" Rupert asked softly. The candlelight made his eyes appear the color of a sunset.

Solange reached across the table and clasped his hand in hers. "How much I don't want to go." She looked him straight in the eyes. "Promise me you'll remember that I didn't want to go. I had to."

Concerned by the desperate tone of her voice, Rupert

squeezed her hand reassuringly. "I promise." He gazed at her a moment, trying to discern what was really going on behind those dark eyes of hers. Her going back home to be with her mother during her operation didn't warrant this kind of emotion. He was learning to know her, though. Perhaps she was given to theatrics when it came to saying good-bye. His own mother, though reticent otherwise, tended to be overly emotional whenever he got ready to go after a visit home.

He reached in his pants pocket and withdrew what looked like a gold coin. Placing it in her palm, he said, "Keep this, it'll remind you of me. My parents gave it to me when I was graduated from Oxford. It's a woman's pendant, although I removed the chain a long time ago. I figured I'd carry it in my pocket instead. They told me it belonged to my birth mother. Besides a few pieces of clothing, this is all she had to give me."

Solange turned the medallion over and read the inscription: *Always, Romeo.* "Romeo?" she asked. "Is that a common Guyanese name for a man?"

"Not that I know of," Rupert said. "I suppose it was a pet name she used for the boy she loved. You know, Romeo and Juliet."

"Tragic lovers."

"Their story ended tragically, too," Rupert said.

Solange knew he was referring to his mother's drowning. But what else was seething inside of him? Did he blame his father for his mother's death?

"Last week I asked if you'd ever tried to find your father and you said no. Is there a reason you haven't?"

"I'm afraid I'd kill him," Rupert said bluntly. He smiled ruefully. "Not wanting to be a part of a Greek tragedy, I chose not to look him up."

"You think he abandoned her?"

"He had to have, hadn't he?" Sometimes his British accent was more pronounced. This was one of those

times. He was upset and was trying not to appear so. For
whose benefit? Solange *wanted* to see the worst of him.
She wanted to experience the gamut of emotions with
him while she had the chance.

"What if he never knew she was pregnant? Would that
change how you feel about him? You know that's a possibility."

"How could he not know? She went through nine
months of pregnancy. He had to have seen her between
the time she conceived and when she gave birth!" Rupert
said vehemently.

"Not if he left the country," Solange disagreed, playing
devil's advocate. "People from Guyana have been coming
to the United States for years now in hopes of making a
better life for themselves. I knew several families who
were from Guyana when I was growing up in Key West.
They assimilated into the black community. Went to our
churches. The children grew up and took black spouses.
Rupert, I don't have all of the answers. I don't have any
idea why your father didn't stand by your mother when
she needed him most. My point is, neither do you. You
can't assume anything. You have to find out the truth. If
he's still living, you should hear what he has to say for
himself. At the very least you'd finally be face-to-face
with someone who resembles you." She paused and
smiled at him.

He had ceased smiling. A deep frown marred his handsome visage. "You should have been a lawyer, not an
archaeologist. You have a contrasting argument for everything. Perhaps I like hating him. It gives me something
constructive to do with my emotions."

Solange laughed. "Go ahead and keep hating him. It
won't answer all the questions you could put to him if
you found him. But I suppose it feels good to blame
someone for all the unanswered questions in your life.
He's a handy scapegoat. He can't defend himself."

The waiter arrived with the coffee they'd ordered. He served them and left. Solange stirred two teaspoonfuls of sugar into the rich, black coffee while Rupert drank his unsweetened.

Solange took a sip of the strong brew and set her cup back on its saucer. She met Rupert's eyes again. "When you told me you had never looked him up, I knew it had to be because you didn't want to. With your skills, you'd probably find him in no time flat. I never broached the subject before because I didn't want to offend you. But now all I want for you is what's best. Your peace of mind. You said it yourself—until you know where you came from you'll never be truly happy."

Rupert's facial muscles thawed in a slow smile. "Do you remember everything I say?"

"Yes!" Solange said enthusiastically. "I remember everything you say and everything you do. I'm storing memories for when we're apart."

"Well, remember this," Rupert said, and leaned forward to plant a long, slow kiss on her full red lips.

Solange's eyes were starry when they came up for air. "I'll never forget that."

She reached for his hand, and having grasped it, turned it palm up and gently placed the medallion in it. "Although it was a sweet gesture, I can't take this, Rupert. It's too precious to you."

"You have to take it. If you take it, it means you will be obligated to return it to me," Rupert told her. His eyes were so entreating that she wound up taking it back.

Two days later they boarded the bus for Addis Ababa. Solange regretted not being able to visit the mysterious granite stelae of Aksum, the rock-hewn churches of Lalibela, and most of all, the church of St. Mary of Zion where the Ethiopians said the Ark of the Covenant was being kept today. Ah well, she would have enjoyed being swept up in the magic of it all. But the longer she put off leaving, the guiltier she felt. Plus there was the question of Tesfaye. She wanted time to inquire about his family, if he had any. It would be wonderful if she could do something to help ensure a happy future for the boy who'd wormed his way into her heart.

It was night when the bus pulled into Addis. They disembarked and got a taxi to take them to the Sheraton. Upon entering the lobby at nine that evening, Rupert spotted Danyael getting off the elevator and heading for the exit. His strong jaw clenched and before Solange knew what was happening Rupert had doffed his knapsack and begun striding purposefully toward Danyael.

Danyael hadn't seen him yet, he was chatting up an attractive brunette who'd gotten off the elevator with him. She saw Rupert first and after Danyael saw the alarm in her eyes, he turned. It was too late by then, though, because Rupert was within four feet of him. Those four feet were no space at all for Rupert's long, powerful legs.

Rupert grabbed Danyael by the collar. "You and I need to talk." He peered at the woman whose eyes had stretched in shock at first but had now returned to their normal size and held something akin to lust in them. She was not in the least concerned with whether Danyael was about to be beaten within an inch of his life. She was more interested in who the hunk was with the bulging biceps and a day's growth of beard on his square jaw.

"Are you with him?" Rupert asked her.

"I've never seen him before in my life," she answered truthfully. She'd been wondering how she was going to ditch the lothario who'd latched onto her in the elevator. His imminent death seemed a surefire way to do so.

She calmly removed a business card from her clutch and slipped it into Rupert's denim shirt pocket. "Call me

when you're done with him. I'm an attorney, I could probably get you off with self-defense."

Solange had arrived by that time and smartly took the
card and handed it back to the startled woman. "If anyone
is going to 'get him off' it'll be me."

The woman snatched the card and walked away in a
huff, muttering "Foreigners," under her breath.

In the meantime, Danyael was withering in Rupert's
grasp. He seemed to have lost the ability to hold himself
up on his own two legs. Rupert had to drag him around
the corner where they would have a bit more privacy.
Solange followed, carrying both her knapsack and Rupert's.

"I'm not going to hit you," Rupert told Danyael
through clenched teeth. "Although I'd probably feel better
if I did. But the lady abhors violence. It bothers her gentle
sensibilities. What I want to hear you do is apologize.
And sincerely. Because if I hear a note of insincerity, I
shall ask the lady to leave so I can pound you in private."

"I'm truly sorry, Dr. DuPree," Danyael said, his voice
hoarse from having his collar cutting into his throat for
the last few minutes. "I let my baser emotions get the
best of me. I offended you, and I am enormously sorry!
Truly I am!" He wore a hangdog expression. He did not
try to look at Solange. He felt his eyes upon her would
further incur the wrath of the huge man who held his life
in his hands. Blast Theophilus Gault for getting him into
this predicament. Here he was, about to pee his pants
while Gault was living the life of Riley in a villa outside
of town.

He did risk looking into Rupert's eyes, however. Your
executioner respected you more when you were able to
meet his gaze. It showed you were a man and not a craven
coward. You would meet your fate with your head held
high. Of course, holding your head high didn't resonate
much in your soul when you were about to get it lopped

off. "I had too much to drink that night. I assure you I don't behave that way when I'm sober. And Dr. DuPree is such a lovely woman. I lost my head." Why did he have to use that terminology?

Solange said, "Apology accepted. Let him go, Rupert."

Rupert abruptly released him, and Danyael leaned heavily against the wall to prevent himself from sliding to the floor. His legs were weak, and so was his bladder.

"Good day to you, Danyael," Rupert said as he turned to Solange and accepted his knapsack. They headed back around the corner to the elevators.

Danyael breathed a sigh of relief and hurried to the nearest men's room on wobbly legs. He'd be glad when this was all over with. Samantha had left for Colorado this afternoon. He was certain Gault would set everything in motion soon. The sooner, the better.

He didn't blame Rupert Giles for defending the honor of his lady. Both Giles and Dr. DuPree were caught up in something neither of them yet knew they were players in. Theophilus Gault was the puppet master pulling everyone's strings. Couldn't Gault find some other way to occupy his time?

In the elevator, Solange and Rupert stood on opposite ends of the car. An elderly Indian couple stood in the middle. Solange would not look at Rupert. She was angry with him for pulling that stunt with Danyael. She'd told him she'd handled the situation, but he had to display his macho tendencies anyway and get his rocks off by scaring the horny little man. Not that she was defending Danyael. Not by a long shot. He was scum as far as she was concerned. It was the principle of the thing. She didn't need a rescuer. Danyael had already been satisfactorily put in his place, by her. Would she ever understand the male psyche?

The Indian couple got off, and Solange remained in her corner of the car as it rose the remaining three floors.

"Don't be like that," Rupert said.

"Like what?"

"Disgusted at my display of machismo. I saw him and I reacted from the gut. There is no honor in beating a lesser opponent. I didn't hit him. Give me credit for that."

"You said you would drop it," Solange accused.

"I never said any such thing. I said I could always pound him the next day. I thought you remembered everything I said. I never promised not to catch up with him at a later date. There was no way I was going to let that pass."

Solange thought back. He was right. She blew an exasperated breath between her lips. "Okay, you did say that," she admitted in a low voice.

"I'm sorry, what did you say?"

Solange spoke up. "You're right. You didn't say you wouldn't pound him."

The elevator stopped on their floor, the doors slid open and Rupert allowed Solange to precede him off the car. "I'm sorry if I scared you. You must have thought I'd taken leave of my senses, dropping my knapsack and charging across the lobby like a madman." He laughed. "I wanted him to know he can't treat women like he does without consequences. I believe we might have rescued that woman who got off the elevator with him from being propositioned by him. She looked relieved when I showed up."

"Relieved is not the word I'd use for the expression on her face. Lust was in full bloom on her carefully made-up mug."

"Ridiculous," Rupert said. They'd arrived at her door.

"Men," Solange said. "Macho *and* dense, what a combination!"

"I'll take issue with that as soon as I've had a bath and a meal," Rupert told her as he turned away to go next door to his room. "Room service in your room?"

"Sounds good," Solange agreed. "See you."

They closed the doors of their separate rooms.

In her room, Solange dropped the knapsack on the chair next to the door and padded across the room to the bed where she flopped down and began untying her boots. To let her feet breathe would be a major treat right now.

In a matter of minutes she'd stripped down to her underwear. She went into the walk-in closet and placed her boots neatly beneath the clothes that hung in there. Then she placed her dirty clothes in the laundry bag provided by the hotel.

Selecting a nightie, this one a lavender number with a plunging neckline, she went back to the outer room and laid it on the bed. As tired as they were, she and Rupert would probably do nothing but sleep tonight. A girl still had to be prepared, though.

As she turned to go into the bathroom, the flashing red light on the phone caught her attention. She had a message? Who would be phoning her? Not her mother. Marie rarely made overseas calls. Too expensive. Rupert?

She walked over to the nightstand and picked up the phone's receiver. She had to dial the message center in order to hear the message. After she'd done so, she put the receiver to her ear, listening.

Danyael's voice said, "I'm mortified by my behavior, Solange. Please forgive me. It'll never happen again." He'd phoned to apologize while she was away.

She replaced the receiver and went into the bathroom to shower. She didn't know what to make of his behavior. He didn't seem the lecherous type.

Danyael had been on his way to the nearest police station when he'd been waylaid by Rupert. His wallet had gone missing yesterday. He'd backtracked, thinking he might have dropped it somewhere. Then he remembered the boy who'd conveniently bumped into him the day before. He didn't hold out much hope that he'd ever see his wallet again, but at least he would have done his civic duty. He felt sorry that the boy was grubbing for a living on the streets, but stealing to get by didn't solve the boy's problem, it exacerbated it. The child should be in an orphanage somewhere, or a foster home. Danyael bet he hadn't spent much time in school. The percentage of children who attended school long enough to make it to college was abysmal.

At the police station, he was directed to the waiting room. People were slumped on chairs with worried expressions on their faces. One man nursed a bleeding forehead that he'd apparently gotten in a fistfight. His left wrist was cuffed to the chair he sat on and a young officer sat next to him, writing down his statement.

Danyael sat there for more than an hour, growing more restless by the minute. Was it really necessary to file a report? He'd already cancelled his credit cards. His driver's license could be replaced. There was nothing of sentimental value in the wallet. More money could be earned. What good would it do to snitch on the little thief? His description would go in a file somewhere, and would soon be forgotten.

Danyael's time, on the other hand, was valuable. The room at the Sheraton was being paid for by Gault Electronics. Danyael had gone to the bank this morning and he had plenty of cash in his new wallet.

He rose, looked around him at the frustrated, hurting, and cornered people in the room, complainants and criminals alike, and decided he didn't want to be one of them. The evening was young. There was still time for a few drinks at a tej beat, or local bar. This time he'd keep his hands to himself if an attractive woman graced him with her presence. At this rate he'd wind up a lonely, bitter, middle-aged man like his employer.

"Hello?" Marie's voice sounded as though Solange's call had awakened her.

"It's me. How are you?"

"I've been doing pretty well since we last spoke," Marie answered, her tone more normal now. "The worst thing that's happened is your father came to see me yesterday. Said he wanted to see for himself how I was doing. It was nobody but that big-mouthed Esther Johnson who told him about my condition. I'll never speak to that woman again about anything I don't want put in the streets."

"She's your best friend."

"Not anymore!"

"Mama, you didn't cuss him out or anything, did you?"

Marie laughed. "Of course not. I was the perfect hostess. I invited him in and gave him a cup of coffee. The first few minutes were spent spouting niceties: My house was lovely. I always could make a good cup of coffee. I looked good. He looked good. We both looked *good*. Before I knew it we were in bed together and having the best sex of our lives."

"You didn't!"

"No, I didn't. Just wanted to know if you were still listening," Marie said, laughing.

Solange laughed, too. Her mother had never said anything so bawdy, so human to her before. "So what did you talk about?" she asked, once she could speak again.

"He explained that he'd come to apologize for cheating on me all those years ago. He said the least he could have done was apologize. If he had been more humble when he got caught, maybe our marriage could have been repaired. But he didn't. And because he didn't, I divorced him."

"You mean you would have stayed with him even after he'd been with another woman?"

"I loved him. He's the only man I've ever loved. If he had been sincerely remorseful, yes, I would have forgiven him and stayed in the marriage. But he was not. He acted like a fool. It's not easy to forgive that. Not when he'd promised to love me forever, the same as I'd promised him. I kept my end of the bargain and he didn't. I'm putting all that behind me now, though. Hate is a parasite that feeds on your soul."

Solange was so pleased to hear her mother talking like this, she wore a broad smile as she listened. "I'm glad you're letting that go."

"Enough about me," Marie said. "How about you? Are you okay?"

"Yes, I'm fine. We spent the last few days exploring the area north of Addis. We just got back in Addis tonight."

"We?" Marie asked pleasantly.

"I met a man," Solange explained. "Actually, I met him in Miami. He happened to be here at the same time I am and we decided to go around together."

"Him?" Marie inquired. She seemed to be stuck on one-syllable words.

"A man."

"Yes, a man. Does he have a name?"

"Rupert Giles."

"That's a lovely name. Strong and masculine."

Solange was sitting on the bed wearing her nightie. She'd thought she'd phone her mother to briefly say hello, but the conversation was getting more interesting by the second, and she realized how much she'd missed having chats like this with her mom. It's one of the things she envied about Gaea and her mother, Lara's, relationship.

They could talk about anything and remain respectful of one another, never doubting the other's love and devotion.

"Mama, can I tell you something important? And if it's too much for you to take at this moment, please tell me, because I know you should avoid stress. If what I'm going to say makes your blood pressure rise, just stop me, okay?"

"Do you know how long I've wanted you to feel comfortable enough with me to tell me something truly personal about your life? I've been hungry for it," Marie said. Solange thought she heard her mother's voice break. "I don't care what it is. Tell me!"

Now that Solange had her mother's permission to speak freely, she didn't know where to begin, she was so excited. "I'm in a quandary. If I had my way I would marry Rupert in a heartbeat. But I know it would never work."

"Why *not?*" her mother immediately asked. Her voice was low but the passion in it spoke volumes. She feared for her daughter. She feared that Solange would never be able to get past her inability to conceive and would allow one small shortcoming, that she had no control over whatsoever, to stand in the way of her lasting happiness.

"You know why not."

"Shouldn't that be his choice, sweetheart?"

"I've already been rejected by two other men because I couldn't give them a child. I don't know if I could take the pain if Rupert reacted in the same manner. Three strikes, you're out."

"Just because they walked away doesn't mean he will. Look at your father and me, Solange. If we had talked instead of stubbornly ignoring each other's feelings, we might still be together. You have to be brave and tell him the truth. You're stronger than you think. You always have been. Strong yet tender, that's you. Your generosity of spirit used to scare me. I knew you'd wind up hurt by a man, just like I'd been. I tried to make you see you had to be tough as nails to survive in this world. By behaving tough, I became tough. But look where it's got me: There's no man in my life. After your father, I started thinking of all men as pigs. They were all out to *take* from me. It's true, some men do take, but there are others who give as much as we do in a relationship. I was too blind to see that a couple of times. Frank. Remember him? He was a good man, but I ran him into the ground trying to make him prove his love to me. He finally stopped trying. Baby, don't make the same mistake I did. Talk to Rupert. Promise me you'll tell him, and let *him* decide. It's not up to you to make that decision for both of you."

"Okay, Mama, calm down. I'll talk to him," Solange promised.

Rupert gave her little opportunity for talking that night. When he walked through her door, showered and refreshed, all he wanted to do was hold her in his arms and smell her peppermint-scented hair. Solange used a shampoo with natural peppermint oil in it. It gave her hair extra shine and body, plus the aroma was delightful.

He'd put on a pair of button-fly jeans and a cotton polo shirt in baby blue. He hadn't bothered to put on socks with his brown leather Italian loafers.

"Look what was outside your door," he said, and produced a bouquet of red roses from behind his back. Solange reached for the flowers, backing up to let him in. She assumed they were from him but after reading the card that came with them she learned they were from Danyael. *I'm sorry,* the card read. Solange smiled. Talk about apology overkill!

"They're from Danyael," she told Rupert.

A frown crossed Rupert's features but he was soon his

amiable self again. He didn't like any man other than himself giving Solange flowers, but it would be presumptuous of him to tell her that this early in their relationship. He could not even call her his girlfriend. Not until their intentions had been spoken out loud. Sure, they'd said they wished to take things further. But what exactly were they taking forward? *I love her.* There, he'd thought it even if he hadn't told her yet.

How could he tell her? She'd think he was one of those crazy guys who fall in love at the drop of a hat, then become pests who pledge undying devotion and don't want their woman going to the bathroom by herself! She'd already gone through something similar to that with Dr. Nicholas Campion. He didn't want her to think he was another Nick. What he would have to do is simply love her. Love her so well, she'd instinctively know how he felt. And when the time was right, he'd spring it on her with a ring hidden in his coat pocket.

He went to her now and took the vase of roses in his big hand. "I'll put those away for you."

He took them into the bathroom and set the vase in the bathtub, drawing the shower curtain so that they'd be out of sight. "I will not have roses from another man in the room while I'm trying to romance my woman."

"Your woman?" Solange asked, feigning indignation. "When did I become your woman?" Inside, she was amused by his show of jealousy. She stood in the bathroom's doorway, blocking his path.

Rupert bent his head and kissed her soft lips. "Oh, let's see, around the tenth time we made love?"

"Is that a question or a definitive answer?" She pressed her body closer.

"It depends," Rupert said against her ear.

"On what?"

"How you feel about being my woman."

Solange turned her dark eyes on him. "I love it," she said in a husky voice.

"Then you're my woman now, and I'm your man," Rupert said. "It's as simple as that."

It was in the aspect of his eyes: the seriousness behind his declaration. Solange's spirit was so buoyed by this turn of events, she figured this was as good a time as any to tell him about her condition.

"Rupert, there's something I should . . ."

Knock, Knock. Someone was at the door.

"Oh, I forgot to tell you, I ordered dinner for us. They had fresh lobster and I know how you love that. No butter, I didn't forget. Mixed salad and fruit."

"Would you get the door?" Solange said, inwardly deflated. She kept smiling, though, because Rupert was in such a good mood and she didn't want to spoil the evening for him. She watched him as he crossed the room, wondering if his mood would be that elevated after she told him she was barren.

She was torn between doing what she knew she had to and wanting to remain in this blessed moment. She'd seen love in Rupert's eyes. She knew it. Seeing that in a man's eyes had been such a rare occurrence in her life, she was not liable to misread it. That, above all else, prevented her from saying anything. It would rip her heart to shreds to see the love light in his eyes go out.

The waiter quickly converted the table that sat by the window in the room to a dining table. Replete with tablecloth, china, cutlery, and crystal wineglasses. Then he took his leave.

Solange came out of the bathroom where she'd been hiding in her skimpy nightie, and Rupert acted the gentleman and held her chair for her. After they were both seated, she said, "It was so late, I figured you'd come to my door in your bathrobe. I should have put on fresh clothing after my shower. I feel naked sitting here across from you in this."

"Would you feel better if I removed my clothing?" he asked, his eyes glittering with humor.

"That would be entirely too distracting," Solange told him, smiling.

"We'll talk about mundane things," Rupert suggested. "It'll take your mind off your half-naked state which, by the way, I'm quite enjoying."

Solange twisted off a chunk of her lobster with the tiny fork provided and dabbed it in lemon juice. "I was thinking the American Embassy would be a good place to start in my search for help for Tesfaye."

Rupert was nodding as he chewed a mouthful of salad. "Even if they can't help you they can point you in the right direction."

"Then I'll go first thing in the morning."

"Not too early, sweetness. I'm worn out. I feel as though I could sleep until noon tomorrow."

"I'll tell you what," Solange said. "If you're not awake, I'll go alone. If I run into any problems I'll phone you."

"All right," Rupert agreed. "You'll go alone if I'm sleeping like the dead in the morning."

The day was beautiful and bright. Solange strode out of the Sheraton and right into a waiting cab. She'd worn the only attire she'd brought with her that could pass muster as a business suit, an off-white slacks suit made of a durable cotton material. The jacket was double-breasted. On her feet were a pair of brown leather low-heeled dress boots. She pulled on her sunglasses before requesting of the cab driver, "The American Embassy, please."

The American Embassy, on Entoto Road, was an ultra-modern building with a fence around it. The gate was open at this time of the day, and the driver put Solange out at the curb. She gazed up at the building. There were two armed American Marines standing guard on either side of the door.

"Good morning, ma'am," one of them greeted her.

Apparently they weren't silent guards as the British Royal Guard were. "Good morning," Solange said pleasantly. The marine who'd spoken held the door open for her. "Thank you," she said.

"My pleasure," he returned.

The air in the building smelled like an office, Solange thought. It wasn't unlike the smell of the building where she had her office on the campus of the University of Miami, with the recognizable odors of paper, books, and copier fluid.

She walked down a rather long corridor, looking at the pictures and plaques on the wall as she did so, until she arrived at a huge mahogany desk behind which sat a woman who appeared to be in her late fifties. She was tall and thin with dark blue eyes and blond hair in a bouffant hairdo. Solange supposed she was one of those people who found a hairstyle and stuck with it, no matter how many decades passed in the interim.

"Good morning, may I be of service?" the woman asked, with a smile that didn't reach her eyes. She looked at Solange as if she were trying to guess the nature of her business.

"I was hoping you could direct me to someone who could help locate the family of a street child I've grown fond of," Solange said succinctly. It was obvious the woman had a lot of work to do and she didn't want to keep her from it for too long.

Solange's eyes swept over the woman's desk, looking for a nameplate. She spotted it behind a clear-glass vase of thick-stemmed sunflowers. She peered closer. There were goldfish swimming in the vase.

Beatrice Anderson regarded Solange with an amused expression. "You're another one of those do-gooders who comes here and thinks she can change things." She sighed resignedly. "Take it from me, Ms.—"

"Doctor," Solange said. She tried to keep the imperious note out of her voice, but failed. This woman had attitude in spades. "Dr. Solange DuPree from the University of Miami. And you are?"

"Mrs. Beatrice Anderson from Kenosha, Wisconsin. I've been here for ten years, Dr. Dupree. Nothing ever changes. The people like it that way. They can document their history for five thousand years. Big whoop-de-do! I don't mean any disrespect, I have a great deal of love and respect for this country. Believe me, I wouldn't be here if I didn't. My point is, some parts of this country still seem to be in the Dark Ages. Your question about helping that child? My answer would be, don't even try. You'll be caught up in such a paperwork hell, you'd end up pulling your hair out and knocking your head repeatedly against a brick wall just to get some relief from the headaches.

"Oh, I know you mean well," she continued, having gotten her second wind. "But I'm telling you, if you value your sanity you'll drop this madness right now and return to the University of Miami. The child has survived without your help for years and he'll continue to survive without it. Now, if you're still intent on getting involved . . ."

"I am," Solange told her, her position on the matter implacable.

Beatrice smiled at her. This time it reached her eyes. "I thought so. Okay, here's my advice: If you really want to do something for that child, I say begin adoption proceedings as soon as possible because the only way you'll help him is to get him slam out of this environment. Now, I know what you're probably thinking: Wouldn't he be better off with his own people? The fact is, if he's on the streets, he probably doesn't have anyone who wants him. Many children languish in orphanages for years without any living relative coming to claim them. Some of those orphanages are worse than the streets, which is why children often run away from them. They prefer the streets."

Solange felt as if she had sensory overload. When Beatrice got started there was no stopping the depressing statistics that poured from her mouth.

"Adoption? I haven't even given that any thought. I assumed Tesfaye has family somewhere in Ethiopia!"

Beatrice pointed at the row of upholstered chairs lining the southern wall. "Tesfaye. That means *My Hope.* Pull up a chair, would you, Dr. DuPree?"

Solange went and got a chair and sat down across from Beatrice. "Tesfaye is at least twelve years old. He's got a mind of his own. He might not *want* to come to the U.S. and live with me."

"He's a difficult child, huh?"

"I met him when he tried to pick my pocket."

Beatrice laughed. "They've got to survive some way."

Solange leaned closer. "I need to cover every base before talking to him about adoption. You guessed right when you said I'm concerned about his missing out on his culture. A person needs to know where they came from."

"Indeed," Beatrice readily agreed. "You're a doctor of archaeology, you can bring him back to Ethiopia on one of your research junkets."

"How did you know my field of study?" Solange asked, bewildered.

"I went to the University of Miami's Web page and looked you up while we were talking," Beatrice confessed. "The photo on your page doesn't do you justice."

Solange smiled, shaking her head. She didn't like that photo either. "Okay, so you know I was telling the truth.

Can you direct me to someone who can get the ball rolling?"

"Absolutely. That would be Mr. Tan, I'll check whether he can see you now." Beatrice brought the receiver to her ear and punched the button for Mr. Tan's extension. Her eyes didn't leave Solange's face as she spoke. "Mr. Tan are you extremely busy? There's an American citizen here who needs your advice." She listened a moment. "All right. Thank you, sir."

She met Solange's eyes. "He can give you ten minutes. He has an appointment with someone else soon. It's the third door on the left." She pointed. "Down that hall."

Solange rose and extended her hand. Beatrice took it and they shook. "Thank you, Mrs. Anderson," Solange said.

"Best of luck," Beatrice said, and meant it.

Mr. Tan was a trim, neatly dressed Chinese-American in his early forties. His black hair was combed away from a high forehead and he wore round spectacles that gave him an intellectual appearance. His nameplate read, *James Tan, Consular Officer.*

Solange offered him her hand upon entrance. "Mr. Tan, so good of you to take the time to see me."

He gestured to the chair in front of his desk. Solange sat down. "We always try to accommodate our people visiting here in Addis," he said. He had a lean, attractive face. "What can I help you with?"

"There's a street child whose relatives I'd like to locate, if I can."

"The easiest way to do that is to start adoption proceedings. In the course of the process an orphan investigation will be conducted. That will tell us if he has anyone left in Ethiopia who is able to care for him. If so, and they're willing, they will have first dibs on the child. We prefer the child to remain in Ethiopia when at all possible. If not, and the child's willing, your adoption request may go through."

"There is no way I can find out if he has any living relatives without starting adoption proceedings? I've never even discussed the subject with Tesfaye."

"I'm trying to save you time, Dr. DuPree. Social Services does not generally give out that kind of information to just anyone. If, however, you're a prospective parent to the child, the orphan investigation will be done as a matter of course. It's your choice. I'm just here to facilitate things for you."

Solange thought for a moment. Bureaucracy. A confusing maze that not even those who were supposed to be well-versed in it were sure of. Okay. She was willing to play by their rules.

She sighed. "All right, Mr. Tan. I hereby officially file for adoption of Tesfaye Roba. What's our next step?"

Mr. Tan smiled and began typing on his computer keyboard. "Tesfaye Roba, did you say? I wonder why that name rings a bell. Tesfaye is a very common name, but Roba isn't so common. Wait a minute, I'm checking the archives of one of the local papers, the Addis Tribune. It's privately owned and less likely to suppress news that shows the government in a bad light. Hold on. Yes, here we are."

He crooked a finger at Solange, indicating that she should come around his desk in order to peer over his shoulder at the computer screen. Intrigued, she did so.

"Teachers Hailu Roba and his wife Terunesh were on their way to an Eritrean refugee camp when they were gunned down by Eritrean soldiers. The Robas had two children, a boy, Tesfaye, who was nine years old at the time of his death, and a daughter, Desta, who was five. A caravan found the girl several days after the death of her family, still close by their bodies. She had survived by eating the food the family had brought with them for the trip and drinking rain water from puddles nearby."

James Tan looked up at Solange. "I suppose that name stuck in my head after all these years because the incident occurred the first week I was in Ethiopia. Plus, my own parents are teachers, so it felt personal somehow."

"What happened to Desta?" Solange asked.

"She would have gone to relatives."

"And if she didn't have any relatives?"

"In that case Social Services would have been in charge of her fate."

"She would have gone to an orphanage?"

"Yes."

Solange cocked her head to the side and regarded James Tan with determined eyes. "I know you're pressed for time now, Mr. Tan. But when you get the chance would you find out from Social Services if Desta Roba is still in their system or not? I suspect she's living on the streets."

Mr. Tan's features mirrored his distaste at hearing her theory. "I certainly hope not. I'd like to imagine Desta in a good home, being taken care of by loving adoptive parents."

"Yes," said Solange, her frown matching his. "So would I."

Ten

"Daniel is traveling tonight on a plane. . . ." The strains of Elton John singing one of his classics came over the car's sound system. In the back, Danyael wished *he* was on a plane to Spain instead of returning from the villa with instructions to bring Dr. Solange DuPree to meet with Theophilus Gault, even if he had to abduct her.

He tried to remain calm. How much did he want to keep this job, anyway? Theophilus Gault was not the man he used to be. In his position as the family's butler for the past twenty years, he'd gained the confidence of all of the Gaults. He'd adored Francesca Gault, and she was the one who'd insisted Theophilus hire him in the first place. Danyael had come to the United States by stowing away on a freighter. He'd managed to live by working one menial job after another. He was only seventeen when he arrived in America, and he'd looked it. He also had a thick accent, which made it difficult to even apply for a job. Plus, there was the matter of not having a visa or a green card. He was deathly afraid of being found out and deported.

In Washington, D.C., he was working as a dishwasher at a swanky restaurant. The owner was fully aware he had illegal immigrants working in his kitchen, but being in the black was more important to him than obeying the law. One night a private party was booked and Danyael was at his regular post of dishwasher when the owner threw a jacket at him and said, "You. We need some extra people to serve tonight. Think you can handle it, Einstein?" The owner facetiously referred to anyone he thought was intellectually inferior to him as Einstein.

Handle it? Danyael had dishpan hands and a constant ache in his back from bending at the sink. He also thought that machine they called a dishwasher wanted to kill him. Each time he placed dishes in the rack and went to close the metal door, the door would come crashing down. He had images of his hand being amputated at the wrist.

The evening ended disastrously, at least for the restaurant owner. Danyael spilled soup in the lap of one of the female guests. She was none other than Francesca Gault, who chaired the national committee for AID TO ETHIOPIA. She had traveled to Ethiopia on numerous occasions, and the moment she laid eyes on Danyael she knew where he hailed from. Her soup-spattered dress forgotten, she started talking to him in Amharic. So shocked was Danyael at hearing his native tongue that he immediately responded. Before the night was over, Danyael had been hired by the Gaults and the restaurant owner had been written up for hiring an illegal immigrant who didn't have a green card. Through some wangling, Francesca managed to help Danyael get his green card even though he'd entered the country illegally.

She started him out as a gofer around the house, working closely with their butler, Simon, who was elderly and could use the help. Simon taught him everything he knew and when he retired Danyael moved into the position.

Danyael grew to love the Gaults. He'd been as devastated by Francesca's death as Theophilus and Samantha had been. The house became a dismal place with Francesca gone and Samantha away at school. When Theophilus said he was going to Ethiopia and inviting Samantha, Danyael had thought it a wonderful idea until Theophilus told him what he planned to do. What Theophilus was planning would make Danyael a traitor to his people if they got caught in the commission of the act. In the annals of Ethiopian history his name would be synonymous with Benedict Arnold.

Danyael was caught between his loyalty to the Gaults and his love of country. Which would have his devotion in the end?

When Rupert heard the tapping on the door, he was standing at the sink shaving, a towel wrapped around his waist. He walked barefoot across the room and peered through the peephole. Tesfaye.

He opened the door and stood aside for the boy to enter. "If it isn't Mr. Roba, our favorite guide. Please come in."

Tesfaye looked beyond Rupert into the room. He hadn't budged an inch. "Is Solange here? I would like to speak with her."

"Solange is out," Rupert told him. He thought it best not to tell him where she was, as Tesfaye might not be pleased that they were checking up on him. "She should be back shortly. You can come in and wait, if you like."

Rupert thought he saw a fleeting expression of alarm in the boy's eyes at the mention of coming inside. Maybe he didn't trust him the way he trusted Solange. Rupert wouldn't be surprised. He hadn't been very welcoming to him.

"Listen, I know we haven't always gotten along but if Solange thinks you're an okay sort, then so do I."

Tesfaye looked astonished by his words. "She, she likes me?" he stuttered.

"I think it's safe to say she's quite fond of you, yes," Rupert said grudgingly. He couldn't fawn over the boy. His turnaround in behavior would scare him off faster than outright rudeness.

Tesfaye turned away. "I shall wait for her downstairs."

Rupert didn't argue. "Very well."

Outside, Solange's cab was pulling up to the Sheraton. When it stopped she automatically reached for the door's handle and opened the door. The driver got out anyway and held it open for her. Solange placed several Birr notes in his palm. "Thank you," she said, walking off.

"My pleasure, Madame," he called after her upon noticing the generous tip she'd given him. Solange tossed a smile over her shoulder and kept walking.

"Solange!"

She turned. Danyael was getting out of the black Mercedes she'd seen him in a number of times. A voice in her head told her to pretend she hadn't heard him, but she figured nothing untoward could happen in broad daylight with all these people as witnesses. The walk in front of the Sheraton was fairly populated with pedestrians, and the revolving door of the hotel was getting quite a workout, too, so she felt relatively safe standing in the bright sunshine conversing with him.

What could he have to say to her? He'd already apologized profusely. There was nothing left to say. If he was going to try to ease his way back into her good graces, she'd have to tell him pointblank that she no longer considered him trustworthy and even a cup of coffee alone with him was out of the question. He'd ruined their budding friendship when he'd touched her inappropriately.

She was standing perhaps four feet from him. He was still at the car, bending down and saying something to the driver that she couldn't hear.

He straightened up momentarily and gave her a brilliant smile. "Solange, did you get my flowers?"

"Yes, I did. They were lovely. Thank you."

"Then you accept my apology?"

Solange removed her sunglasses and looked him in the eyes. "Danyael, what you did is not something a woman easily forgives. I do forgive you if you're sincerely sorry you did it. Conversely, I have to tell you I don't feel comfortable enough with you to be alone with you anymore."

"I understand," Danyael said, his tone regretful.

"Good," Solange said. She didn't want to be rude, but it was vital that she return to her room before Rupert awakened. "Good day to you, Danyael."

"Now!" Danyael yelled to the driver.

The driver, a strapping fellow with arms and legs like tree trunks, quickly got out of the car. Solange reacted by stepping backward. She wanted to keep her eyes on the hulk moving swiftly toward her.

"Solange!"

Hearing Tesfaye's voice, Solange looked back for a moment and the driver grabbed her around the waist with one beefy arm and clamped his baseball-mitt-like paw over her mouth with his other hand.

"Help! Somebody help her!" Tesfaye yelled as he ran full speed down the steps of the hotel, heading for the horrifying scene unfolding before his eyes. Solange tried to bite, stomp the foot or instep of, or kick the muscle-bound freak who had her in a steel vise. She twisted her head, but only succeeded in straining her neck muscles.

Danyael had climbed onto the back seat and was motioning frantically for the driver to force Solange inside. "Give her to me, you dolt. Then get in and drive! Come on, hurry up."

The big man gave Solange a great shove and Danyael grabbed hold of her and held on with all his might. "Don't struggle, Solange. We mean you no harm. My employer would just like a word with you. Then you'll be free to go."

Both of Solange's arms were imprisoned at her sides. She could not get her knees up in order to put a well-placed knee in his groin. The only part of her body left to fight with was her head.

"Danyael?"

He leaned in closer.

Solange bent her head and quickly came upward, right beneath Danyael's chin.

"Dammit, you made me bite my tongue," he said, his words muffled because of his injured tongue.

Solange heard the engine turn over and her heart fell. There was no telling what would happen to her once they got her to where they were taking her.

"Ay ya ya ya yaya . . ." A shrill war cry arose all around them. The sound was so disturbingly high-pitched and unexpected that it momentarily froze all three adults in the car. Accompanied by the trilling, Danyael suddenly felt as if his hair was being pulled out by the roots. He realized, too late, that the driver had gotten behind the wheel of the car without dealing with the boy who'd been racing to Solange's rescue.

The boy had hurled himself through the open back window and now had a handful of Danyael's thick hair in his fist. Panicked, Danyael loosened his hold on So-lange and the first thing she did with her free arm was poke him in the ribs with her sharp elbow.

The driver looked over his shoulder at the free-for-all in the back with a frightened expression. He was confused as to what to do next, drive away or offer aid to Danyael.

"Drive, drive!" Danyael yelled.

The driver burned rubber, pulling away from the curb and into the mid-morning traffic.

"Let her go," Tesfaye shouted menacingly.

"Stop the car," Solange demanded.

"God, help me," Danyael pleaded, one hand on his right side where Solange had elbowed him, and the other on top of his head, trying to dislodge the boy's grip. "If you don't make him stop at once, I'll have the driver stop the car so he can be dealt with, permanently," Danyael warned Solange. "It's you my employer wants to see, not a rabid street rat."

His threat gave Solange pause. Only for a moment, however. They were fighting for their lives, she couldn't listen to his lies. She tried to poke him in the eye. He turned his head just in time and her finger went in his ear instead.

"Ow, woman!"

"Let us out of this car now, Danyael, or I'm going for the jewels next," Solange threatened, a seriously deranged gleam in her eyes.

"The jewels!" Tesfaye confirmed, looking as bloodthirsty as Solange did.

"I swear, Solange, Theophilus Gault only wants to talk to you about the Ark of the Covenant. He wants your opinion on whether or not you believe the Ethiopians are truly in possession of the authentic article. He read your paper on the subject."

Theophilus had instructed him not to say anything to Dr. DuPree; but if divulging why she was being taken to Theophilus Gault saved his ability to father future children, he was willing to face his employer's wrath.

Solange squinted at him. "Gault Electronics?"

Danyael tried to nod but Tesfaye still had hold of his head. That minute movement had caused him excruciating pain. "Yes, yes," he cried. His eyes watered.

"Then you weren't lying about working for an electronics company? Why didn't he come to see me himself? A phone call would have been preferable to this method."

"He guards his privacy," Danyael said. "I know this is unorthodox. He's an unusual man. But, I swear, he sincerely only wants to talk to you."

"I don't believe you," Solange said, and grabbed his privates.

* * *

In the meantime, back at the Sheraton a woman who'd been walking by when Solange had been forced into the Mercedes was hysterically reporting the incident to the clerk at the front desk.

"This gargantuan man grabbed her and *threw* her into the car and while a smaller man held on to her, the big man got behind the wheel of the car, it was a late model black Mercedes by the way, but before he could drive away from the curb, a boy—a street kid from the looks of him—launched himself through the window, yelling, 'Let her go!' It was the bravest thing I've ever seen. The dear boy!"

The clerk was looking at her as if she'd forgotten to take her medication that morning. Those dotty British. They were worse than the Americans when it came to dramatics.

"Did anyone else see this?" he asked. No one besides this woman had reported the incident. The hotel had a reputation to uphold. Still, he should phone the police anyway and tell them about it. What if it truly had happened and one of the guests turned up missing? He wanted the hotel covered, just in case.

"Yes, I'm sure others saw but they kept walking, probably not wanting to get involved," the woman told him. The excitement had gone out of her pale green eyes. It occurred to her that the clerk didn't believe a word she'd said. Prudence Bellweather could also use words that were quite cutting when she needed to be taken seriously.

"You can believe me or not, young man. But when a guest of yours turns up dead, her body cast along the road somewhere, it will be on *your* conscience! I tried to do something about it. My conscience is clear. Now I shall be on my way."

She turned her back on him and began walking toward the exit.

The clerk cleared his throat. "Wait, Madame. The police will want to take down a description of the victim and the assailants."

Prudence Bellweather smiled. It had faded by the time she turned back around.

"If you insist," she said pleasantly.

In the car on the way to the villa, Danyael was taking a beating. The driver twice pulled the car over to disentangle Solange and Tesfaye from a limb of Danyael or his hair. But the moment he got behind the wheel, again the fracas commenced. Danyael was exhausted. So were Solange and Tesfaye, but neither of them thought of giving up.

In the tussle Danyael inadvertently knocked off Tesfaye's head wrap and long, dark luxuriant hair fell around the boy's startled face. He let go of Danyael to pick up the unraveled material. His eyes met Solange's. Tears glistened in them.

Solange let go of Danyael as well and pulled Tesfaye into her arms. "It's all right, baby," she cooed in a soft voice. She shot daggers at Danyael with her eyes. "Look what you did, you brute!"

Danyael didn't know what to make of it. She was calling *him* a brute when she'd spent the last twenty minutes or more biting, kicking, punching, and grabbing his crotch while he'd done nothing but deflect both her blows and those of the child.

Solange rocked Tesfaye in her arms. "Are you Desta?" she whispered in his ear.

He raised his head to peer into her eyes. In them he saw the kindness he'd been seeking in an adult's aspect ever since he'd been left to starve to death on the road to Eritrea. He sighed and buried his face in her chest, nodding in the affirmative.

Solange responded by hugging her tighter. Tears rolled down Solange's cheeks. "Don't you worry. I'm not going to let anything happen to you."

For his part, Danyael had no idea what was transpiring between the two of them. He was just happy for a reprieve. For the remainder of the ride to the villa he sat as far away from the both of them as possible.

"How do we find out if a guest is missing?" the clerk asked, confused. "Do we go from room to room throwing the guests into a panic?"

The hotel manager, a tall erudite gentleman with rather large brown eyes, frowned at that suggestion. They were sitting in his office: the police detective, the witness, and the clerk.

"I believe it would be wiser to wait until someone asks after a guest," the detective put in. He was in his late twenties, impeccable in his uniform. He had the air of someone who rarely lost his cool.

He turned black eyes on Prudence Bellweather. "Madame, are you certain you didn't hear a name called in the midst of the struggle? You recalled hearing what the boy said when he went to the woman's rescue. Could you have possibly heard a name, too?"

Prudence racked her brain but wound up sadly shaking her head. "No I don't recall a name. I wish I'd gotten the license plate number, but I was not wearing my prescription sunglasses. I was wearing a cheap pair I bought when I got here. I forgot and left my good ones on the bureau at home. And that sun is a killer."

"Too bad," the detective said. "A name would help lead us to the missing guest, if indeed the woman was a guest here." He got to his feet. "At any rate, we will alert all mobile units to be on the lookout for a black, late-model Mercedes."

"I'm sorry I couldn't be of more help," Prudence said regretfully.

"On the contrary, Mrs. Bellweather, you have been a great help. You reported what happened."

Mrs. Bellweather rose, too. "I shall worry about that woman and the boy until they've been found. If only I had been closer when it happened, perhaps I could have done something to prevent it."

"Oh no, Mrs. Bellweather, it was best that you did not try that. You may have fallen victim to the kidnappers as well."

A chill ran up Prudence's spine. She had traveled the world ever since her Rodney passed away four years ago. Rodney had not enjoyed traveling very much. He preferred his garden in Bath to any place else on earth. She'd buried him in it and moved the next day. She enjoyed living in a flat in London now and taking trips to exotic locales around the world. Danger was a part of living. This intrigue-filled day would not deter her from going anywhere she wanted to go.

Rupert was finishing his second cup of coffee that morning when he overheard a couple of guests talking about the abduction that had taken place in front of the Sheraton that morning. They were talking in whispers as if the news were a juicy piece of gossip, so he had to strain to hear.

"I heard it was a woman and a little boy who were snatched off the street in broad daylight. Imagine. You're not even safe taking a stroll down the street anymore."

A thrill of fear shot through Rupert when he heard the words "woman" and "little boy." He had been trying to chalk Solange's lateness up to a harmless diversion like getting a sudden impulse to get in some shopping, hoping that she'd just lost track of the time.

He motioned for the waiter. He saw the waiter pause at his station to collect his payment clipboard. Good. Rupert wanted to leave as soon as possible after he got a bit of information.

The waiter approached, offering Rupert the clipboard with his check on it. Rupert hastily signed. The amount of his order plus a tip for the waiter would be added to his bill. The waiter was then prepared to go. Rupert stopped him short with, "Is it true someone was abducted right in front of the hotel this morning?"

The rattled expression on the young man's face was all Rupert needed to see. He uttered an expletive and hurried out of the dining room straight to the front desk.

There were no employees in sight. He rang the bell repeatedly until the very same clerk who'd been skeptical upon hearing Prudence Bellweather's account of the abduction put in an appearance.

"Yes, sir," said the man. "What can I do for you?"

"The woman I'm staying here with, Dr. Solange Du-Pree, hasn't returned to the hotel in some time now. Have you seen her? She's a petite African-American woman with short black hair. Very attractive."

The clerk went ashen beneath his brown skin. His eyes were haunted. He beckoned to Rupert with bony fingers. "Come with me, sir. The manager would like a word with you."

Rupert swallowed hard and followed. He'd been praying all along that his suspicions were unfounded. His stomach muscles constricted painfully. If anything ever happened to Solange he would go mad with vengeance and take it out on the person who'd harmed her. He'd comb this country from one end to the other until he found him, and then he'd take his time torturing him. He'd derive great pleasure from it.

But now, the thing to do was find out whether all that would be necessary. Perhaps Solange was running late. He steeled himself as he strode into the manager's office.

Fifteen minutes later, the police detective who'd taken Mrs. Bellweather's statement, was again in the manager's office taking down Rupert's. The two men, though both wanted the same results, were immediately at odds. Rupert knew how time could be wasted by following procedure. The detective, on the other hand, felt compelled to go by the book.

Rupert had told him everything he could about Solange and where she'd gone that morning. He'd also told him about Danyael Abate's advances and how he'd threatened him to make him stay away from her.

Upon hearing this the detective asked, "Do you think he would have done something this desperate?"

"I don't know the man well at all," Rupert told him. "He was infatuated with Solange. He went as far as to ask her to drop me for him. It was after that that I threatened him with bodily injury if it ever happened again."

"He might do this as a kind of revenge, then," the detective surmised. "To get back at you for humiliating him."

"It's a possibility," Rupert said, weary with the questioning. He was a man of action. He needed to get to work tracking down the black late-model Mercedes the detective had told him about. There couldn't be many cars that fit that description in the city. Danyael's car had . . . "Hey, wait a minute. The car that Danyael Abate used was a black Mercedes." Why hadn't he thought of that before now? Could it be his brain was malfunctioning due to worry? The woman he loved was gone. He'd failed her. He should not have let her go to the American Embassy alone. *Get it together, Giles.*

Before the end of the session the detective reminded

Rupert that they hadn't made a positive ID of the victim yet. "Do you have a photograph of Dr. DuPree?"

Rupert remembered the photos he'd taken of Solange at Blue Nile Falls. He reached into his coat pocket. "Yes, we had some developed in Bahar Dar. I have a couple here."

"Wonderful," Detective Mulatu said. "Give them to me and I'll take them for Mrs. Bellweather to take a look at them. She's a sharp one. We should know in a matter of minutes whether or not your Dr. DuPree has been taken or is, perhaps, delayed for other reasons."

Rupert's heart reached for the hope implied in the detective's words. If only Solange were, indeed, somewhere else, haggling over the price of a carpet.

Desta wept for a long time. Sometimes her weeping was convulsive, at others no more than a whimper. Solange held onto her throughout the cleansing, rocking her, speaking consolingly to her.

From his corner of the back seat, Danyael watched them with suspicion.

"Here's the turn off," the driver announced, startling all three people in the back.

Danyael stopped leaning on the door and straightened up. "Let me reiterate, Solange: No harm will come to you or the child. We're here for a friendly chat and nothing more." They were on the half-mile-long drive that lead to the villa. The road was lined with eucalyptus trees. Seeing them reminded Solange of the night she thought she'd seen a bat when returning from dinner with Rupert in Addis. Rupert. Her heart ached. He was probably climbing the walls by now. Someone must have seen her being shoved into the car in front of the hotel.

She regarded Danyael with dispassionate eyes. "After

what you've done, don't ever expect me to believe anything you say."

Danyael looked away, his gaze taking in the arid countryside.

The drive was not paved, and the Mercedes' tires left a trail of dust in their wake. By the time the Mercedes was brought to a stop in front of a villa inspired by Italian architecture it was covered in a fine layer of pale dust.

Danyael got out of the car on the right side and walked around to open the door for Solange and Desta. The two of them got out and stood at the side of the car, shielding their eyes from the sun. Solange had dropped her sunglasses when the driver had grabbed her.

"Hello, hello!" came a hearty welcome from the direction of the entrance to the villa. Solange turned her gaze in the direction of the voice. She blinked, hoping to clear her vision, for she could not be seeing what she was seeing.

The man who had come out to greet them was at least six-foot-four and a tad over two hundred pounds. He had a broad chest with incredible pectorals for a man his age. Solange guessed he was in his mid-fifties. However, black men tended to look good well into their seventies if they took good care of themselves. He could be older.

He was wearing a loose-fitting tunic over slacks, both made of white Egyptian cotton, and brown leather slippers. Apparently he'd decided to adopt the dress of the locals. His short, wavy hair was gray at the temples. He had a big square head, high cheekbones, a broad, proud nose, and a full, well-shaped mouth. Solange noted that his chin had a dimple right smack in the middle of it and when her eyes finally met his gaze as he approached, she gasped softly. They were large, expressive, thickly-fringed eyes the color of burnt caramel. Golden with brown striations.

Her hand went to the medallion she'd hung around her

neck on dental floss. It was safely under her clothes and she'd tied it with a double knot. She'd meant to buy a chain for it sometime today. She probably wouldn't get the chance to do that now.

"Dr. DuPree, hello," the big man said again. "I'm Theophilus Gault. I hope your journey here was a pleasant one."

Solange had to shake off the shock and surprise that had seized her at the sight of him. They said there was a twin for everyone somewhere on earth. She'd just come face-to-face with Rupert's. Theophilus Gault's uncanny resemblance to Rupert was only a coincidence, she told herself, and she had to treat it as such.

"It was not a pleasant trip at all, Mr. Gault," she said witheringly. Her dark eyes swept over him as if he were so much rubbish. "If this is how you treat someone you would like a chat with, I hesitate to ask how you treat people you truly detest."

Theophilus's eyes were on Desta. "Who is the little person?" He directed his question to Danyael, who momentarily closed his eyes and blew an exasperated breath between his lips. "She jumped into the car after we'd already gotten Dr. DuPree inside. We had no choice but to bring her along."

"You had a choice," Theophilus corrected him. "You simply weren't thinking." He sadly shook his head at Danyael's incompetence, then brightened. "We can worry about that later. Follow me, ladies. You look parched. A drink will refresh you."

He regarded Danyael. "Pay the driver and dismiss him," he said.

The driver's brows drew together in a frown when he heard he was going to be let go. He had done everything they'd asked of him for the past three weeks. If they were firing him, they'd better make the severance pay worth keeping his mouth shut. He'd been a participant in a kidnapping. He intended to be well-compensated for his efforts.

Danyael went to do Theophilus's bidding.

Solange and Desta followed Rupert's doppelganger into the villa. They hung back. "He looks like Mr. Giles," Desta said in an awe-filled whisper.

"Yes, he does," Solange replied softly. "Keep your eyes and ears open, Desta. I'm relying on your street smarts to help get us out of this."

Desta seemed to gain strength from knowing Solange had such faith in her. She didn't lean on Solange at all as they walked onto the shaded veranda of the villa.

"I had you brought here to discuss your comments in your *Archaeology Today* article," Theophilus said to Solange. He was looking back, smiling at her. "I thought it was fascinating."

Solange cringed inwardly. "That article was written on a dare," she told him. "A colleague challenged me to publish views that would be resoundingly laughed at by most of the scholars in our discipline, and I did. We all got a good laugh, and that was that!"

As they stepped into the villa their voices took on an empty-well sound. Both Solange and Desta peered up at the more than thirty-foot ceiling. Their footsteps echoed on the flagstone of the veranda, then on the marble of the floor inside the villa. Solange held onto Desta's hand.

"It doesn't matter to me why you wrote it," Theophilus Gault said. "You wrote it, and it made sense to me. You see, I've studied the Ark of the Covenant for nearly thirty years now. I, too, believe that it's somewhere here in Ethiopia."

"Did you read to the end of my article?" Solange interrupted him. "I quoted Jeremiah chapter three, verses sixteen and seventeen, where it says there would come a time when the Ark would not be in use and Jerusalem itself would be called the throne of God. To me that meant

Jehovah God had taken his favor from the Ark and had impressed upon the Jewish people the need to have faith in Him rather than rely on signs and portents. The last mention of the Ark in the Bible occurs in the eleventh chapter of Revelation, nineteenth verse, where John speaks of seeing the Ark in Jehovah's temple sanctuary in heaven."

They walked on until they arrived in a great room with a comfortable grouping of leather sofas and chairs. The walls were lined with books. Theophilus gestured for them to have a seat, then he walked across the room to a fully stocked bar, choosing from the bottles lined in the built-in wall unit behind the counter. "Water, orange juice, Diet Coke? My daughter makes sure we have a good supply of that on hand."

"Orange juice?" Solange asked Desta.

The girl nodded. Her dark fall of hair was still loose about her head and her cheeks were tinged red from the tussle in the car and her crying jag.

"Are you hungry?" Solange asked. She was hungry, having skipped breakfast that morning. She'd hoped she would return to the hotel in time to breakfast with Rupert.

"A little," Desta answered, her voice barely a whisper.

Solange peered across the room at Theophilus Gault, who was pouring orange juice into three tall glasses. "I know we should wait to be asked. You may not feed your prisoners, but we'd both like a bit of sustenance, if you don't mind."

"Of course not," Theophilus said magnanimously. "Where are my manners?"

"From all indications you don't have any," Solange said without cracking a smile.

Theophilus had the uncanny ability to raise one eyebrow while the other remained in a fixed position on his face. The only other person she'd ever seen do that was Rupert. Theophilus smiled at her as he rejoined them, handing them glasses of orange juice. "Come, ladies. There is plenty of food in the refrigerator. Before she left this morning, for a two-week vacation in France, my housekeeper, Mary, put fourteen casseroles in the freezer and, if I'm not mistaken, there is half a roast from last night's meal in the fridge."

They followed him down a long hallway until they arrived in a spacious, professionally appointed kitchen. He went and opened one side of the double-door stainless steel refrigerator. "Let me see, said the blind man as he picked up his hammer and saw."

Solange pointed to a nearby table. "Have a seat, sweetie," she told Desta. "I'll make you a sandwich."

She came up behind Theophilus and cleared her throat. He moved out of the way. This was clearly woman's work. He had not spent much time in the kitchen over the years. The kitchen had been Frannie's domain. Now it was Mary's. She'd been with them since Samantha was five years old.

He went to sit at the table with Desta, who would not meet his eyes. Her lips were pressed together in a thin, tense line. "What are you called, child?" he asked.

She did not respond. In fact, he hadn't heard her utter a word since she'd gotten there.

"Can she speak?" he asked Solange.

"And hear," Solange said as she removed the pan with the roast in it from the fridge and set it on the nearby counter. She found a jar of mustard in the door of the refrigerator. "Do you like mustard?" she asked, looking at Desta.

Desta nodded again.

"Oh, come now," Theophilus said, laughing. "I'm not an ogre. I didn't bring you ladies here to harm you in any way. I just need your expertise, Dr. DuPree."

"I heard you the first time," Solange said as she sliced what she hoped was roast beef with a knife she'd found

in the drawer next to the gas stove. She turned, holding
the knife aloft. "If we're not prisoners, I'd like to phone
my friend, Rupert Giles, and tell him where I am. He'll
be worried about me."

"I'd rather you didn't do that just yet," Theophilus
hedged. "I don't have you in my confidence yet and you
may decide to turn me in for kidnapping, which is exactly
what my incompetent butler did to you."

"Butler!" Solange couldn't hold back the laughter.
"Danyael is a butler? This is priceless. The butler did it!"
She shook her head in amazement. "Okay, Mr. Gault,
win me over in a hurry because Rupert Giles is not the
sort of man to allow me to go missing for very long
before taking the law into his own hands and causing
quite a ruckus. Believe me, I've seen him in action. You
don't want him angry with you."

She continued building two sandwiches while Theophilus talked.

"I was in Italy two years ago where I visited a rare
bookstore. I collect books, among other things. I came
across a handwritten journal by an Italian soldier who'd
been among the invading troops to enter the Ethiopian
capital in October of 1935. He wrote sensitively about
the cruelty of the Italians, saying the Ethiopians had nothing to fight with. Yet they kept fighting. Sometimes they'd
be coming at you with a stick when you had a rifle in
your hands.

"He also wrote about the orders to take everything of
value when they came across it. They stole jewelry, art-
work, holy scripture written on papyrus and golden
crosses. The Orthodox Church boasted opulent finery and
ceremonial chalices from which the anointed drank the
blood of Christ. This soldier had a flash of ingenuity and
didn't stop at stealing the churches' treasures. He decided
if they had such riches above ground then they must be
hiding even better things below ground. He got together

with three trusted friends and went down into the cellar of St. Mary of Zion Church. Down they went. Soon they came to catacombs. They followed the well-beaten path until it came to a cave, and in that cave he says they found a room whose walls had been painted with murals of religious figures. In the center of that room stood an altar. In the center of the altar sat a large object covered with a velvety purple cloth. At that point he said a wizened old man appeared out of the shadows and frightened them all because he was so ancient they thought he was a ghost. But then he spoke in halting French, for he thought they were Frenchmen. He had been below ground for so long that he hadn't heard about the invasion. The writer of the journal spoke French, so he understood the old man. The other three did not. "Beware!" the old man said. "Take anything you wish from above but do not touch the Ark, for you shall surely die.

"The writer of the journal translated this warning for his comrades, but they laughed at the weak old man's assertions. Unwilling to have come so far without taking something back with them, they approached the object on the altar. They did not trust each other, and all three of them touched the covering of the object simultaneously. Fire, wrote the soldier, flew out of the object like a living thing and leaped onto the hands and arms of the three who had touched it. It spread rapidly to every inch of their bodies and they went up in an eerily contained conflagration. Eery because nothing else around them burned. Only the bodies themselves. It was as if they'd burned from the inside out. The soldier was so horrified he ran madly back the way he'd come but got lost in the catacombs. He found his way out some three days later, and once he was free he went AWOL."

"And you believe that?" Solange asked, incredulous. She and Desta had nearly finished eating their sandwiches. She pushed her plate aside and regarded Theophilus with sober eyes. "That account jibes with the myth that if anyone comes near the Ark, supposedly kept in the walled St. Mary of Zion Church compound near the Northern Stelae Field, they will burst into flames." She laughed. "You're an accomplished man, Mr. Gault. I read about you in *Black Enterprise*: You own the most successful black-owned electronics company in the world. Are you sitting there telling me that you believe the real Ark of the Covenant may be underneath the St. Mary of Zion church in that walled compound?"

"Yes!" Theophilus said enthusiastically. "And I'm going to get it, then you are going to carbon date it. Imagine, Dr. DuPree: You will go down in history as the archaeologist who unearthed the greatest treasure mankind has ever known."

"I'm telling you, it's a myth the Ethiopians have been perpetuating for centuries. They've been telling that tale for so long, they believe it themselves."

"But what if it's true?" Theophilus asked. "Wouldn't it be cunning of them to hide it in plain sight?"

Solange sighed wearily. It was becoming evident to her that Theophilus Gault was intent on locating the Ark of the Covenant. The question was, why? It had to be more than the monetary value of the Ark that fed his compulsion.

"The Israelites looked to the Ark for guidance and wisdom," Solange said. "Is that what you're looking for, Mr. Gault? Or are you looking to harness the legendary power of the Ark? In some Biblical accounts it's described as a weapon of war. Jewish legend says that the Ark was so powerful that it literally lifted its bearers from the ground. At the battle of Jericho, when the Israelites simultaneously held it before them and blew their horns, the walls of Jericho came tumbling down."

She paused for effect. "Now, why do you suppose the Living God would allow a weapon of that magnitude to remain on earth to fall into the hands of unscrupulous men?" She shook her head. "I don't believe He would. I *believe* the account in Revelation where John says he saw it in heaven."

"There is evidence that Hitler searched for the Ark of the Covenant," Theophilus said, his eyes shining with excitement.

"Too bad he didn't find it and touch it before he had six million Jews killed," Solange said seriously. She looked him straight in the eyes. "Why do *you* want to find it, Mr. Gault?"

He ignored her question, again.

Seeing that Desta was finished eating, Solange rose and took their plates and glasses to the sink. She rinsed them. When she was finished she turned around and faced Theophilus Gault. "I don't care about fame and fortune, Mr. Gault. You couldn't pay me enough to steal the Ark from the Ethiopian people. I don't believe they're in possession of the real thing, but that doesn't matter to me. *They* believe it. More than a thousand years of their history is based upon it. The Lion of Judah, Emperor Haile Selassie, claimed he was descended from Solomon and his claim would be null and void without the belief that Menelik the son of Makeda, Queen of Sheba, was sired by Solomon. And it was Menelik who brought the Ark to Ethiopia hundreds of years ago. History is a funny thing. It changes on the tongues of its tellers. Your quest for the Ark is a selfish thing when your taking it could collapse the faith of a people who have been relying on its existence for hundreds of years. I wouldn't want that on my conscience."

Eleven

"That's her," Prudence said quietly. She smiled and handed the photo back to Rupert. "She fought like a wildcat. I bet the smaller man is battered and bruised by now. The boy was also giving it to him when the driver sped off."

"Speaking of the driver, can you describe him for us?" Detective Mulatu asked. He, Mrs. Bellweather, and Rupert Giles were all sitting around his desk at the police station. He was behind the desk busily pulling up data on the computer. The other two sat on chairs opposite him.

"He was a mountain of a man," Prudence said. "Bulging muscles. Even bigger than yours, Mr. Giles. He was at least a foot taller than the other fellow and his skin pigment was darker, too, like the Karo people's in the Omo valley."

"He could be from any number of groups in the country or he could be from one of the border countries: Kenya, Somalia, Sudan, or Yemen. Whoever he is, he has to be caught," Detective Mulatu said fiercely. "Did he have any unusual features? Scars, moles, unusually large teeth?"

"He was bald," Prudence recalled. "And he had markings on both his cheeks. He reminded me of that lovely recording artist, Seal."

Rupert sat there thinking he should be doing more.

Momentarily he got to his feet, forced a smile for Mrs. Bellweather's benefit, and said, "Ten to one, the driver worked for a car service here in Addis. It's Monday afternoon. I say we should check them all to see if any of them have a man working there fitting the driver's description."

Detective Mulatu rose, too. The men's expressions were equally hostile.

"I'm handling this investigation, Mr. Giles. *You* will not be doing anything except providing information we may be able to use in locating Dr. DuPree and the boy. You are a guest in our country. I suggest you tread carefully if you don't want to be detained for your own safety."

Rupert took a deep breath and exhaled, calming himself down. From what he'd observed, the police department was sorely understaffed. Detective Mulatu appeared sincere in his desire to do a good job, but what could you do when you didn't have the resources? Time was running out.

"Okay," Rupert said. "I apologize for suggesting I get involved in the investigation. It's just that that's what I do, investigate. It's difficult for me to sit here wondering what's happening to Solange and Tesfaye, two people I care about. They could be being tortured. As we both know, time is of the essence. What harm would it do if I lent my time to checking out the car rental agencies?"

Dawit Mulatu had only recently made detective. He could not afford any screw-ups; however, he sensed the coiled rage inside of Rupert Giles and figured asking questions at car rental agencies throughout the city might keep him out of trouble. "All right, Mr. Giles. You're to inform me immediately if you find anything relevant to the case."

"Of course," Rupert said, offering his hand.

The men shook on it.

Prudence listened to this conversation with interest. If Mr. Giles were permitted to lend a hand she should be, too. She waited for either of the men to ask for her help. After all she'd provided every one of the leads they had so far.

Instead of asking for her help, though, Detective Mulatu smiled warmly at her and said, "Thanks once again, Mrs. Bellweather. You may go."

Prudence rose slowly. Young people invariably expected her to have aching joints. She didn't want to ruin their image of her. Her joints were perfectly fine. However, other people's perceptions could sometimes work to your advantage.

"Good day, then," she said to Detective Mulatu. To Rupert Giles, she said cheerfully, "Dr. DuPree seems like the sort of woman who can take care of herself. She's a fighter. She'll figure a way out of this."

"Thank you for your kind words," Rupert sincerely said.

Prudence smiled her pleasure, turned and left, softly closing the door behind her. From the police station she went straight to the public library where she knew she'd be able to find a phone directory whose pages hadn't been ripped out.

It was dark already and they had not been released. That fact, alone, had Solange antsy. She and Desta had each been shown to a spacious bedroom. But she didn't want Desta out of her sight for any length of time, so she and Desta would be sharing a room for the duration.

Theophilus Gault had told them Danyael would be preparing dinner for them and in the meantime they should rest in their rooms. Danyael, not knowing they would have two guests, had shopped for Solange, guessing at her size. She would find several changes of clothing, lingerie and toiletries in their proper places in her bedroom. The thought of Danyael handling items of clothing that would eventually touch her body gave Solange a creepy feeling. However, she couldn't refuse to wear the clothes. She had nothing else to put on. The seam in the arm of her jacket had been ripped in the melee with Danyael and Desta in the back seat of the Mercedes. And she had to think of Desta, who could use a change of clothing. The clothes would be a bit large on her, but at least they were clean. The first thing she and Desta did when they got in the room was search for a phone. They found a phone jack adjacent to the desk near the window, but there was no phone plugged into it.

"There must be a phone somewhere in this place," Solange complained.

"Probably where he sleeps," Desta said, her dark eyes once again revealing the sharp intelligence Solange had always admired in the girl.

"Yes," Solange agreed. "He probably removed all the rest and locked them away; but he'd want one in use in case he got a business call. And he mentioned a daughter. She might phone."

Desta nodded, walking around the room, looking at all the luxuries the owner of the villa had spared no expense on. A Persian carpet on the marble floor. A four-poster antique bed with carved lion's feet for legs with a matching bureau, dresser, and nightstands on either sides of the bed. In less opulent surroundings the furnishings would look grotesque, but here in this huge house they appeared perfectly suitable.

"What we've got to do is not worry. Rupert will find us, I'm sure. But while we are waiting we have to be thinking of a way to escape. In the meantime, let's freshen up, shall we? It's been a long day. We're both sore from beating up Danyael."

Desta giggled and it was the most beautiful sound to

Solange's ears. "You first," she told the girl. "Into the bath with you."

"Ah," said Desta, the thought of a bath rendering her voice wistful. "I shall die from joy."

Solange smiled, thinking that if Desta were still in her role as Tesfaye, staying true to character, she probably would have balked at a bath. Now, however, she was a twelve-year-old girl, and a bath sounded like a heavenly prospect.

"Don't die yet," Solange said. "Let me get my hands on that hair first. I'll wash it for you, then I'll plait it before you go to bed tonight."

Desta spontaneously hugged Solange. "Oh, yes, thank you!"

Solange hugged her back, feeling tears prick the backs of her eyes. She was getting entirely too sentimental in her soon-to-be middle thirties.

"Where did you learn to speak such good English?" Solange asked as she sat on the side of the tub shampooing Desta's long, thick hair. She tried not to rub the child's scalp too hard, but it was clear from how dirty the water in the tub was becoming that her hair hadn't been washed in a long time.

Though Desta's weight was slightly lower than a normal twelve-year-old girl's she was far from emaciated. Somehow she'd managed to eat on a regular basis while on the streets. "From Sister Laura at the orphanage," Desta said. "She's British. She taught me to read and write it, too. She's one of the people I miss from the orphanage."

"Why did you leave?" Solange asked softly.

"There was a boy there who was always trying to touch me. He was older, probably sixteen or seventeen. He threatened to kill me if I told on him. I believed he would so I kept quiet."

"How old were you?"

"I was ten at the time."

"So he kept pestering you," Solange said, encouraging Desta to talk.

"He would follow me everywhere. The other girls were afraid of him, too. One of them had stolen a knife from the kitchen and she gave it to me so I would be able to protect myself. I guess he got tired of waiting. Late one night after he knew the staff would be sleeping he crept into the room I shared with five other girls, caught me while I was sleeping and put his hand over my mouth so I couldn't scream. He was much stronger than I was. He lay his body on top of mine. I couldn't move. I couldn't breathe. Then he did something, he raised up off of me so he could reach down and open the drawstring on his pants. That was when I put my hand under the mattress and got the knife. I cut him below the waist. I don't know where I cut him exactly. It was as if I was not *me*. I can't even remember how many times I cut him. All I know is that when the nuns came in and turned the lights on there was blood everywhere. I was covered in it. The bed was soaked, and he was screaming and holding that place below his belly."

Solange and Desta were silently crying, Desta remembering the pain, and Solange experiencing it for the first time. She went on gently massaging Desta's scalp. The physical contact comforted both of them.

"They took us to the hospital," Desta continued. "I'd cut my right thigh in several places, but the cuts weren't bad. Turns out his wounds weren't deep either. The next day I was told I was going to another orphanage. It was a place for bad children, the ones they were afraid to let live in the 'good' orphanages in case they corrupted the other children. I tried to explain that he had attacked *me*. None of the nuns asked why he was on top of me in my own bed. The day they were planning to take me to the other orphanage, one of my friends—the girl who'd given

me the knife—started a fight and practically all of the
other children joined in. In the confusion I slipped away
and I've been living on the street ever since."

Rupert was dead tired when he got back to Solange's
room at the Sheraton that night. He'd been to ten different
car rental places. He hadn't imagined there would be so
many in Addis. But like many Westerners, he'd underes-
timated the sophistication of the city. *He* wasn't like most
Westerners, though, he thought. He was an ex-spy. He
should have made more progress by now.

He'd come back to Solange's room because he wanted
to lay his head on her pillow. The smell of her peppermint-scented shampoo would lull him to sleep.

He walked over to the bed and pulled the bedspread
back. The maid had made the bed, of course. He picked
up Solange's pillow and sniffed it. The faint smell of peppermint assailed his nostrils. He hugged the pillow and
wearily sat down with his back against the headboard.
When he did that he heard the crinkling of paper. He felt
beneath him. He was sitting on a sheet of paper. He pulled
it free and peered down at it, reading: *Rupert, I'm sorry
I can't be the woman you need in your life. I would not
go if I didn't love you. But, I do. And because I do, I have
to give you back. It would be selfish of me to keep you.
Please don't ask me why. Forever, Solange.*

Rupert read the note four times before it registered.
She'd left him.

He quickly got up from the bed and went to check her
closet. Sure enough, all her things were gone. He'd had
no reason to go into her closet that morning. His things
were lying on chairs, and all the toiletries he needed were
in the bathroom. He didn't exactly know how to feel at
that moment. Like an utter fool for believing in her?
Used, because they'd had such great sex together? But in

that case, who had used whom? They'd both gotten satisfaction. And they'd both fallen in love. He knew it! He'd never been more certain of anything in his life.

And that cryptic note: She'd had to let him go because she *loved* him? The tone had suggested sacrifice. Why did she believe he'd be happier without her? Because that's what she was saying, wasn't it?

He went back into the bedroom, the crumpled paper still in his right hand. He placed it on the bureau's top and began undressing. He could not allow himself to mourn the passing of their love affair when he now knew for a certainty that she loved him and it wasn't solely passion between them.

He stripped down to his sleeveless T-shirt and his boxers and got in bed and lay on his side, the pillow with her scent on it beneath his head. He lay there a long time with his eyes open praying for Solange and Tesfaye's safety. And cursing his ineptitude. He should have dealt with Danyael more severely when he'd had the chance.

As for Solange's betrayal, he didn't know why she'd decided to leave him. He was going to find out though. Very soon.

He closed his eyes. He needed to be alert tomorrow.

"Sir, I'll give you twenty dollars if you'll let me get in line in front of you," Samantha said to the hefty man in front of her at the American Airlines desk in Boulder, Colorado.

He smiled and grabbed the twenty. She moved ahead of him.

"Madame, I'll give you twenty dollars if you'll let me get ahead of you in line . . ."

Samantha worked her way up in line until she was standing in front of the ticket agent. She handed the woman her return ticket to Addis. "Ethiopia," she joked.

"And step on it! I've got to see a man about an *old goat.*"
Namely, her father.

The woman laughed and began typing on her computer
keyboard.

Prudence Bellweather had a knack for being in the
right place at the right time. She'd just walked into the
Thrifty car rental store on Bole Road and was treated to
a shouting match between the owner and a disgruntled
employee.

She did not understand all of the exchange because
her Amharic was a bit rusty. However, she didn't need to
understand a word of their conversation—the angry employee, who was being asked to turn in his car keys and
name tag, so to speak, was none other than the driver of
the car that had driven away with Solange DuPree and
Tesfaye Roba two days ago. Prudence backed out of the
shop and went up the street to a tej beat. Inside the bar
she frantically searched for a phone. Finally, she spotted
one in the back. Hurrying to it, she picked up the receiver
and waited for a dial tone that never came. She walked
up to the counter, forcing herself between two Ethiopian
men to do so. Both gave her curious glances but simply
moved over a bit further to accommodate her. "Tele-
phone!" she said to the man behind the counter.

He pointed to the one in the back of the bar.

Prudence pounded her hand on the counter and shook
her head in the negative to denote the phone was out of
order. Sensing her dilemma the man said, "Boulangerie."

Prudence recognized that word. It meant bakery in
French. "Merci," she said, and left.

All three men gave great sighs of relief. They were not
used to women, especially white-haired white women, in
their watering hole.

The public phone inside the bakery was in working

order and Prudence phoned Detective Mulatu. She waited on the line for several minutes. No Detective Mulatu. Next she dialed the Sheraton. She looked at her watch. It was nearly four in the afternoon. Mr. Giles was probably out doing the same thing she was, casing the car rental joints. She loved American lingo.

"Hello?"

Prudence crowed with joy. "Mr. Giles, I'm at a bakery across from the bus station only about a mile from the Sheraton." She gave him the exact address. "I just saw the driver of the Mercedes at a car rental outfit called Thrifty. I'll meet you there." She hung up, not waiting for his reply.

In his room at the Sheraton, Rupert had just returned from pounding the streets all day long. He'd been discouraged because Detective Mulatu had told him that although they knew Danyael Abate's room at the Sheraton had been charged to a Gault Electronics corporate account, and what's more the account number was valid, there was no Danyael Abate working for Gault Electronics out of Washington, D.C., and never had been.

Rupert's weariness didn't stop him from putting his shoes back on and grabbing his keys and his coat and rushing back out into the November chill. If Mrs. Prudence Bellweather had actually seen the driver, he had no time to waste.

Once out of the elevator in the hotel parking garage he ran to the car he'd rented two days ago at the very first car rental place where he'd questioned the owner. It was a Saab. Ten years old, but still in pretty good condition.

He spotted Mrs. Bellweather right away. She was wearing a chartreuse trench coat and holding an umbrella in the same shade. She was shaking her hands as though she were trying to cool them off, she was so anxious for him to stop the car and get out.

As soon as he stopped the car at the curb, she ran over to it. "Hurry, hurry. He's still in there arguing with the poor man behind the counter."

Rupert pointed to the car. "Wait in the car, Mrs. Bellweather."

Mrs. Bellweather took one more peek at the assailant and decided she'd feel much more comfortable waiting in the Saab, and she climbed inside and shut the door.

Rupert decided the best way to handle the situation was with directness. He walked into the small shop and cleared his throat. The big man wouldn't stop his verbal assault of the shop's owner. He was so livid, he didn't even bother to look at the person who'd entered the shop.

Rupert sized him up. The assailant appeared to be at least thirty pounds heavier than he was, but his middle was soft. His arms and legs were powerful, however. His strength lay in his punches. His weakness was his midsection. From the look of his face he'd been hit a lot. He could probably take it on the jaw, too.

"Excuse me," Rupert said.

The big man turned his head to glare at Rupert. "We were talking, bloke!"

Perfect English. Without an African dialect anywhere in the intonation. He was from England—via *where*, Rupert had no idea. But that didn't matter now.

"No. *You* were talking. He was getting a headache from your blathering."

A flicker of pique, a squinting of his eyes, a tightening of those massive jaws. Then his brain sent a message containing an appropriate comeback, but by then Rupert had moved in and slammed his mighty fist into his stomach. The big man doubled over and Rupert chopped him on the back of the neck rendering him unconscious. It was over within a matter of seconds.

The owner of the shop clapped his hands with glee.

"Beautiful, beautiful," he said over and over again. It was probably one of the few English words he knew.

Rupert didn't have time to accept accolades. He went around and grabbed the sack of malice under the arms and dragged him out of the shop, popped the car's trunk and shoved him inside.

Prudence had watched it all from the car. "Very well done, Mr. Giles," she said when Rupert got in the car and started it. "I hate violence," Rupert said.

"But you do it so *well,*" Prudence said. She settled back on the seat, getting comfortable. "Where to now?"

"I don't know, Mrs. Bellweather. Where shall I drop you off?"

The sixty-two-year-old pouted like a two-year-old all the way to her hotel.

"Thank you, Mrs. Bellweather. When this is over I'm going to treat you to dinner," Rupert promised when he dropped her off.

"Good luck, Mr. Giles. I would like to meet Dr. Du-Pree after you've rescued her and the boy."

As he drove off, Rupert wished he had as much confidence in his abilities as Prudence Bellweather seemed to have.

Rupert had always been the type of operative who could use anything lying around to take the place of whatever it was he didn't have on hand. He needed rope to tie up the big man in the Saab's trunk. Being without it, what he did when he'd driven out of town to a deserted spot was strip the man and tie him up with his own clothing.

He was as naked as when he'd come into the world, spread-eagled on the ground next to the Saab when he finally came to. It was dusk by then. Rupert crouched near the man's face. A smelly sock was tied around his head preventing him from speaking. Rupert imagined it didn't taste well at all.

"Just nod. Up and down for yes. Side to side for no," Rupert said. "Do you want to live?"

Up and down.

"Do you want your testicles to remain on your body?"

Vigorously up and down.

"Are you going to tell me what I want to know?"

Slowly up and down.

"That's all I wanted to hear," said Rupert.

He cut the nasty sock away with a knife and the man started spilling his guts. After which he literally spilled his guts, vomiting from the stress of the moment and, likely, from the presence of the malodorous sock in his mouth.

"Then when can you get here?" Theophilus shouted into the phone.

It was a cordless phone and he was standing in the garden of the villa. For three days he'd been holding Dr. Solange DuPree and the child against their will. For three days he'd been trying to get this show on the road.

The helicopter pilot and the two men he'd hired to go in and get the Ark were having trouble with the Ethiopian Airforce. The helicopter had nearly been shot down over Ethiopian airspace, and they were holding it until the pilot could prove he had not stolen it. One just like it had been reported missing from an airfield just outside of Addis.

"Did you steal it?" Theophilus thundered.

"Well, yes," said the pilot. "My chopper is out of service at the moment."

"Your services are no longer required, Mr. Addison," Theophilus cut him off. He hung up and went inside the villa through the garden door which led to the kitchen.

In the kitchen Danyael, Solange, and Desta were preparing breakfast. In the past two days, Danyael had told Solange all his troubles, beginning with the moment he'd met Francesca and Theophilus Gault. After listening to him, she'd begun to have a grudging understanding of the put-upon soul. She still didn't trust him as far as she could throw him, although she could fathom the level of loyalty he felt for the Gaults.

Theophilus strode into the room, his commanding presence immediately felt.

Startled, Solange turned around too quickly and the glass of orange juice she'd been drinking slipped from her fingers and shattered on the tile floor. When she bent down to collect some of the larger pieces, the medallion came out of her blouse and caught Theophilus's attention. Something stirred faintly inside of him, then began to grow until it blossomed into a full-blown memory.

He moved as though in a trance toward Solange, stepping on the glass as he did so.

"May I?" he asked, as he reached for the medallion. His hand glanced Solange's throat as he grasped the medallion in his right hand.

"Wait, you can hold it," Solange said. She pulled it off and handed it to him.

Theophilus Gault's eyes watered as he gazed down at the cheap gold-tone medallion. On one side was an olive branch, on the other the words, *Always, Romeo.*

He bit his bottom lip in an attempt to bank his emotions. "Where did you get this?"

Solange backed away from the mess on the floor. She touched Theophilus's arm and led him to the side. Danyael immediately set to work cleaning up the broken glass and mopping up the orange juice.

Recognizing this was a solemn moment, Desta went to sit at the kitchen table and watch from a distance. Observing people was her strong suit.

Solange peered into Theophilus's eyes. "The man I

love gave it to me. His adoptive parents gave it to him. They told him it belonged to his birth mother."

Theophilus's hands suddenly started trembling. He clasped one with the other, the medallion between them, to stop their shaking. "I don't believe this. There can't be two exact pendants with the exact same endearment on the back." He looked deeply into Solange's eyes. "H-how old is Rupert Giles? That is who you're referring to?"

Solange nodded. "He's thirty-eight."

Theophilus frowned. "If she had been pregnant when I left, the child would be thirty-eight now." His breath was becoming labored. "I can't believe this! Where is he? I've got to meet him."

"He's in Addis at the Sheraton."

"No, sweetness, I'm standing right here," Rupert said from the kitchen doorway.

Danyael started at the sound of Rupert's voice and went to move.

"No sudden moves, Danyael," Rupert said. "I'm wound pretty tightly and with any encouragement, I may go off." He looked at Theophilus Gault and it was like looking in the mirror at himself twenty years in the future.

He'd heard everything that had been said. He'd been standing there unnoticed for the past five minutes. So many emotions were vying for attention inside of him: relief at seeing Solange and Tesfaye (he guessed that was Tesfaye) unharmed; the desire to crush Solange against his chest and feel her body heat against his; the leftover anger with Danyael and the need to hit him in the face; and finally, the shock at seeing someone who looked like him looking back at him. He'd come face to face with his heart's desire and felt paralyzed with indecision.

Solange was not confused as to what to do next. She flung herself into his arms and wrapped her arms around his strong neck. Desta followed, clinging to Solange's waist.

"I'm so sorry," Solange cried.

"Sorry for what?" Rupert asked. He met her eyes. "Sorry for loving me?"

"No. Never for that!" Solange vehemently denied. "I'm sorry for not telling you I'm not whole. I can't conceive, Rupert." She was so relieved to see him, she didn't care who heard her confession. She was not keeping it a secret anymore. She held on to Rupert with one arm and Desta with the other. "I was on my way back to you that morning because of this child's bravery. I'd found out from the consul at the American Embassy just what she'd been through these past seven years since her family was killed. And I felt ashamed I couldn't tell you about my condition. I felt like a coward, and I had to go back to you and tell you everything. But then Danyael and some hulk showed up and Desta and I wound up here."

"Desta?" Rupert said.

Desta peered up at him with her love for him shining in her dark eyes and he put his arm around her, too. "Desta, *destiny*. I guess it suits you." He smiled warmly at her. Then his eyes fell on the man across the room. His father. Even thinking the word hurt. *Father.* Some father!

"Excuse me, ladies," he softly said to Solange and Desta.

The two Gault men locked eyes, and horns, from across the room. Solange feared they were going to butt chests or something, there was so much testosterone flying in the air in that room.

"You abandoned her, you son-of-a-bitch! She's dead because of you!" Rupert shouted so loudly Solange thought the windows would surely rattle in his wake.

"I didn't know she was pregnant. I never would have

gone to America without her if I had known. I loved
her more than my own life. I must have, her father
warned me he'd kill me if I didn't stay away from her.
But I couldn't. She was so beautiful, so delicate. But
strong. Don't you see? She didn't tell me she was pregnant because she wanted me to go. It was our only
chance to be together. And, then, when I wrote to her
and I didn't hear from her, I wrote and asked my mother
to go to see her for me. My mother wrote back and told
me Maryam had drowned. Drowned! No one in my family knew she'd given birth. If they'd known they would
have told me."

Rupert went absolutely still. Could it be that his mother
had never received his father's letters and because of that
she'd been distraught and in her depression had drowned
herself? "Her father," he said. "He probably never gave
her your letters. She thought you'd abandoned her. She
gave me to a couple who worked as missionaries in Guyana and she killed herself."

Theophilus let out a wail so pitiful, Rupert could not
deny his father the embrace of a long-lost son. He put
his arms around him and let him sob.

It was this scene that Samantha walked in on. She
looked from her weeping father being held in the arms
of a perfect stranger, for she couldn't see Rupert's face,
to the familiar face of Danyael, whose eyes were glassy
from watching the emotional reunion of his employer and
son, to Solange, whom she recognized from The Hard
Luck Café, then to Desta, who looked like the sweetest
little girl in the world, and said, "I'm too late, aren't I?
He's already done the crime and I'll be visiting him in
prison for the next thirty years."

The Gault men parted and she finally saw Rupert's
face. "Oh, my God! It's you!" she cried.

"Hello, sis," said Rupert.

Whereupon, Samantha fainted dead away.

Samantha revived almost immediately. Rupert carried her to a nearby room where he gently put her on a couch. When she opened her eyes the first things she saw were the faces of her father and newfound brother, wearing nearly identical worried expressions.

Solange was there pressing the rim of a cold glass of water to her lips. "Here, drink."

Samantha drank deeply. She could not take her eyes off Rupert. "I danced with you."

"Yes, at the Hard Luck Café." He smiled, remembering.

"This is too spooky. I wanted to meet you that night because you reminded me of my dad. And now here you are. My *brother?*" Her gaze moved to her father. "How?"

Theophilus knelt beside her and told her about Maryam. How they had been in love and how he had gone to the United States to try to make something of himself. He'd intended to send for her later.

There were tears in Samantha's eyes when he concluded with Maryam's drowning.

"I never knew Rupert existed until today," he said, his voice catching. He swallowed hard and looked at his son standing only a few feet away from his daughter. He had *two* children. He ran a trembling hand through his hair, trying to compose himself.

Samantha sat up on the couch, peered at Rupert and patted the space beside her. "Sit down, let me have a good look at you."

Rupert sat. Samantha turned toward him and clasped one of his hands in both of hers. She simply observed him for a long while, taking in the shape of his head. How his ears lay flat against it. Large eyes the color of a sunset on an autumn day. Even the texture of his hair, though it was shorn close to his head, was like her father's: thick and wavy.

Sensing this was a private moment, Solange took Desta by the hand and led her away. Danyael, who had been caught up in the moment, too, followed them out of the room.

When she, her father, and Rupert were alone, Samantha smiled warmly at Rupert and said, "There's no doubt about it, you're definitely a Gault. God help you!" To which she and Rupert laughed.

"What is that supposed to mean?" Theophilus inquired, taking umbrage. "You haven't suffered too badly with the name, young lady."

Samantha, still holding on to Rupert's hand, gestured to the chair next to her. "Sit, Daddy. I am not going to crane my neck looking up at you."

Recognizing the tone in his daughter's voice as irritation nearing the boiling point, Theophilus sat. "I'm sitting."

Narrowing her eyes at him, Samantha went on to explain why she'd tempered her welcome to her brother with a warning. "How did you happen to meet Dr. DuPree, Father?"

Theophilus knew he was in for it now because she'd called him "Father." She never did that unless she was really ticked off.

"I had Danyael bring her here," Theophilus said, his voice no more than a mumble.

"Speak up. I don't think Rupert heard you."

"I had Danyael and another fellow bring her here," Theophilus said louder.

"You *had* Danyael bring her here," Samantha repeated. "Against her will!"

"Well, yes." Her father had the good sense to look contrite.

Feeling much better now, and knowing that if she

didn't hammer home her point her father would feel justified in his actions, Samantha released Rupert's hand and rose. Pacing, she continued. "That's kidnapping."

She locked gazes with her father. Hers was accusatory, while his was sheepish.

"In Ethiopia, you can go to prison for life for kidnapping. That is, if you don't get shot by a firing squad." She looked at Rupert. "The police, I take it, know about the abduction?"

"Of course," Rupert said. He did not hasten to add that he'd acted independently of the authorities when he'd come out there to stage a rescue attempt. That was beside the point. Detective Mulatu would have to be told a very convincing story if their father and Danyael were to escape punishment for their crimes.

Theophilus looked alarmed when he heard that the police knew Solange and Desta had been forcibly brought to him. "I would never have harmed them."

"They didn't know that!" Samantha vehemently said. Her eyes sought Rupert's again. "What do you think? Should we let him go to prison, or try to pull his fat out of the fire?"

Rupert had to consider that question a while. It was more than a minute before he spoke. "I think the wronged parties should decide what becomes of him."

Samantha turned on her heels and started walking in the direction of the kitchen where she could smell the aroma of coffee brewing. Danyael had probably put the coffee on. Perhaps Solange and Desta were in the kitchen, too. The men followed.

When they entered the room, Danyael, who was reaching into the cabinet to retrieve coffee mugs, stopped and turned, his attention on them. Solange and Desta were sitting at the kitchen table, their heads together in conversation. They, too, gave the trio their attention.

Rupert went to Solange, pulled out the chair next to

her and sat down. "Sweetness, we were trying to figure
out what to do about Mr. Gault, here." He looked at his
father. Though Theophilus Gault might be his biological
father, it would be a long time before he would be able
to refer to him as such. If ever. Too many years had
passed for the transition to be a painless one. "The discovery that he is my father has come as a shock to us
all. But we can't forget how you and Desta were snatched
off the street. What do you and Desta think his punishment should be?"

Solange saw the seriousness in his eyes, and the realization that he was giving her and Desta the final say in
the matter made her heart swell with love for him.

She peered at Desta who was attired in a purple sweat
suit that was too large for her. Her long, dark hair was
in a ponytail. "What do you think, Des?"

Desta leaned forward, indicating she wanted to whisper
something to Solange. Solange bent down. After a few
moments, she straightened and said, "The orphanages in
Addis could use funding." She smiled in Theophilus's
direction. "A million dollars sounds like a nice, round
figure."

"This is highway robbery!" Theophilus bellowed.

Rupert laughed. "Take it, or leave it."

Theophilus took it. Danyael, standing nearby, released
a huge sigh of relief.

Two hours later they were all leaving the police station
in Addis after swearing the kidnapping had been a practical joke on a son by his father. Detective Mulatu, upon
seeing Rupert and Theophilus together, was immediately
convinced of their relationship to each other. Besides,
once Jeffrey Graham, the driver who'd assisted Danyael
in the kidnapping, had managed to work his bonds loose
he'd cut his losses and headed for the border. There was
no one left to testify that their story wasn't true.

They parted in the parking lot of the police station,

Desta going back to the villa with Samantha for the night. The two had taken an instant liking to each other, and Samantha had agreed to care for the girl until suitable accommodations at an orphanage could be arranged. Solange had contacted James Tan who was delighted at the turn of events and promised to do everything within his power to place Desta in a good facility.

In the meantime, Rupert and Solange had some things to discuss. Things that were best said in private. They went back to Rupert's room at the Sheraton.

Behind closed doors, Rupert stood watching Solange as she wearily walked over to the bed and sat down. He was torn between the desire to comfort her, or angrily lash out at her. Their eyes met and held across the room.

She would not lower her gaze at the sight of the pain in his. No matter what was to come next, she would not flinch. Her mother had been right. She should have told him. Plain and simple.

Rupert reached into his pants pocket and retrieved the note she'd written to him. He walked over and handed it to her. Solange accepted it. She rose to stand directly in front of him. "I'm a coward."

"You're the bravest woman I know," Rupert said, his voice husky. "You saw a child who needed you and you did something about it. You were forced into a car by a man who could have broken you in two and you fought him. You would have died before you would have allowed anything to happen to Desta."

Solange held the crumpled piece of paper in the palm of her hand. Her eyes glistened with tears. "But this. I hurt you."

Rupert pulled her into his arms. "You were frightened. Thinking that I'd reject you, you left me first. But you were coming back to me. That's what counts. That you came back." He kissed her forehead and held her face between his hands, peering into her dark eyes. "I don't know what our future holds. All I know is, I want you beside me. If we want more children after Desta's adoption is final, we'll adopt more."

"But . . ."

"Don't fight me on this, woman. I'm not letting you off the hook so easily. I should have been given the opportunity to decide my own fate in the first place! Haven't I told you about making decisions without my input?"

"Yes, but . . ."

"Don't 'but' me. You're going to marry me, dammit, and that's that!"

"Marry you?" Solange said, shocked down to her toes. "I told you, *I can't get pregnant.*" She raised her voice a little to make certain he'd heard her.

"I'm not deaf." Determined golden-brown eyes bore into hers. "If you think, for one minute, that I'm going to give up a woman like you just because she can't give me a kid that looks like me, you're not as smart as I thought you were. I've been looking for you all my life. Give a guy a break, and say yes already!"

"Ask me again in six months," Solange managed to say before bursting into tears, turning and running toward the bathroom, with Rupert right behind her.

She outpaced him this time and had locked the door before he could reach her.

He jiggled the doorknob. "What is this? I ask you to marry me and you start sobbing? That kind of behavior isn't good for a man's ego," he said calmly.

In the bathroom, Solange put the seat down on the toilet and sat. "You're asking me to put aside years of conditioning myself to be alone the rest of my life. You're asking me to believe in something I knew would never happen to me. I'm scared, Rupert."

"You don't think I'm scared?" Rupert asked. He put his shoulder to the door. It was not solid wood like the room door. One good shove and he'd be in there. He would not force his way inside when she was in this state, though.

"I love you, Solange. I love your passion and your naivete about certain things like, everyone has the power to make a difference in someone's life. Hey, that belief may not always pan out, but sometimes it does. As in Desta's case, for example. I love the way you comb your hair. I love the way you eat pasta. I love you when you're drunk. At least you're not a belligerent drunk . . ."

Solange laughed.

Encouraged by this, Rupert went on. Smiling, he said, "I love the way you look first thing in the morning when your hair's sticking up all over your head, and your eyes still have sleep in them. I live for the smell of you fresh from the shower. I love your feet, sweetness. I would kiss them now if only you'd come out of there."

He waited, hoping to hear her unlocking the door. Nothing.

Then, the shower came on and Solange called, her voice clearer now, "Door's open."

When Rupert entered the room he saw Solange's clothing hanging on the hook behind the door. She'd closed the shower stall and he could see the shape of her brown body behind the opaque sliding door.

"Water's fine," Solange said.

Rupert wasted no time peeling off his clothing, leaving it piled on the floor.

Solange pulled the door open just as he was removing his T-shirt, which he'd left for last. "What's taking you so long?" she asked with a saucy grin.

Rupert's heart raced at the sight of that smile. She was okay. Or she was getting there. He smiled back. "I'm going as fast as I can."

"I can remember a time you would have been naked and making love to me by now," she said, her eyes possessively raking over the body she'd been denied for three days.

Rupert stepped into the shower, the water falling on both their heads. "We're not even married yet, and you're already nagging me."

Solange impatiently pulled him down for a kiss that felt like the beginning of something good to Rupert, and the end of a journey for her.

Epilogue

By the time Solange showed up on her mother's door-step in early December, she had already seen Desta placed in a well-run orphanage in Addis and had assured her that she would never be out of touch during the months it would take for her adoption to become final. Mr. Tan had warned Solange the process could take a year or more, but had promised to work diligently to reduce the time.

Solange had come straight from the airport. Her clothes were rumpled and she knew her eyes must be red-rimmed from lack of sleep, but she had to see her mother the moment the plane touched down in Miami.

When Marie opened the door and saw her daughter standing there, she let out a whoop of joy and threw her arms around Solange's neck. Solange was enveloped in Lancome's *Miracle,* her mother's favorite perfume. She dropped her bag and embraced her. Marie's silky cheek pressed hers. Marie rocked her in her arms.

"What a lovely surprise!" Marie exclaimed, holding her daughter at arm's length. Her dark brown eyes fairly danced. "Look at you. You look beautiful."

Solange laughed shortly. "I look *horrible!*"

"You look like new money to me," Marie told her, pulling her inside. She went back herself and got Solange's bag before closing the door.

Solange moved past the foyer into the great room. As

usual, her mother's home was immaculate. Hardwood floors. Expensive oriental carpets. Handcrafted furnishings.

Marie had turned her flair for decorating into a business and was now a sought-after decorator among Miami's well-to-do. She made certain her home reflected her talent and eye for detail. She paid no less attention to her own dress.

The air smelled of cinnamon and other spices.

"Are you baking?" Solange asked, surprised. Her mother sometimes joked that though she was an excellent cook, her work kept her so busy she had forgotten where the kitchen was. Perhaps her circumstances had made her realize there was always time to cook.

"Come on back," Marie said, turning on her Ferragamos and walking swiftly through the house to the kitchen. "I'm making my mother's famous spice cookies. I dreamed about her last night and woke with the urge to make them."

So, that's how Solange found herself at her mother's kitchen nook eating homemade spice cookies and drinking milk while she related her recent adventures in Ethiopia.

Marie smiled pensively at the conclusion of the tale. "Theophilus went to Ethiopia in pursuit of one treasure and found another, his son. God has a way of throwing a curve, doesn't He?"

"He certainly does," Solange had to agree.

Sitting on a stool across from Solange at the nook, Marie crossed her legs and looked into Solange's eyes. "I'm ready to tell you about Maman now. I figure I should tell you before I go into the hospital in case something happens."

"Nothing's going to happen," Solange assured her. But she was afraid for her mother, even though her doctor had assured her the operation was routine.

"Things happen on the operating table, no matter how competent the surgeons may be," Marie gently insisted. She reached for Solange's hand and Solange grasped hers tightly. "Don't be afraid, daughter," she said. "I'm not going anywhere. I'm going to be around long enough to spoil my new granddaughter." She smiled wistfully and then began her story.

"Your grandfather, Henri, was a healer. He was a good man and had a talent with herbs. People from all around would come to him for their ills. He was what was called a docte fey, a leaf doctor. Your grandmother, Margarete, was also skilled in herbs. They were very much in love. I cannot recall a cross word between them.

"One day Pere went into the highlands to gather herbs and did not return. We never saw him again. Shortly after that a man started coming around trying to court Maman, but she rebuffed him. She was certain Pere would some-day return to her. It was later that we learned he was one of Papa Doc's *tontons macoutes,* the secret police Farn-cois Duvalier used to terrorize the people into subjuga-tion. He was obsessed with Maman.

"I blame myself for what I'm about to tell you now: I was seventeen and very much in love with your father. We would sneak off to be alone together. One late after-noon he saw me home and when we entered the house, it was eerily quiet. I sensed something was terribly wrong. I called out to Maman and there was no reply. I don't know why I went into her bedroom, but I did, and there he was over her body. He'd raped her and then stran-gled her. Probably because she wouldn't stop screaming. I saw him there, struggling to pull up his pants and then the next thing I spotted was the gun he'd placed on the bureau's top. I can still remember the look in his eyes when he saw me. Not panic. Not fear. But amusement. He probably thought he was going to get the opportunity to do to me what he'd just done to my mother. He didn't count on my having the presence of mind to grab the gun and use it on him. But that's what I did. I picked up the gun and shot him right between the eyes. He dropped like a sack of potatoes. I was calm. Unperturbed, really. My father was gone. My mother, lying dead on her bed, her head twisted at an unnatural angle. I knew there was no justice to be had. Especially not when the very man who'd killed her enforced the laws of the land."

Solange had been holding her breath. She exhaled and got up to enfold her mother in her arms. Marie clung tightly to her as she continued in a low, haunted voice.

"Your father and I burned the house down and left Port-au-Prince that very night. A couple of days later, we were on a boat heading for Miami. We were nearly dead from dehydration by the time the Coast Guard rescued us. Back then, in 1966, they weren't as hard on Haitian immigrants as they are now. Georges and I made a pact, we would never talk about our life in Haiti. When you were born in 1969 we saw you as proof that America was now our home. But, now, I've come to realize that no matter where you go, you take your past with you."

She raised her head to look Solange in the eyes. "There you have it, my dear one. Your mother is a killer, and that's the big secret she's been keeping all these years."

Solange wiped her mother's tears away with the pad of her thumb and smiled at her. "Two days ago, Rupert told me he thought *I* was the bravest woman he'd ever known, and now I know where I got it from." She planted a kiss on her mother's forehead. "I adore you, Maman."

Dear Reader:

I hope you've enjoyed Solange and Rupert's adventure in Ethiopia. I tried my best to capture the heart and soul of the Ethiopian people. I have a great deal of respect for them and their beautiful country.

If you'd like to drop me a line or two, you can reach me at P.O. Box 811, Mascotte, Florida 34753-0811, or if you're online you can write me via E-mail at Jani569432@aol.com or visit my Web site at http://www.janicesims.com

Until next time,
Janice Sims

COMING IN AUGUST 2002 FROM
ARABESQUE ROMANCES

__COMING HOME
    by Roberta Gayle   1-58314-282-7 $6.99US/$9.99CAN
When Charlotte's husband left her, she only had herself to blame. Now, years later, he's returned to their hometown. Charlotte asks her friend, Steve Parker, to help her become the woman she knows her ex wants. But when attraction begins sizzling between her and Steve, Charlotte has to decide which man and which life—is the real thing.

__FROM THIS DAY FORWARD
    by Bettye Griffin   1-58314-275-4 $6.99US/$9.99CAN
Cornelia "Hatch" Hatchet's dreams for her future are confined to working the night shift at Super Kmart. Life in her poverty-stricken hometown of Farmingdale, Illinois, just seems doomed to stay the same, until a reporter comes to town and changes everything.

__TRUST IN ME
    by Alice Wootson   1-58314-250-9 $5.99US/$7.99CAN
Linda Durard had fallen for the wrong man and lost everything. Now she's starting over by working at a community center. But first she has to earn the trust of Avery Washington, the center's owner. Like Linda, Avery is struggling to heal an emotional wound. The only chance they have is if they entrust their hearts to a love taken on faith. . . .

__LUCKY IN LOVE
    by Melanie Schuster   1-58314-362-9 $5.99US/$7.99CAN
When Clay meets Bennie, he is both attracted and wary. But after spending blissful days and nights with her, he wants Bennie as his wife. Now, as secrets from the past test their happiness, they must each struggle to put the pain behind them—and claim the future . . . together.

A FAMILY AFFAIR—*Family Reunion Series*
    by Shirley Hailstock   1-58314-366-1 $6.99US/$9.99CAN
Brenda Reid has always been the bookworm—beautiful, but not expected to marry. That is until a romance with Dr. Wesley Cooper inspires her to give into the reckless, passionate side of herself.

Call toll free **1-888-345-BOOK** to order by phone or use this coupon to order by mail. ALL BOOKS AVAILABLE AUGUST 1, 2002.

Name_____

Address_____

City_____ State _____ Zip _____

Please send me the books that I have checked above.

I am enclosing	$_____
Plus postage and handling*	$_____
Sales tax (in NY, TN, and DC)	$_____
Total amount enclosed	$_____

*Add $2.50 for the first book and $.50 for each additional book.
Send check or money order (no cash or CODs) to: **Arabesque Romances, Dept. C.O., 850 Third Avenue, 16th Floor, New York, NY 10022**
Prices and numbers subject to change without notice. Valid only in the U.S.
All orders subject to availability. **NO ADVANCE ORDERS.**
Visit our website at **www.arabesquebooks.com.**